Simon & Schuster

New York London Toronto

Sydney Tokyo Singapore

PARADISE OVERDOSE

A Novel

Brian Antoni

SIMON & SCHUSTER
Rockefeller Center
1230 Avenue of the Americas
New York, New York 10020

SIMON & SCHUSTER and colophon are registered trademarks
of Simon & Schuster Inc.

Designed by Karolina Harris
Manufactured in the United States of America

1 2 3 4 5 6 7 8 9 10

Library of Congress Cataloging-in-Publication Data
Antoni, Brian
Paradise overdose: a novel/Brian Antoni.
p.   cm.
1. Young men—Bahamas—Fiction. 2. Man-woman relationships—
Bahamas—Fiction. 3. Friendship—Bahamas—Fiction.
4. Drug trade—Bahamas—Fiction. I. Title.
PS3551.N768P37   1994
813'.54—dc20   94-19756
CIP

ISBN: 0-671-88426-3

Acknowledgments

I would like to thank my sister, Janine Antoni, for letting me use her art; my agent, Heather Schroder, for believing; my editor, Bob Asahina, for taking the risk; April Krasner and Amy Edelman for support when I needed it most; and my brother, Robert Antoni, for the sibling rivalry without which I probably wouldn't have written a book.

I would also like to thank my grandparents, Mr. Alvin Tucker (Papa), Mrs. Gertrude Zurcher-Tucker (Gugu), and Mrs. Maria Rosario de Medina Antoni (Maina) for all the old stories. It's your fault I wrote a book, so stop rolling around in your graves.

For my mom, Mrs. Lynette Tucker-Antoni,

my dad, Dr. Robert Odillo Antoni,

and the real Robin

Emancipate yourself from mental slavery

None but ourselves can free our mind . . .

Won't you help to sing these songs of freedom

That's all I ever heard

Redemption song

Redemption song.

Bob Marley, "Redemption Song"

Blessed are they that mourn:

for they shall be comforted.

Gospel of Saint Matthew

———————————————————————————————

1

The huge red snapper hangs in the crystal water. Adrenaline shoots. His legs kick, knees locked, the fins propelling him through fluid. He stretches back the sling. Release. Spear streaks through ocean. Dead stop. Shish-kebabs the fish's tail.

The fish flinches, then shoots erratically sideways like a balloon with the air rushing out. He lunges forward, chasing, seeing the spear just inches beyond his fingertips. Bubbles pop. Lungs scream. He blanks out the feeling. Finally his right hand grasps metal, and for a second he's suspended in the fish's lidless eyes. White cocktail onions.

Then the snapper pulls down as he pulls up, fish flesh ripping against slipping spear. Air! Now! He lets go, forgets the fish, fights his way up, no surface, only more water turning Jell-O thick. Panic. A vacuum sucks his lungs. He's stuck. Unyielding void. Pain filling and overflowing, and he's hurtling deeper and deeper.

And he's a child again and he has just taken a shower and he stands soapy-smelling next to his mother's bed and she breathes in and says, "Mmmm, something smells so good. Soooo good. I wonder what it is." And he answers, "It's me, Mommy. Me!" She opens her arms, long and milky, and he hugs her, and he's on the bed with her and he buries his head into her side, nestles in the spot beneath her arm, next to her breast, and it's so dark and warm and he hears the soothing far-off ocean sounds inside of her and it smells of her, and he feels so good. He holds his breath because he never wants to leave, but he has to breathe and she giggles and says, "Stop breathing hot air on me."

Then a current of bright coming closer and moving away, and then around and around and around, spinning, and he tries to focus, and he feels lips on his lips, so soft, and he concentrates on the lips. He feels warm air puff in and cold water pump out. His eyes open. Spots—he's staring into black eyes. Clammy panic shoots. No. No, it's Shark.

"Chris!" he hears Shark scream. He feels so calm and he tries to tell Shark it's all right but his mouth won't move. His body starts to tremble, his teeth chattering, and he can't stop. Then his mouth and nose stuffed full of salt smell and salt taste as he coughs swallowed sea water spasmodically.

He sits up. Everything fades again. Shark grabs him. He forces his eyes to stay open, holding on to Shark, his head falling forward, staring at Shark's smooth black back, feeling Shark's muscles jump under his skin as if they are separate and alive. He breathes. But he just can't keep his eyes open as he remembers opening his eyes two weeks ago. The smell of sweat and piss and rum and come oozed. A scab of dried blood and coke under his nose. Terrible snoring pounding in his brain. His face, inches from a dribbling woman with shiny mauve lipstick. He turned away. Faced a sleeping fat man, hairless, nude, fleshy foreskin pierced twice. Two golden loops. He jumped up, grabbed his jeans, left the hotel room. He walked, then jogged, then ran up the empty beach.

His eyes begin to focus. He shudders, spits again. Salty scum like the goo that sticks to cold boiled okra. He inhales. The air tastes as fresh and clean and sweet as rainwater. He squeezes the words out, slow and hoarse. "I'm O.K.," he says into Shark's ear.

Shark's body relaxes against his. "Thank fucking God," Shark says, slowly letting him go, his hands inches away, ready to catch him if he falls.

The Boston Whaler rocks. Chris places his head between his own legs, feels the blood flow down, feels Shark's hand on his head, stroking.

"Mon, you looking whiter dan white on rice."

"What happened?" Chris asks, confused, trying to remember, gazing up at Shark and then back down at the white fiberglass hull, at the dozen live conchs struggling, stretching out of their pink shells, like fat grey-black thumbs. Waves flop against the boat.

Shark sucks his teeth. "You got some pervert wish to meet the devil early?"

Chris sits up, watches dizzily as Shark wipes drool from his back. It sticks to his fingers. He washes them in ocean. The fuzziness fades.

"What the fuck happened?"

"I see dis mama red snapper. I let you shoot first cause it you birthday. You hit she tail. Den I's catch one breath and dive back down, and you is floating, not moving at all. You get shallow-water blackout. I swim you up and give you mouth to mouth. Save your sorry ass."

"Where's the fish?"

"Under a coral head with your spear jab up she tail."

Chris picks up a mask. "You know what I want for my birthday?"

"Pussy and coke. I means coke and pussy. Dat's the order."

"I want that fish."

"Don't fuck with me, mon." Shark grabs the mask from him.

"I'm gonna get her!" Chris yanks the mask back. It's foggy. He spits in it and the saliva sticks, sits in a clump, thick like egg whites. He rubs it in, cleaning the mask.

"Shit for brains," Shark says, shaking his head.

"That fish almost killed me!" Chris puts on the mask.

Shark grabs the front of it, pulling Chris's head forward. "You's one foolish fool!"

Chris pulls away. The mask snaps off his head, yanking his hair. "Fuck!"

"You ain't getting dat fish. I am!" Shark puts on the mask, snorkel, flippers, flips over backwards. A white splash and he's a black shimmering spot swimming down through turquoise. Ripples spread along the surface as Shark disappears. And it hits him. He starts to tremble, seeing the cotton-candy pink coffin, thinking that he almost died, and he hears Shark saying coke and pussy, pussy and coke. He pictures the words on his tombstone as he hugs his body, shakes his head back and forth. Then stares through the ocean.

A spot separates from the shadow of the coral head, moving up, taking human shape. Head and spears and redfish splash up. Shark dumps the fish into the boat as he blows water out through his snorkel. Spray flies through air.

"Happy birthday," Shark says, climbing into the boat. "You's crazy as crazy-self."

"The pot calling the kettle black," Chris says, laughing.

"I am black. Dat's why I act crazy. I got noting to lose. You white and got money. What's your excuse?"

"Cause there's nothing to gain. I got everything already," Chris says, sliding his spear through the fish's tail and slipping it out the other side. He twirls around the second spear stuck into the side of the fish's head, places one hand firmly on the cold, slimy head, avoiding the sharp, bright red gills, and pulls. The spear comes out trailing strings of translucent flesh. Clotted blood sticks to his fingers. He jabs his thumb and forefinger into the fish's eyes and stands up, holding the fish by its sockets. It's the color of an overripe tomato and about three and a half feet long.

"You said it was big," Chris says, dropping the fish into the back of the boat.

Shark grabs the anchor rope. "Everything look bigger, better, before you got it."

"I'm white and I got money," Chris says sarcastically.

"And I got you, smart ass and all." Shark smirks, struggling, pulling the rope left and then right.

Chris yanks the outboard's cord. The engine sputters, coughs, as the cord is sucked back inside. He adjusts the choke. Tugs again. It starts, a mechanical roar shattering silence.

"Come to Mama," Shark says, cleating the rope, pointing to the left. Chris goes left, gives the engine a little gas. The bow of the boat sinks into the water, then pops up.

"She undone," Shark says, pulling up the anchor, coiling the line around his arm. Anodized aluminum gleams in sunlight.

The boat slips through the flat blue, trailing a foamy white wake tail. They head for shore. The sun burning down dries Chris as pearls of salt water vanish, leaving almost invisible salt crystals. Vibrations from the engine massage his body as he looks up. Another stretched skin of blue. No clouds. Then a thin white jet-exhaust line pierces sky like a needle, cuts sharp at the point, its tail spreading, turning crooked and cottony, then fading away. Chris sings,

> If I had the wings of a dove
> If I had the wings of a dove
> I would fly
> Fly away

And Shark sings,

> Fly-I-I-I
> Away-A-A-A
> And Be-E-E-E

Shark and Chris sing,

> Like the rest.

"It was like sex," Chris says, hugging himself.

"Sex?"

"Shallow-water blackout. Like coming. Coming back. That sticky after-sex feeling. Only there was no one to get rid of."

"Boy, you sounding white!" Shark says with exasperation. "When last you jucked?"

"I don't remember."

"You turning tutti-frutti on me? Fucking fun. It don't hurt no one."

"I'm twenty-fucking-five. A quarter of a century old. Reef diving by day. Muff diving by night."

"Remember when we was kids and dere was a storm? I would bodysurf, ride dem waves, and you be standing in the surf punching dem before dey's break. You still punching dem waves."

A line of pelicans flap and then glide in the sky, each bird in the back of the line flapping when it reaches the spot where the first bird flapped.

Shark chants, "The bestest bird be the pelican. He beak can hold more dan *he belly can.*"

The lead bird stalls, drops down, a feathery spot of brown, out of sky.

"He beak can hold enough food for a week. And I'll be damned if I can tell how the *hell he can,*" Chris chants.

The bird's wings fold inward as it collides backward with the ocean and is swallowed by splash, and then it bubbles up, sits on the water, a fish dangling from its beak, until it drops with a soundless slurp down the pelican's pouch.

Chris looks at Shark's smile, remembers the smile on his face when he went to visit him last Christmas because he couldn't get off work. He walked into the Club Med dining room, heard the soft calypso music,

It's better in the Bahamas
Where the happy natives sing.
It's hip to hop to the Bahamas.

mixed with talking pierced by alcohol-laced laughter. He searched for Shark, passed the endless buffet of salads of every vegetable imaginable, and then breads—baked brown and crispy, loaves and buns and muffins and sticks—and pale yellow curlicues of butter riding in swans of melting ice, a slippery plate of pink tongue, goose liver formed into the shape of a goose, bleeding roasts of beef, lamb, ham in a coat of canned-pineapple slices with red cherries in the center, and then a sea of seafood, a Christmas tree made out of crawfish, a candle burning at the top, a bowl of caviar like teeny black eyeballs staring at the large lard sculpture of snow white Santa Claus with fat "Ho! Ho! Ho!" smiling face. Chris wondered where the dessert was as he looked around the room at happy red faces, tourists decked out in their casual formal resort-wear best, invading colonist whites fighting with the let-it-all-hang-out-and-go-native patterns, mixes of floral and tropical prints, bold neons, gold-buttoned sport coats, one too many sailor suit, and enough Banana Republic to make you gag. The lights dimmed and the Club Med theme song screeched through the sound system,

. . .

Stand up, Baby hands up
Give me your love
Give me, Give me,

and Shark walked out, slow, nearly naked, a sheet of tinfoil wrapped around his waist. His black muscles cut, greased and glowing. Peopled oohed and aahed, gasped and gawked. Clapped. His arm held high over his head, up into the air. Black biceps, triceps bulged. Orange-blue leafy flames licked and flicked at the mountain of snow white egg white in his hands. The look on Shark's face, the smile, burned into Chris. He led the other waiters, blacks dressed in starched whites, around the room. Burning Baked Alaska lighting up the Caribbean night. Shark went up on the stage. Chris looked at Shark's Afro armpit because he couldn't look at his face. People shushed one another. "Please follow me to the patio for dessert," Shark said in a clear voice. And then the sound of chairs scraping, and flip-flops flopping, and sneakers squeaking, as the other waiters followed Shark and the hundreds of guests followed the waiters, and the management people, panicky and red-faced, gave up trying to stop the procession and they followed too. Shark led everyone away from the Club Med, out into the back, to the staff dining room. The staff's heads were bowed as they held hands, saying grace. They looked up in fright as Shark walked in with the burning dessert followed by twenty-five other waiters carrying burning desserts and the crowd of Club Med guests. Everyone stood silent as they looked at the staff's Christmas dinner of spaghetti with Hunt's catsup and a hard-boiled egg.

A flying fish, its tail twitches, fin-wings spread. Then it glides silver through the air.

"Hey mon, what dat?" Shark asks, pointing toward the beach.

"It's a bird! It's a plane! It's Superman!" Chris says.

"Not the fish, Holmes. The beach."

Chris squints, takes off his mirrored sunglasses. "What the fuck?" A section of the beach looks as if it has been dipped in color. Painted red and yellow and blue. As they get closer, the colors get brighter.

"It's not the beach that's colored," Chris says, turning off the engine. "It's the water between the ridges of sandbar in front of the beach." The engine sputters, stops, as the boat glides forward, stops. So silent.

"Wow," Chris says, walking from the water onto the stretch of sandbar. The colors. So many. Separate, bold, solid, and then running together, mixing to make many different hues in the water between the endless ridges of sand. Like multicolored ribs glistening in the sunlight. Chris runs, excited, his feet sinking into the sand, smashing the ridges, joining the wet streams, causing colors to flow together, making new colors.

They follow the colored sandbar beach around a corner, walking together. There's a woman at the end of the painted beach. She's on her knees, next to a camera on a tripod and jars filled with concentrated red and yellow and blue. Chris walks slowly toward her, squinting behind his Bollée's, his eyes slipping up smooth, long, tan legs, bouncing off her ripe bikini-accentuated bottom, settling on the nape of her neck. He looks down, adjusts himself in his black Speedo so it looks bigger, better. She turns. Chris yanks his hand out of his pants. She drops the turkey baster. Red-dye drips fly. She glances up at them from beneath the brim of a white Panama hat.

Shark flexes his body. Defining. Chris looks at her, feels nervous, retracts, looks away, remembers seeing her on the beach after running away from the fat, shaved man and the dribbling woman. The sun was rising. She was naked except for a bathing cap covered in rubber daisies. One arm across her chest, one arm held straight out. Golden skin glinted with sweat as she tangoed on the breaking waves. The expression on her face serious. And he wanted to know her, and it was a new feeling or an old feeling he forgot. He turned, ran until he could run no more. Then dived into the cool.

"Talk bout finding treasure at the end of the rainbow." Shark flirts. Chris feels jealous, wants to scream at him, I saw her first, and then feels ridiculous.

"You're painting?" Chris asks. He digs his toes into the sand. "Like the beach is your canvas? Right?"

"There's a relationship to painting," she says, and the look on her face shifts slightly. She looks less preoccupied and he's encouraged and he doesn't know why he cares but he does.

"It's beautiful," Chris says.

"Ahhhh!" she screams, her hands clenched into fists. "That's the problem."

"It's more . . . ," Chris says.

"Beauty? A problem?" Shark interrupts, shaking his head dramatically.

"Like when something's beautiful, you don't want to get behind it, get inside . . . Right?" Chris asks, hesitantly, wanting to smooth the wrinkles on her brow.

"You got dat upsided down, it's when it looking good dat you wants to get inside." Shark makes a fist, bends his arm as if it has become a giant hard-on, looks at Chris as if he's urging him to punch a wave.

"Not get inside in a sexual way, like if it's only beautiful it's shallow, like when you get in it's empty."

She looks at them, amused. Stains of muted shades of the beach colors stretch from her kneecaps to her toes. "Parsley," she says seriously. "This piece is just parsley."

"You're being too hard on yourself. It's more than decorative. There's more than garnish going on."

"Like what?" she asks, folding her arms, really looking at him for the first time.

Chris takes a deep breath, feels stage fright. "I never noticed the way the ocean carves the beach. Not the ridges themselves. But the actual process. The colors are making me see." She leans toward him.

"Why you don't do someting dat last? When the tide rise up, it gone."

She stretches, stands, paces, pointing the turkey baster at them. She stops. "It's alive. It has a life. It dies."

"Kinda like a flower," Chris says.

"Like a rainbow," she says.

"A butterfly," Chris says. She starts to relax.

"Like a Hallmark card," she says.

Shark smiles with his eyes, winks at Chris. "Like fuck me baby I'm sensitive."

A brief pause and then her little lips stretch into a big smile. Perfect lickable white teeth.

She sits cross-legged, next to the jars, squeezes the bulb of the turkey baster, and it sucks up some of the red liquid. Red, like red-red wine.

"Yeh mon, it's kind of like you ain't doing noting. The ocean's the one painting the picture," Shark says as the red bleeds into a streak of blue turning violet. "Carving up the beach."

"I want to do it," Chris says, standing. He grabs Shark's hand, pulls him up. "With who?" Shark smirks.

She hands the baster to Chris. He inserts into the blue dye, walks away and stops and pinches the baster's bulb. Squirt. Blue, the color of the deep ocean off the continental shelf, runs into the clear water stream between the ridges. It bleeds into yellow and turns greenish. "You're like taking Christo one step further. His surrounded islands. You're not just putting something in nature, you're intervening in it. Working with it."

"You know about art?" she asks, surprised, turning, looking at him with curiosity.

"No, just conch," he says, sarcastically.

"And about decorative tourist gals," Shark says.

They all laugh together and he has this tremendous urge to hug both of them.

"I was in Miami when Christo wrapped those islands. I was blown away," Chris says. "That turned me on to art. Led me to Duchamp. Sort of ass backwards."

She looks at him and he can tell she's impressed and he feels good. "What's your name?" she asks, as if she's just meeting him.

"Chris," he says, "and this is Shark."

"Today's Chris's birthday," Shark says.

"I'm Robin," she says, shaking Shark's hand, and then she holds out her hand to Chris. "I guess the painted beach is your birthday present."

Chris grabs her hand and tries to catch her eye. She looks down.

He looks down. His eyes stop at her lips. She tries to smile. Her lips tremble. His hand tingles as he holds hers. She squeezes tight. He feels it between his legs, lets go.

"A rainbow and a redfish. You can't want more dan dat," Shark says.

"I want a photo," Chris says.

She detaches the camera from the tripod. "Walk into the colors."

They look at her and at each other and she starts to snap. Shark jumps on Chris's back. Snap. Snap. Snap. They fool around and pose like men in muscle magazines.

"You two look exactly alike, but in opposite ways," she says.

Chris laughs as he feels Shark yank his bathing suit below his knees. "Fuck you," he says, grabbing for his suit, tripping, falling back onto the sand.

And she's above him, her face hidden behind the snapping camera, shadowed by her hat. As he pulls up his Speedo he thinks he sees her lick her bottom lip. The colored water cools his sun-warmed skin, and he stares up at the sky, at the sun burning into him. And he imagines fucking her on the flat rainbow, imagines Shark taking pictures of him fucking her on the flat rainbow.

Then Shark is standing above him, laughing. Chris stares up at him. The colors of the water stick to his white bathing suit. He grabs Chris's hand, pulls him up. "Now she got one picture of where all dat art bullshit coming from."

"You're the one with a dick for a brain," Chris says.

"I want one with all three of us," Robin says. "I have to get the tripod."

"I like her," Chris whispers to Shark.

"I do too," Shark says.

"More," Chris says.

"No shit, Sherlock," Shark says. "She remind me of you mother."

"How?" Chris asks, frowning.

And then she's back, setting up the camera on the tripod.

"We models don't work for free," Shark says. "You have to buy us a drink at the Tipsy Turtle tonight."

Robin runs back from the camera and stands between them. Shark puts his arm around her and Chris puts his arm around her, touching Shark's arm. He feels Robin's arm wrap around his waist at the same time as he feels Shark squeeze his butt. He yanks down Shark's bathing suit.

The camera snaps.

2

Chris walks through the lobby of the Holiday Inn, taps the sign on the door:

Welcome to the Tipsy Turtle
No Shoes, No Shirt, No Plat Head
Dress to Impress!
P.S. LOAFERS, PROSTITUTES & PIMPS READ & RUN OR ELSE?

He plunges in, feels darkness devour as he inhales the familiar nutrient—jock smell. Raw beat throbs. A current of rhythm. Pulling. Stronger and stronger. The heat from the moving mass on the dance floor hits. Robin. He can't stop thinking of her. His eyes adjust to the dark. He focuses. Scans the club looking for her, looking at but not seeing the Saturday Night Fever cum Caribbean decor, a mix of worn shag carpet, tinsel curtains, pitting mirrors, plastic bamboo chairs, fading tropical prints. His heart beats hard.

"It limbo contest time. Stand up an bend you spine," the bandleader screeches. The microphone hums. The band plays,

Limbo, limbo, limbo, like me
Dance till the music set you backbone free
Jam you ting into the air
You in the Bahamas so have no fear

• • •

Chris walks to the music, searching for Robin. An endless stream of nameless, fuzzy faces flows through his mind as he pictures pumping away his adolescence innocently, gymnastically, as they tell him, "Try putting your legs here—your tongue there—can we turn over—that's right, stud—oh God—I'm coming!" It feels so good—so gooood—and then nothing. The tourists go back to where they come from. He goes back for more.

Contestants in the limbo contest wind and grind to the music, then bend under the pole easily. They lower it another notch.

Chris sits at the corner of the sticky formica bar, the one with the best view of the door. He looks at his watch. Ten o'clock. The door opens. The bright light from the lobby flashes. The door closes. He fights the feeling that Robin's not coming as the door opens and closes again and again and again. It stings all over, icy numb. He craves rum to calm it. His mother told him that when he was a baby they used to put rum in his bottle to make him sleep. Rum became his pacifier, the pacifier of his family—his grandfather, buried in a cask of rum in accordance with his will—pacifier of the Caribbean, the history of fragmented nationalism mixed with alcoholism, like a rum and Coke. What wrong with you, boy, you West Indian or not? And he's a boy again watching his father's red sunburned face turn redder as he took big gulps, saying, "Take a mouthful of rainwater—rainwater sweet, boy—put the rum bottle to you head, take a big mouthful of rum—rum sweet, boy—a bit more water, so dat the rum be cushion."

He wanted to spit it out, the burning, but he kept it down, to be a man, to be a West Indian. Choking as his father choked on his own laugh, saying, "How I could produce such a sissy-boy?"

"What kind of rum you want tonight, Angostura?" the bartender asks. "Teenager, old man, or dead old man?"

Chris tries to say Perrier as he tastes the Vat 19, the Añejo, the 151 in his head. What the fuck. "Give me a dead old man full of rocks."

Happy birthday, he thinks, gulping. The cold hot burning so good. Wishing he could inject it directly into his brain—go, quick, dive through that stomach lining, swim into those veins and chew on those brains. He takes two more gulps and looks around for Robin again. Only tourists and more tourists. No doubt they saved all year for this packaged paradise—seven days at the luxurious Holiday Inn on beautiful Lucayan Beach, manager's welcome cocktail party with more freeloading locals than tourists providing plenty cock and tail, love juice served free by the glass, if you don't like my mixture, you can kindly kiss my ass, free tours of the Angostura bitters factory, ten dollars in casino chips and a complimentary conch shell.

A woman, slightly Rubenesque in the personals, body and posture hinting of a blowfish future, scrutinizes him, taps the woman next to her with the little paper umbrella from her drink. They look, toothy smiles of invitation. Chris looks down, away, crunches the ice hard. Feels his mouth freeze. Feels it through his teeth. Feels for the missing piece of the puzzle that will make it all make sense. Pictures the painted beach. He takes another gulp and another and another. He feels the rum cloud float into his head, calming him. One drink after another, he tries to picture Robin, analyze her beauty, break it down into parts, but he can't. It doesn't make sense: big wide-set eyes, little nose, little mouth. Her head too big for her elongated body. He pictures Betty Boop, but without the innocence.

Only three contestants left in the contest. Frat boys in Sigma Nu jerseys. So young and scrubbed looking. The limbo pole is about three feet from the floor. People yell, "How low can you go!" Two of the boys make it under. A cheerleader type bounces up and gives them each a Beck's. They chug them. Chugalugalug and then one of the frat boys tries to bend under, knocking the pole, and it wobbles, falls as he yells, "Fuck!" The last boy pulls off his shirt and hands it to the girl. His thighs shake as he pushes his groin under, stomach muscles tense, and one shoulder is under the pole and then the other, his face straining, and he makes it. A smile spreads on his face as people cheer. He holds his arms into the air. The other frat boys pour beer all over him. Gold bubbling white drips down from his yellow blond hair over his naked, hairless chest.

Chris finishes his drink. The door opens and light flashes. No Robin! Fuck. Chris catches a glimpse of a woman all dressed in black with white peroxide hair shining like snow in the light from the lobby.

He orders another drink, flinches as he hears the scream "Uga! Buga-buga!" A man dressed in imitation zebra skin G-string shakes wildly, jamming to the beat, his face covered in white, two burning batons in his hands. He jucks his midsection in and out, down and around. Orange-blue flames crawl along blue-black skin. The fire eater lowers the pole another notch, pours rum, lights it. He bends impossibly at the waist, contorting under the pole, stopping halfway. Zebra skin pulls tight around his genitals, a clenched fist between his legs. He goes lower, pushes his midsection under, folds in half, his head touching floor. He's under. The crowd claps. The band plays,

> Baby you see my ting-a-ling
> It does carry quite a sting
> It may be small but it can make you bawl
> Make you feel, Hot! Hot! Hot!
> Hot! Hot! Hot!

"Fucka Uga Tooga," the fire eater screams, picking up a rum bottle, drinking.

The bartender brings Chris a tumbler full of rum. "On the house, bitter. You look like you need it," he says. Chris swallows as the fire eater dances, spitting stream after stream of fire, rubbing his stomach, fanning his midsection. Then a tablecloth bursts into flames. The bartender jumps over the bar, a fire extinguisher in his hands. He sprays a stream of white froth. The frat boys yell, "Let the motherfucker burn!" The flames smother. A plump man wearing a "Sit on My Face" T-shirt sits covered in white foam. People clap. He climbs on top of the table, pulls down his pants and moons the crowd. Spotlighted marshmallow ass smiles. Red crack. A woman wearing an "I'm with Stupid" T-shirt leaves the table.

Chris looks at his watch. Twelve o'clock. His birthday's over. Fuck Robin. Fuck Shark. He finishes his drink, orders another, picturing his brain in his head like an olive in a martini. And he thinks how sick he is of the same shit, of doing nothing. He feels stuck, trapped in a picture postcard. Coke and pussy. Pussy and coke.

"Come on, all you sexy gals," the bandleader announces. "It time for the sexiest woman contest."

Chris hits back the glassful of 151, no longer tasting it. Stands up, feels the rum buzz, not enough, not numb enough. He walks around looking, pushes his way up to the dance floor. The band plays:

> Dat gal look so sexy, shaking dat fat bumsy
> Lord I want to jam she, right in her fat juicy
> You make me scream,
> You make me bawl,
> You make me bamboo one feet tall.

Chris stares at the group of women trying to be sexy, bumping-winding-pumping-grinding, screwing the air, making it feel shame. Each trying to outdo the other. Frenzied men jeer and hoot and leer, their eyes begging. "Show your tits!" A woman with a big mole on her chin yanks off her shirt. Breasts bounce lopsided and sagging as she gyrates then shoves her midsection in and out as if she's trying to throw it across the room. Chris starts to walk away until he sees the woman in black dancing with her eyes shut in front of a mirror. Black lips, black nails. White peroxide hair with black roots glows in the black light. He wants to touch it. Her bubblelike breasts are squashed by a black sequin tube top exposing her naked navel—like a doorbell. He wants to ring it. He feels the urge. Imagines tangoing naked with Robin on broken waves. White hot exploding into the cool blue. The woman dances, moving her hips smoothly like she has ball bearings in her waist, seductively, in slow motion. She opens her eyes. Stares back at him for a split second. Then she tugs the tube top up higher and looks down, away from him. Chris follows her averted eyes and stares at her toes, flattened by black open-toe high heels. The little toe hangs perilously over the edge of her shoe, wrapped in Band-Aid like a pig in a blanket. He wants to suck it. She dances over to him grinning and he pictures the women in those peep shows, where you can see them but they can't see you as they play with themselves, looking in the mirror as you mirror their movements, play with yourself, but the curtain always closes too early, leaving you on a desperate search for the other dollar you don't have. Your shoes stick to the floor as you leave.

And now the woman in black is dancing just for him, her body touching his, and people are staring and he feels lost in a black hole. He looks up at the mirrored disco ball turning around and around, reflecting little colored spots, spinning around and around. She jams harder against his body and then puts her arms around his neck and pulls him to the middle of the dance floor. People hiss. He hears someone yell, "Get her, pale!" He looks in the direction of the voice and then, through the spotted dark, he thinks he sees Robin on her way out of the club. The door closes as he extracts himself from the woman in black, walking quickly to the door and out into the lobby, but she's not there. Only a huge black man that Chris vaguely recognizes as a dealer, dressed in a white linen suit and a white shirt and a white tie, clutching a white woman. Chris walks up to him, staring at his inflated chest draped in gold, Jesus on a medal the size of a small frying pan next to a diamond-encrusted coke spoon.

The man puts his finger on his nose, sniffs.

Chris nods, walks to the men's room. The man follows.

"How much white, white?" the man asks.

Chris pulls out a fifty.

"Just for you, cream," the man says, handing him a Baggie. Brass-knuckle-sized rings on his fingers. He leaves.

Chris enters the first stall. It's clogged, full of shit. He enters the second one. The seat is all covered in gluey, stinking, yellow pee. Pink polyester pants pushed down around patent leather shoes protrude from underneath the last stall. What the shit, he thinks as he re-enters the first one. Tries to flush but the thick cucumber shit just swims around in a circle. He takes a deep breath through his mouth so he won't have to smell it, pulls down his pants, sits, strains, as he pictures little crabs, herpes, gonorrhea, AIDS jumping from the mammoth turd and grabbing onto his asshole hairs and climbing into his ass. He snorts.

Numb. First the teeth, then the lips and then the head. He soars higher than the alcohol cloud, higher than himself, artificially inseminating his brain.

The music plays louder as he re-enters the Tipsy Turtle from the bathroom, and the happy rushes inside and outside and he feels inside out as so many thoughts race. I don't need you, Robin. He wants to sing, dance. It's so good—great, even. And it's his toy, his putty, silly putty. Go-now, walk-slow, don't-sniff, take-what-you-want, the coke orders.

The woman in black sits at a table by herself, stirring her drink with her finger and then sucking it. He stops, touches her lightly on the back, flashes his Chiclets. She flinches, looks up at him standing over her. Hostile. His smile turns to grimace. "I thought you ran away," she says.

"My name's Chris," he yells over the music, not hearing her.

"What?" she answers-asks, her chalk white face pinched.

"What's yours?"

"What's my what?"

"Name!"

"I don't like to play games."

"Name!" Chris shouts, bending forward, just as the band stops.

People stare at him. He wipes the sweat from his face. He sniffs. Don't sniff, he tells himself.

"Pam's my name."

"Nice to meet you." He reaches his hand out. She looks at it as if he had just wiped his ass with it. He sees her see his Rolex watch, and he thinks it's his seal of quality, one hundred percent prime rich, because it's just as easy to fall in love with a rich man as a poor man and he thinks he can see it in their eyes as they watch the watch, the Sold sign nailed over the For Sale sign. Her eyes now flash VACANCY. Labels showing. Gucci, Pucci and Versace, the money honeys to death, because it's a material world and she's a material girl, so you've got to sell dat pussy, sell dat pussycat, oh yeah, because money talks and bullshit walks and I'm full of both.

"I won," she says, forcing a tight beauty-queen smile, shaking his hand.

"You are the sexiest."

"Yeah?" She masturbates the prize bottle of cold duck. The band bellows:

> When I gave she number one and drove it home,
> drive it home
> When I gave her number one
> She say, The fun's just begun
> Put your lips close to mine and drive it home.

He crouches down in the aisle next to her chair. She bites the cherry stem off the cherry, sucks it into her mouth. "I can tie a knot with my tongue."

"Cool," Chris says, his mind racing, trying to think of things to say, teeth to pull. "I'm from here," he says.

"What?" she shouts, leaning in to hear.

"I'm from the Bahamas."

"Wait," she says. She opens her mouth. Her tongue trembles, the tied red stem sitting on the pink tip. Then she swallows it, moves closer to him. He smells hair spray.

"No white people are from here."

"I am."

She opens her purse, takes out a stick of gum. Sticks half of it into her mouth, offers him the other half, chewing loudly.

"I don't like taking candy from strangers." He sniffs. Feels the coke dripping out his nose, feels his nose dripping off his face, his brain dripping out his ears.

"Oh, you only like candy up your nose?" she asks, smirking.

He opens his mouth. She inserts the gum. He bites down. Chews as the band plays:

> When I give she number two and drove it home,
> drive it home
> When I gave she number two
> She say, Dis can't be true
> Put your lips close to mine and drive it home.

He feels someone bump into him. He turns, his face is in the crotch of a waitress dressed in a mini uniform that looks like she forgot her pants.

She looks down. Her face fleshy, nose from cheek to cheek, laughing eyes. "Angostura, just because you in here every night don't mean you own the aisle. Haul ya rich ass?"

"What's wrong, Cedella, no tips, or you late again this month?"

She puts her hands on her hips. "Boy, only black peoples and packaged tourist in here. Black peoples too smart to tip and package tourist too cheap. As for my time, you want one fat lip on you fat lip?"

Chris laughs, tips her a five. She licks her lips.

Pam stands up, grabs his hand. "Teach me to island dance, Bahama boy," she says, pulling him to the floor.

The heat and sweet sweat smell swallow them. She grabs him hard around the neck. He holds on and works his body into an S shape so he can stick his groin up against hers. Her breasts hit his breast like bumpers, holding him off. And he's moving to the soca beat, swaying back and forth, smooth—like the casuarina trees blowing in the wind—in and out. And she starts to squeeze his ass and he thinks of Monsignor beating his bare ass in the sacristy for eating all the hosts, cassock pulled above his waist, short pants below his knees. And he remembers the time when he woke up in the Holiday Inn to an incomplete past, with an amazing pain in the ass, after taking some unidentifiable pills for some unidentifiable high from some unidentifiable leather queen. His ass hurting like when he was a child and Shark stuck the tire pump air hose up, pumping him up, his stomach bloating bigger and bigger, and then pushing and lighting, releasing a chorus of firework farts.

The music travels through his head, through his body. He slides with her, his midsection slicing into her, swelling to the music. Dick straining against fabric.

When I give she number three and drove it home,
drive it home
When I gave she number three
She say, Make love to me
Put your lips close to mine and drive it home.

He feels her feel it as she cracks her gum extra hard. "You're not gonna run away now, are you?" she whispers, throaty. Chris stares at her razor hair, at the peroxide ends and the dark black roots; he touches the sharpness with his hand.

> When I give she number four and drove it home,
>   drive it home
>   When I gave she number four
>   She say, Darlin give me more
>   Put your lips close to mine and drive it home.

"Is it really better in the Bahamas?" she asks as the music plays,

> When I give she number five and drove it home,
>   drive it home
>   When I gave she number five
>   She say, Darlin I'm so alive
>   Put your lips close to mine and drive it home.

"What?" he asks, even though he heard her.

"You got any more nose candy?"

"Is this the Bahamas?"

"Party!" she says. "Let's go!"

"Give me a chance," he says, trying to force himself down.

"Oh, what have we here?" she asks coyly, touching the lump, laughing, pulling him off the dance floor. The bulge dissolves.

In the car, Chris feels like he's playing one of those driving games, and he's staying still and the scenes are going by. He can't get home fast enough. He snorts deeply, hoping that some of the coke has attached itself to his nose hairs and will now go up to his brain, because he can feel himself losing it, losing his balls.

He parks, leads her down the dock to his yacht.

"*Paradise Overdose*," she says, reading the name on the transom of his boat. "There's no such thing." Then she follows him on board, says, "Wow!" her eyes wide open as they dart over the carpet, the sleek teak, the chrome of his Hatteras. "It's like fucking *Lifestyles of the Rich and Famous*. How big is it?"

"A little under sixty feet and I'm around seven and one-fourth inches." He takes the bag of coke out of his pocket.

"Baby!" she says excited.

Let's get to the coke and get it over with, Chris thinks, sticking in the CD.

> When I give she number seven and drove it home,
> drive it home
> When I gave she number seven
> She say, Darlin I'm in heaven
> Put your lips close to mine and drive it home.

He pops the prize bottle of Duck, sits down on the couch next to her, empties the remainder of the bag onto a silver dessert tray. Doesn't bother to chop it or cut it into lines, just rolls up a crisp Bahamian hundred-dollar bill. He snorts but can't get enough up and it starts coming out of his nose when he breathes. He tries to keep it in, vacuuming up the feeling powder, forgetting her until she says, "What about me, baby?"

Then he hands her the rolled-up bill and focuses on black nails contrasted by white coke as she snorts and snorts, and he thinks, There must be a God because he invented coke and women, wondering what came first, coke or women or the chicken or the egg, thinking coke must have come first because nobody would be able to get any woman if he didn't have any coke to give her first and who cares about the chicken or the egg.

He dips his finger into the coke and rubs it all over his teeth, gums and tongue.

> When I give she number eight and drove it home,
> drive it home
> When I gave she number eight
> She say, Baby I can't wait
> Put your lips close to mine and drive it home.

Chris starts to kiss her and their coked-up mouths feel like a down blanket as he sticks his tongue into her mouth. He's so high, so high—flying. He gets lost in the feeling of her mouth, swallowing it, swallowing the thought that she's kissing the coke and not him. She pulls away and snorts some more.

"Meeting you was sure a stroke of luck," she says, stroking his thigh.

He snorts as much as he can suck up, breathing it in, and it hits his head like breakers on the reef, crashing, leaving a whitecap swirling around in his brain. He feels himself start to get hard again, an outbreak of self-assertion, as he thinks how he spends his life begging it to stay down or praying for it to come up, never calling it his, because it has a life of its own, and he thinks how women are so lucky to have their sex hidden on the inside, no exclamation point. She stands up, coke eyes lit up. She pulls off her clothes quickly, without shame. No strain. Chris undoes his belt, unzips the zip, and it pops out fast. He takes off his pants and shirt. He gets on the floor and looks up. Up into her. Right between her legs. Raw. Lips glistening. Peroxide pubic hair shaved into a Mohawk. He takes a deep breath. And another. And she gets down on the floor. She's high and she's grabbing and she's rough. And Chris looks at the anonymous porno-movie dick between his legs and feels good. It feels too good: just to be close, to be touched. He kisses her breasts, then licks the rings around her nipples, his tongue circling around and around and around. Then he sucks.

Chris sticks his hands between her legs and he thinks about the first time he stuck his hands between a woman's legs. It was like sticking his hands between his own legs but there was nothing but a hole, and he felt castrated and stupid. Because he didn't know what to do. But now he does. And he starts to do it. Wetness forms on his fingers. Coke nail caressing clitoris.

She moans. He dives between her legs, picturing Robin. He wants to get in and suck and lick and eat. Can't get enough. He searches between her legs, tries to jam his head right up. Every time he moves, the drug sends a rush to his head. Every time she moans, the sound sends a rush to his midsection.

She pulls his hair, lightly at first and then hard. The pain from her pulling makes him feel good. He slides up slowly. His face is covered in her and her hair is sticking in his throat and between his teeth, and he feels like his face has now become a part of her as he starts to kiss her mouth, feeling her taste herself on himself as she spreads her legs. Then he tries to enter her slowly, to savor, to get lost, but her pelvis pushes up and swallows him too fast, spoiling it. And her body, his body. He's going as slow and as deep as it can. He enters, he exits, he goes left, he goes right, he goes in, he goes out almost all the way, then in all the way, no almost. Then it starts to take over and he starts to feel the pleasure. It takes him back and he's a child again and Tantie Evalina is giving him and Shark a bath together and the water is filled with Mr. Bubble and they are playing. They held their birdies in their hands, pretending they were guns and they were firing make-believe bullets at each other. "Ready, aim, fire," Shark said.

"Pow! Boom!" Chris yelled, bringing his arms down into the water splashing Evalina, who laughed and said, "God help the gals when younna learn to play proper with you toeties," and then Shark covered himself with white bubble froth and said, "Look, I's white as you now, so I gets to live in big house full of toys."

Then Tantie gave them a perfectly ripe mango and they ripped off the green-red skin with their teeth and took turns sinking into the perfect pudding-orange tart sweetness.

He can see the juice running down Shark's face and feel the sticky juice running down his own face. He thinks how they always shared everything and it's always him and Shark together, like the time when they were sixteen with the tourist in the Tipsy Turtle, who was feeling him up under the table and he didn't know she was also feeling Shark under the table and they took her back to her room and took turns, shared her. And everyone got enough and he remembers her juice running down Shark's face and felt her sticky juice on his face and he thought that they were really making love to each other. And she said, "Whoever made me come, thanks."

"God!" Pam moans and Chris starts to feel afraid, too turned on, and he's outside his body, watching it, so many body parts, reading yet another sex manual, turned off, as the fucking machine goes into self-drive. He pictures himself in competition with the feeling, fighting to control the bang of banging. The masculinity judges are scoring his technique. So he forces himself to feel nothing. Remembering when he had to put that Stud stuff on it, to anesthetize it, but now he has learned to Novocain his dick with his brain.

Thighs slap against thighs. Balls slap against bottom. Tide slaps against hull. And then he feels himself pushed off from below. She sits up. Chris catches his breath, confused, stage fright.

She grabs the plate and snorts more coke. He looks at her. She catches the look and pushes him away with her eyes. She hands him the rolled-up bill. Chris sucks and sucks. Then she gets on all fours. He's sure she does this so she won't have to look at him. So he can't see her, her ass in the air, pussy staring at him like an eye. The fig leaf moved to her face.

He enters her from behind. She starts to moan. And then she lets out the "Ohhhh!" so loudly he can feel it run through his body like a tremor, making him feel not exactly alive, but at least not dead. Her orgasm inflating his ego, allowing him to be a man, and he pictures her orgasm a big golden O that he places on his head like a crown. She falls forward. He holds his breath, trying to squeeze the passion back inside, but it's like trying to squeeze water from a rock. He moans dramatically, faking it, dry-convulsing into her body.

> When I give she number nine and drove it home,
> drive it home
> When I gave she number nine
> She say, Oh, You're right on time
> Put your lips close to mine and drive it home.

Chris panics, pulls out, a plug from a sink. Draining as it drains. Her sweat sticks to his sweat, sour and biting. He shrivels up, small and pathetic, his world comes back, pathetic and small.

Then the other lady takes over because he just wants cocaine running through his brain. He gets up off the floor, finds the dessert tray. There's no more. He starts to lick it. Nothing! Fuck it!

"Got any more?" she asks, sitting up off the floor.

"No, sorry."

"Can you drop me back?"

Chris dresses rapidly, thinking, Why do I do it? Knowing exactly why.

They get into his white Jag and drive back to the Holiday Inn. She doesn't look at him as he walks her to her room, number 409, and it's goodnight-kiss time as they fumble like teenagers, like it was the very first time. Lips meet as he looks into her eyes, black spots floating like tar in blue-blue sea. She shuts them as she pushes her tongue between his lips as he pushes his tongue between her lips as he feels her chewing gum. Good night and goodbye. "I'd love to see you again if you get more coke," she says, and then the creak of closing door. Period.

He goes back to the Tipsy Turtle, walks around the club looking for coke. He spots Shark leaning against the bar.

"What it is?" Shark asks. "You finally reach?"

"Fuck that shit," Chris answers. "I was here earlier. I left." Tooth-like cowry shells plaited to Shark's hair like a closed jaw form a part down the center of his head.

"Where you was? Find pot of gold at the end of the rainbow? Aye, Chrisy-boy?" Shark teases.

"Robin didn't show. You didn't show."

"So where you was?" Shark asks, as a woman, expressionless face, a mask of ruddy skin like a plucked chicken, places a wrinkly hand on Shark's ass.

Shark smiles at her as if she's the most beautiful woman in the world.

The woman's drunk, watery eyes like coddled eggs focus on Shark as she slurs, "Wanna dance, honey?"

"It be an honor," Shark answers. He flutters his eyes at Chris as he leads the woman by the hand to the dance floor. Chris sits down on the bar stool, watches Shark place one finger on the small of the woman's back, plug himself in, and take over the woman's body. Watches Shark's ass, like an overripe mango ready to drop. Yet it rises up, proudly defeating gravity, as it jucks to the music.

So sweet and juicy
Where you get that sugar?
Mon, dere ain't no ting sweeter
Give me the bum bum
Sugar Bum, Sugar Bum

Shark saunters up to him. "I sorry I late. I's involved in a major transaction," Shark says, excited. "No more niggering around with nicky nicky coke shit. I's gotta talk to you bout it."

"Tomorrow," Chris says, "I can't deal . . . Robin . . . She didn't show."

"Don't preoccupy. She just jacking you around. She like you too bad."

"Maybe it's you she likes."

"Dat's one wave you don't have to punch."

Chris smiles weakly.

"Gotta go," Shark says. "Can't let Yankee nose go unpowdered."

"Got any on you now?"

"Do niggers have big dicks?" he asks, reaching into his pocket and placing a Ziploc bag in Chris's hand. He pushes the bag into his pocket.

"Thanks," Chris says.

"What friends for?"

Shark leaves as the bandleader announces, "We have one special request, from Shark to Chris." He sings,

Happy birthday to you, Happy birthday to you
Happy birthday, dear Chris
Happy birthday to you.

Chris leaves. Drives back to his yacht. Goes into his stateroom, pulls the coke from his pocket, pulls off all his clothes, drops them in a pile, picks up the silver tray and walks into the bathroom. He crouches down next to the toilet, empties the bag onto the tray and cuts the coke into twenty fine lines.

Chris snorts. Sucks up one line. Inhale. Exhale. Then the next

and next and next. Line after line after line. Until he has done it all
and the feeling takes over. All full and sexy as he touches his chest,
following the streak of black like black mangrove banyans down to
the nest of pubic hair. To his birdy, when soft. Dick, at half mast.
Cock, when hard as rock stone. And penis in science class. Planting
sucker, follow the root. He grabs it, looks it straight in the mouth, or
is it another eye? He squeezes it, wants to beat it into submission.
He shakes it and it shakes its head back. His pride measured in
inches. He remembers waiting for it to grow, praying desperately to
Jesus that it would grow, because he would understand, because he
was a man. Chris pictures the ruler in his hand, checking the
growth, puberty no explosion, in slow motion, suspended animation, dropping, growing like a stalactite, each drip crystallizing after
years of concentration, and quick looks downward in steamy locker
rooms, always at the guy exhibiting the big one.

He spreads aloe gel on his hands, pictures Evalina's shining blue-
black hands covered in clear aloe gel. Stroking his feet. Down and
up. Strokes. Up and down. Soothing. More coke hits his brain as life
enters into it, as he thinks of Robin, the colors, blossoming Bahama
breezes, as he concentrates on the subtle pleasure, as the blood
starts to enter like an inside-out orgasm. Reflex action. And he
thinks of the white jelly inside the young green coconuts he used to
eat every Monday morning to get rid of worms. His mother mixing
the coconut water with Beefeater and drinking until she had the
courage to fight with his father.

He feels the chilly aloe jelly on his feet, the slimy coconut jelly in
his throat, and hears his parents' huge adult voices screaming. And
he would stick his fingers into his ears.

"Get out," he tells himself now. Whenever those thoughts enter,
he shoves them out. Stops them. His hand stops. Dead. He's gonna
beat it.

He licks the tray. Feels himself coming down, wonders why he
can no longer come in a woman.

Chris goes up to the galley, grabs a bottle of Añejo, returns to the
bathroom and turns on the shower. He sits on the bathtub floor, his
head on his knees, his arms hugging his legs. The shower pulsates

against his head as he tries to forget. But he feels the coke draining from his brain as he remembers burying his head into her side, and he breathes in deeply, inhaling water. Chokes. Just as his starched white collar choked him, felt like a fish bone caught in his throat as his charcoal black tie burned his neck in the burning hard-boiled-egg-yolk-colored sun. His feet hurt in his new black shoes as he walked next to the grotesque, cotton-candy pink coffin. He sucks on the rum bottle. Then another gulp and another. More and more rum until the room starts to spin. A dizzy blur. In the shower, he scrubs to wash his dick off. Hard and harder. God must have been a woman, he thinks, because no male God would have given men dicks. And he pictures cutting it off. Robin. Why? The razor blade and the slice, and the red. Drip. Drip. Drip. And it will finally stop, and he would feel. He would live. And then dripping out his nose: he looks. Drip. Drip. Drip. His broken tap of a nose. Another fucking nosebleed. He chugs the bottle of Bacardi. A drinking contest, competing with himself. And he thinks of his dog Hercules, how they put him to sleep because he got incurable mange and his body turned into an oozing sore, and he asked his mother why they don't put people to sleep and she hugged him and said, "People ain't brave enough." And he tried to be brave, but the tears escaped as he tied the two sticks cut from the mango tree into a twisted cross as he thought, Big boys don't cry. He remembers standing over his mother's grave as the preacher voice, pasty—"I am the resurrection and the life. He who believes in me shall never die"—unrolled like linoleum and then they slid her down and then the rocks were shoveled and he could only think of her body already rotting and oozing, being battered by the stones, and he was ashamed because he couldn't cry, because men were allowed to cry now.

3

Semiconscious, Chris hugs his body.
He feels marinated in mucus. The boat rocks. His head rolls. Seesaw. The usually soothing submarine sounds, whalelike, of the water sloshing against the boat grate on his nerves, as the rope from
the dock grates against the bow. He feels sick as last night hits. "Oh
God, no gonorrhea, no VD, no herpes." And he thinks of AIDS,
thinks that he has now slept with everyone she has slept with, picturing a stadium, standing room only, stuffed full of assorted erec-
tions, and he remembers his pack of assorted rubbers, all lubricated
and unlubricated, spermicided and unspermicided, the lambskin
and Tahiti colors and that kind with the ribs "for her pleasure."

He hears a noise, opens his eyes, sees the black hand on the
shower faucet. Shark's face flickers. Then a rush of cold water.
"Fuck you," Chris screams, bolting upright, grabbing Shark by the
knees. He trips, tumbles down on top of him. Chris pushes Shark
off. Shark lies in the shower, fully clothed, laughing hysterically and
then choking on the water.

Chris gets up, shivering, wraps himself in a towel, crawls into
bed, pulling the covers over his head. He wants it all to go away.

"Chrisy, come out, come out, wherever you are!" He feels the
sheets pulled off him. He buries his head in the pillow. Then Shark
tickles his toes. "I'm gonna kill you," Chris says, turning over, open-

ing his eyes. Everything flickers, like in an old home movie.

"You play, you pay." Shark laughs, taking off his wet clothes, throwing them on the floor. "I gotta talk to you," he says, putting on a pair of his underwear, his jeans, his T-shirt.

"I feel like I'm getting a migraine," Chris says from under the sheet.

"I'll help you," Shark says, leaving the room.

Chris gets up, stumbles around the cabin searching for his migraine pills, licking the scum on his teeth. He finds the bottle, fights with the childproof top, opens, pours—two more. Thank fucking God, he thinks. He pops the pills, picking up last night's leftover bottle of Duck, swallowing. He wills them down. But up they come. He kneels, head over the toilet, spitting. Spit and pills. And something black. Blood? No, it has legs. A dead cockroach.

He tries to ignore the pain, hearing his Granny Maria telling him about her debut in Trinidad French Creole society when she was invited to the bon soir at Mille Fleurs, the plantation of Monsieur and Madame de la Bastide, "who claimed to be the Marquis of Bon Bon or something stupid so. Dey tink dey so high-whitey-mighty dey shit don't stink, when in truth dose frogs does stink so bad cause dem don't bathe, dem stinking like toilet, no matter how much eau de toilette dey does dab on dey privates. Well, I was beautiful den, you see my legs still beautiful for a woman of ninety. Anyway I's playing uppity knowing dey does call we crème de cacao behind we back, and the good Lord vex at me because I letting the Bon Bon monkey heself pet me pussy under the table, getting he so excited dat he poor me a glass of special Rotchile champagne, an I gulp it down like sweet drink. Dat drink stick in me throat and I tink it be the bubbles and den I feel it's a cockroach crawling in me mouth. I too shame to spit it out. If dat don't teach me, when I shit dat cockroach out, she legs scratch me backside up so bad I think I sitting on stinging nettles. Papa God does work in mysterious ways. So watch youself, boy."

"You O.K.?" Shark asks, concerned, placing his hand on Chris's forehead, supporting his head, then pulling his sweaty hair back off his face.

"There was a fucking roach in the bottle," Chris says. Shark laughs, says, "I'm sorry." Chris gets up, stumbles back to bed, shuts his eyes. He feels Shark sit on the bed next to him, smells Limacol. He remembers the last time he was sick he went to his mother's and she put him in her bed and when he slipped under her satin sheets he felt so much better. His mother fussed and fussed, bringing him little sandwiches with the crusts cut off and bowls full of plump purple grapes, which she peeled and removed the seeds. The lines on her face smoothed out as she filled her Lalique bowl full of crushed ice, then adding a squirt of Limacol, the fresh smell filling the room. He would laugh and point at the Limacol label that said "A Breeze in a Bottle." He would ask her how they got the breeze in the bottle like he did when he was a child and she would smile. She would place her silk scarf into the Limacoled ice until she thought it was cold enough, and then she would pull the scarf out and place it gently on his forehead. He swore to himself that he would give up the coke and the alcohol and he did for almost eight months. Then she died. He couldn't stop dreaming about her, gasping for breath, gasping for him, choking on her own vomit. He woke up grinding his teeth, copped just one line, swearing that was all he would do. And that was it.

Shark takes the cloth from a plastic bowl of ice water he brought from the galley. He removes the cubes and squeezes it out. Ice smoke rises. He places the frigid cloth on his forehead. Chris shuts his eyes and concentrates on the rush of cold. Pain goes into deep freeze.

"Thank . . ." Chris says, and Shark puts a finger on his mouth, muffling the "you."

"So, what can I do for you?" Chris asks.

"Noting," Shark says, shifting on the bed next to him. "It can wait till you better."

Chris opens his eyes. "I'm better. O.K. Talk."

Shark takes the handkerchief from his forehead, squeezes it, puts it back into the ice water. He struggles. "I need . . . want to ask you for . . . Well I got dis one opportunity . . ." He looks down at his hands.

"What?" Chris asks, exasperated, sitting up. His head stabs.

"Green, mon. I need to borrow more money."

Chris pulls the sheet over his head, shuts his eyes, wishes everything would go away. He remembers last year, a couple of months after Christmas, after Shark got fired from Club Med. They were on Shark's Cigarette, the *Black Thunder*, doing massive amounts of coke, and Shark was pacing, sniffing, excited. "I owe it all to you and cocaine," he said, sticking his middle finger into the pile on the silver tray, snorting, licking his fingertip, then rubbing it on his gums. "I find square groupers on dis boat floating with everone kill up and I's sell dat and I's buy some pure white from Pappa Lick, dat albino nigger. Me and dis dude name Blade—cause he skinny as grass blade—put the coke in rubbers and we's slicks dem with oil and swallow dem and bus to Miami. Before I's even shit the shit out, spics at the door trying to score. I drink milk of magnesia till me belly full. I sweat till I start to shit coke-filled dick skins. But dem stick up in Blade gizzard. Fuck me if I know what to do."

And Chris remembers he was so high, and Shark was talking so fast, as if the words were rushing out. "Dis dude called Muerto makes one deal to buy the product for ten thousand. By dat time Blade be freaking. Muerto tell him he gots choice of waiting for the rubber to rot and pop in he stomach or to off heself. And I's not sure whether Muerto's gonna give me the money or shoot me till he asks if I knows the water round Boiling Rock. I's tell him dat I knows every slit and slip and hole and reef like my own dick. He pay me a next ten thousand, to act as a 'pez,' a fish, for him. To guide he boat. Muerto hand one revolver to Blade and he sticks the gun in he mouth and he head turn hamburger. And Muerto pull out one long knife and open Blade gut up, like he cleaning hog or fish, and pull out the coke. Dat very same night, I guide Muerto's Cigarette to Boiling Rock for a pickup. And dat run teach me I born to run and I takes the money Muerto pay and borrow the rest from you and buy me boat. It cokomatic automatic on the *Black Thunder* from dat. Capital E, capital Z, money. E-Z money. I owes it all to you!"

He feels Shark get up from the bed next to him. Chris opens his eyes, pulls the sheet down. Shark is about to leave the room. "Stop," Chris says, thinking, I don't need this shit; I'm not healthy enough for this shit.

Shark turns around, folds his arms tightly in front of him. "You white and you got money."

"Not that fucking shit again."

"Fuck you," Shark says. "Mon, you don't know how hard it is to ask for something cause you got everyting. I work myself up for weeks to ask you for something and you bury your fucking head."

"Oh God," Chris says, sniffing. He rubs his face, breathes deeply. "I don't want to kill you," he says weakly. "Shark, I . . . "

"Who's talking about killing me?" Shark says, exasperated.

"I feel guilty about the money I already lent you. I'm the one getting you further mixed up in the drugs. You gonna end up dead."

"Dat's the ting. You got it upsided down. I want out. I want to buy the Black Pearl space, turn it into the hottest club around, call it the Studio 69. I almost got enough money."

"You're not shitting me?" Chris asks, massaging the indentations on the side of his forehead.

"I's wanna go legit, get out. I don't want you to give it to me. I want you to be my partner."

And there is a slight pleading tone in Shark's voice and this hurts Chris and he asks, "How much?"

"Thirty thousand."

And Chris thinks, What the fuck, it's not like I did anything to get the money, and he thinks, I should give it all away, I don't deserve it, and he knows Shark is telling the truth, knows Shark is probably fooling himself. "O.K.," he says, "I'll be your partner on one condition."

"What?"

"Dat you get the fuck out of here. Let me suffer for my sins in peace."

Shark grins, relaxes on the bed.

"Grab my checkbook from the desk," Chris says, shutting his eyes.

Shark gets the checkbook, brings it over to the bed.

Chris writes out a check, gives it to Shark.

Shark takes the check, folds it, slips it into his back pocket.

"Don't worry. You's gonna get it back plus."

Chris shakes his head. It stabs.

"Thank," he says, and Chris touches Shark's lips, stopping the "you." He feels Shark's hot breath on his finger.

Shark stares at him, his face softening, and Chris thinks how his face usually reveals nothing. He feels for him. "Ever wish I was a girl?" Shark asks.

"What?" Chris feels the blush on his face, avoids his eyes.

"I was just tinking how great it would be if you were a gal . . . If I can find a gal like you. Den we wouldn't, I wouldn't need nothing, no one else."

Chris hugs him clumsily. Shark hugs him back lightly, then tighter. Chris feels his strength, his warmth, feels good, and then afraid. "You promised me you'd fucking leave," Chris hears himself saying as he forces himself to let go, to lie back down. Shark squeezes the handkerchief out, puts it on Chris's forehead. He feels cool all over. He shuts his eyes, hears Shark leave.

Then the pain, like drinking something icy too fast. He wants to take an ice pick, jab it above his left eye. He touches the blood vessel. It twitches like a fish.

More pills, he thinks, as he forces himself up, receiving a direct hit of nausea. He searches. His head pounds. In the medicine cabinet. Toothpaste and toiletries fly across the bathroom. He gives up, tries to pick up the melted gobs of regurgitated pills from the floor. They dissolve in his hands. He licks them, walks back to his bed and pulls the cover over his head, retreating into his own cave of pain. And he hopes Shark is really getting out. And he pictures Shark dead, head blasted like Blade, and he hears the words "I owes it all to you." He grabs his head. I have to get pills, he thinks, have to get to the hospital, as he forces himself up and out.

He drives along Queen's Highway, trying to hold his head still, picturing barefoot boys, all black as tar, he the one white, with skinny arms, feet melting into the road like toasting marshmallows, bravely fighting the pain to prove he's one of them. He feels the burning tar in his head, as hot and soft as the inside of a baked potato, remembering when there was only one paved road on the island, paved by his father's construction company, from pitch shipped from the pitch lake in Chacachacari, Trinidad, where his father told him, "Dere's a lake of tar as big as the sea and stuck in the pitch are dinosaurs and some of Columbus men, who fell in when dey was getting pitch to repitch the *Santa María*." He feels to vomit again, swallowing to keep it down, tasting the bitter after-Bacardi, after-coke, after-sex taste.

He arrives, parks, struggles to the front desk of Angostura Hospital. No one's there. He rings the bell. The sound penetrates his ears as he stares ahead at the plaque that says,

THIS HOSPITAL DONATED TO THE SICK OF THE BAHAMAS
by SIR ODILLO ANGOSTURA

Chris stares at the Disney World haunted-mansion portrait of his father. His father's face, his face, stares back at him. The face that everyone keeps telling him is beautiful. The result of minor members of the European aristocracy arriving in Trinidad with land grants in their hands mixing with multiple major European criminals, chains on their hands. His mouth: ripe lips, watermelon red. His nose: perfect, inherited from a heavy dose of East Indian blood kept securely skeletoned in the closet. The story of his grandfather's grandfather, the governor of Trinidad, decadent aristocracy with a crest to prove it, with the motto PERSEVERANCE WITH JUDGEMENT. He persevered with judgment to rape the fourteen-year-old East Indian servant girl fresh from Calcutta as she served afternoon tea. Maidenhead marmalade spread on freshly honey-buttered crumpets.

Finally he sees his eyes staring back at him from his father's portrait. He sees the look that cut, that his father would give him for no reason, saying, "Boy, if you was half the man I is, if you could do half what I do." And Chris scans the Angostura Hospital waiting room, thinking of everything he accomplished, thinking if his father could only have been as good to him and his mother as he was to everyone else. Chris's head stabs as he hears a noise pulling him out of the daydream. He looks up at He-she, the island's most famous nurse and drag queen. His nurse's cap is perched on top of a bouffant of multicolored sponge curlers. He-she winks and asks, "What happening, Baby Bitter?"

Chris tries to smile, staring at the tiny powder-covered bumps on He-she's face where his beard and mustache should be.

"Pussy got you tongue, handsome? Speak."

"Nurse, I got a migraine. I need pills."

"You sure some big boy didn't give you ram-goat batism?"

"I'm not fucking around."

"Boy, how you could vulgarize me? You got perscription?"

"No."

"You's got to see the doc." He-she takes out a compact and applies some rouge and a fresh layer of lipstick.

"Give me a break."

"You wants me to break the law and end up in Fox Hill jail? I would get stick more dan pin cushion."

"O.K., where's the doctor?"

"Doctor Baboo be at the cancer club," He-she says. "And if you ever wants a woman with a dick bigger dan yours, I's waiting," he snaps and swishes away.

It will only be seconds, minutes, until I get the pills, he tells himself, grabbing his head. He walks across the street to the immunology center. He feels each step deep in his brain. He opens the door, scans the lobby quickly, looking for the doctor. Faces stare at him, spin, then flit like cells through a microscope. He sits, queasy, the greasy vomit rising inside. Sweat pours from every pore. He takes deep breaths. Puffed-out necks, distorted heads, he feels trapped in a carnival sideshow. Trapped on a carnival ride, everything spins faster and faster. The birds are singing, the flowers are blooming, the sun is shining and everyone is dying of cancer. He runs. He leans against the big mango tree, his head propped against the trunk. His eyes fill with water. His mouth fills. The vomit projects, up and out, splashing, clinging to him, in his mouth, on his chin. It keeps coming out.

He feels someone behind him and then hands touch his head, as soft as cashmere. One nestles in his hair. The other touches his brow. He thinks he's imagining it.

"Let it out," the voice says, stroking. The retching continues. It's dry now, but the retching continues. His guts want to follow the poison. "That's good, that's good."

Robin opens a little square packet, the type that comes with lobster at fish restaurants. She rubs the cool wet paper cloth on his forehead. He breathes the smell. Thinks, breeze in a bottle.

"I'm sorry," he says, his voice wobbly. He recovers, feels shame ripen and rot. He shakes his head, looks up at Robin. She lowers her eyes. He feels a cloud pass over the sun as he looks at the tiniest shadow of little freckles on her little nose. He wants to touch them, count them, eat them.

She removes her hand from his forehead. Pain pumps.

"You all right?" she asks.

He tries to speak, smells-tastes his own vomit, shakes his head *yes* as he holds the *no* inside. She walks away fast.

4

Chris walks along the beach, searching for Robin. The scent of suntan oil grows as he approaches the crowd of tourists, oiled pink skin on bright white sand. The Holiday Inn frames them—a pink pastel prison fringed in gingerbread and coconuts. The beach band plays,

> Let me tell you bout a man name Fred
> Poor fisherman, barely kep' he family fed
> Den one day, he be cooking up some chowder
> And down from the sky fall Colombian powder,
>
> Coke dat is, White gold
> Well the first ting you know, old Fred's a millionaire
> He kin folks say, Fred move away from dere
> On Lucayan Beach, to the row of millionaire.

Chris sucks in his gut, stares at the tourists. Two perfect naked breasts stop him. He looks, unable not to look, at dark nipples like eyes staring back. He spots Tweed schooling around the women. Tweed has an overdeveloped, elongated torso and skinny, short legs. His pencil-eraser hair stretches up from his small head.

"It's action Tweed, guaranteeing satisfaction," he says, sauntering up to Chris, cupping his genitals. "My lips sugar, my dick honey, but you ain't getting none, less you got some money." Tweed sticks out his hand.

"I don't want none of that chicken drumstick," Chris says, shaking Tweed's hand the normal way, never knowing the ever changing latest hip handshake.

"What kind of shakes dat is?" Tweed asks, laughing. "You hip starting to drip, you getting queer on me, you turning square."

"I need blow," Chris says.

Tweed sits on a lounge chair. Chris sits next to him on the wet sand, feeling the cool white surf push and pull against and between his legs.

"I got some reef, chief. But, mon, I's out the coke business. Dey bust my brother Harris. Dey say he been dealing and they gets their lackeys to start squealing. I miss Harris. Blood thicker dan pee. Dey bust him coming out the water."

"Why would he have coke in the water?" Chris asks, confused.

Tweed sucks his teeth. "Police got more games dan the Olympics. You got to be born again to keep up with dem."

Then they both turn in the direction of screeching noise.

"Younna tourists gonna singe in hell! Before younna came, dis island was solid rock, rock of Jesus. Now it be cocaine rock," a young man yells through a portable microphone. His face sunglazed, red-black and pretty. He has on a flame-colored jogging suit, looks like he should be rapping on MTV.

The band gets louder. The preacher gets louder.

"In the name of the Lord. Stop shipping coke through we country and perverting we youth with car, an stereo, and wall-to-wall carpet," the preacher yells, waving his arms dramatically.

"Dat dude sound like he head base out bad as mad," Tweed says.

"It's not better in the Bahamas, it's louder. Aye, Tweed?" Chris watches the tourists pretend to ignore the commotion.

"See Sister Ev and her band of bigoty Bahama mamas over dere," Tweed says, pointing at the straw market vendors. "She in charge of God on dis beach."

"That's my Aunt Evalina," Chris says, staring at her. She looks away from the preacher, out to sea, her plump face pinched. She sits regally on a Spam box under a Beck's umbrella, her hands working straw automatically, surrounded by colorful straw hats and dolls and bags. About ten other straw vendors form a line up the beach.

"If dat you auntie, I's queen of England," Tweed says, standing.

"Catch you later, Your Majesty."

"Cool!" Tweed struts away.

Chris runs into the ocean. When the water reaches his knees, he falls forward into it, a slap of a splash. He stands up, flicking his hair back, and then walks out of the water and up to Evalina.

"My sugar dumpling." She stands up, her face lit up, opening her arms.

Chris reaches his arms around her and hugs. She feels like a giant marshmallow as he squeezes her harder and then picks her up, her sweet thatch smell swallowing him up.

"Put me down, boy," she says, laughing, as he feels her belly roll.

"Pay no mind, he white and I's dark as the moon backside. Dis my chile," she says to the other straw vendors. "I mind he when worm would make he man-snake shame." The straw vendors chuckle.

"Enjoying the sermon?" Chris teases Tantie, sitting next to her on the box.

"I vex too bad," she says, squishing up her face. "Botheration for so!" She sucks her teeth, putting down her straw work. "I fighting to make a living and dis flat-nose bad-john has to come playing messiah to speechify my clientele. Too much hypocrite!" she yells, pointing at the preacher.

Chris laughs loudly, looks at the preacher, shakes his head. The preacher makes eye contact with him, starts yelling, pointing at him. "I means you, white, Conchy Joe. Quit pushing drugs up you nose-thrill. Push you nose in Bible."

"Push your nose in your own business," Chris yells. His left leg starts to shake.

Evalina yells, "Sisters! Can the congregation say, 'Praise the Lord'?" Her thick bottom lip trembles.

"Praise the Lord!" the other straw vendors repeat, all standing at once. They are all sizes, ages and shades of brown, dressed in bright skirts and fading T-shirts.

"Thank you, Jesus," Tantie replies, raising up a yellow parasol and walking toward the preacher with the other straw vendors behind her, humming "Onward Christian Soldiers."

The formidable group surrounds the preacher. The band stops playing and walks over to watch. Chris follows. The preacher and Evalina stare at one another. It's very quiet. Only the sounds of waves breaking. Everyone waits.

Finally the preacher wipes the sweat from his face and asks Evalina, "What you want, or is it you like staring up people's faces so?"

Tantie frowns. "You see dat white boy dere?" she says calmly, pointing at Chris. "He's mine, even though he ain't black, and what you call the son, you call the mother. Praise the Lord."

"Praise the Lord," the group replies, forming a tighter circle around Tantie and the preacher.

Chris wishes he could bury his head in the sand as he pushes through the group to Evalina. "Don't worry," he tells her. She puts her hand on his shoulder and says to the preacher, "He be as good as me, cause I raise him Christian, an he would have been a preacher if he didn't want to sex every woman he meet. Pitch stone at him an you pitchin' stone at me! He who ain't got he no sin, pitch the first stone." Her lip stops twitching.

The preacher stares, a dramatic, shocked look on his face, yells, "My heart does burn up dat you high-basted exaggerate self could bawl like twenty Tarzan at the good Lord's servant."

Chris stares at the preacher's black gums. "Leave her alone," he says, grabbing Evalina's hand, trying to pull her away, and she squeezes his hand and then explodes. "Ragamuffin, I was God servant when you black ass was still in diapers! You still got mama milk stuck round you mouth!"

"A woman who son Shark does be the biggest devil-pusher on the island does have the conspunction to mouth my ministry," the preacher stammers.

The vendors look stunned as Evalina walks forward, her big

hands clenched into fists, until she is only inches from the preacher's face. She cuts her eyes at him. "God don't like ugly!" Evalina preaches, sticking her finger in the preacher's sweaty face as one of the vendors pitches backward as if her legs have been kicked out from under her. Her body lies still, dead weight, as everyone watches, waiting. Spit dribbles out of the corner of her mouth, and then she makes a gargling noise; her eyes roll; her nostrils flare. Evalina rushes to her fallen sister. The preacher skulks away. "All you preacher's falseness has worked Obeah-Voodoo on poor sister Blossom," she yells at the preacher's back. Blossom twitches, slow and subtle at first, like if she's shaking a fly off her body. Then she convulses. A group of tourists have now joined the audience. A lady says, "I think it's a native show." Evalina begins to work the crowd. "See the body move as if it ain't ever hear of gravity," she says as the sisters surround Blossom, trying to hold her down. "It the devil self jucking she so." Then Evalina sits on top of Blossom as her body explodes upward, carrying Evalina with it. Blossom grunts and moans and barks.

Evalina places her hand on Blossom's forehead, going into a trance, chanting: "Ten, ten, the Bible ten—the devil is in her legs—we's command you in God name—out! It in her stomach now! Out!" With this, Blossom's stomach starts to convulse as if she's having a baby. She twists and gasps, her skirt tangled above her waist. She's covered in sweat. The vendors chant, "Out, Satan! Out!"

"Out of the dark hole, out the dark side to white darkness. Devil, you'll take no zombies here," Evalina shrieks, her eyes glazed over until Blossom farts. Members of the congregation hold their breath and their noses and then make the sign of the cross, a sign of relief. Chris smiles as the smell of rotten eggs drifts out to sea. Evalina and Blossom recover together to a chorus of alleluias.

The tourists clap loudly and give Evalina money. She stuffs the money in her pockets, saying, "I's ask you tourists for anyting?" Then she grabs Chris's hand and says, "Let we go cool out."

They walk up the beach in silence, sit down under a cannonball tree. Sun shines through the blowing leaves of the tree, shimmering shade and sun spots as if blowing across Evalina's face. She tries to smile, her round cheeks plump plums under her eyes, black lips pulled tight across too many eggshell white teeth. He looks into her eyes. He aches. "Dat false preacher right," she says, picking at her fleshy arms. "My Shark. A pusher. And he want to buy me tings. I tell him, I ain't want no blood money."

"He's getting out of the business. He's opening a club in the old Black Pearl space. I'm his partner. I've been helping him. He's gonna have the best club in the whole Bahamas." And Chris thinks of visiting him last night at the 69, sees himself and Shark snorting and then smashing. Heavy sledgehammers in their hands, they slammed them against the wall over and over, slabs and chips and concrete powder flying and falling, white power up their nose, floating down covering them. They pulled off their shirts. The powder stuck to their sweat, slowly coating them as the coke coated their brains, and they laughed and screamed, and Shark yelled, "It's snowing. We're finally seeing snow," and it felt so good, the destruction, and they smashed until they could smash no more, and snorted until they could snort no more, and they collapsed together in front of the demolished wall and Chris remembers yelling, "Shark, you finally turned white."

"Thank You. Praise the Lord," Evalina says, her face relaxing as she says, "My beautiful boy-baby," squeezing him tight, and he remembers hugging her, not letting her go, when he was a child.

"Please, take me home with you, Evalina," he begged.

"But Chris, you ain't belongs to me. I ain't you mama," she answered. Then she picked him up and held him in front of her face so they were staring into each other's eyes and she said softly, "No matter where the good Lord put me, you will always be my beautiful boy-baby."

Chris opens his eyes, sees a woman walking on the beach. He takes off his glasses, wipes his eyes, squints. It's her. She sees him, hesitates, then keeps walking slowly.

"Bye, Tantie," Chris says, staring at the woman's back.

Tantie's face flashes hurt and then she follows his gaze and smiles, saying, "Crab gotta crawl if he wanna get fat." He kisses her cheek and it tastes of her, of the big kitchen, of snapper fried in butter and onion.

Chris follows. Maybe it isn't Robin, he thinks. What should I say? He looks down at his big footprints next to her small footprints on the sand. Then her shadow. Then her.

"Robin?" His voice cracks. He feels his heart beat.

She stops, turns. He stares from behind his mirrored sunglasses at her mirrored sunglasses, at the reflection of himself looking at her. He focuses on her needle-prick-sized diamond earring catching sunlight, half covered by a parsley-colored paisley scarf that covers her hair. He takes a deep breath, pictures the multicolored beach. She takes off her glasses. Her brown-black eyes squinting. He wants to run away and clasp her at the same time. They look at each other. Silence. He takes a deep breath.

"You're not going to throw up?" Robin asks, smirking, putting her glasses back on.

"If you want me to," Chris says, smiling.

"I'm not that kinky."

"Pity," he says.

"Most guys don't reveal what's inside so easily," Robin says, starting to walk up the beach. He follows her, feeling himself begin to calm down.

"I'm very sensitive," Chris says.

She laughs. "Yeah, like fuck me baby, I'm sensitive."

"Sugar and spice and everything nice, that's what little girls are made of."

"I'm not a little girl," she says, stopping, playfully pushing out her chest.

He wants to bury his tongue between her breasts. "Wo-man," he says.

"Purrrr," she says. "Hear my roar."

"I'm a little boy," he says.

"I know," she says, challenging.

"No you don't," he says.

"So tell me."

"What."

"Everything."

"You first," he says. "Where were you all week? I looked all over. What were you doing at the cancer clinic?" And then he tells himself to shut up, stop asking so many questions. He bites the skin on his thumb, checking her for lumps, any irregularity.

"My mother's a patient," she says, walking ahead.

He picks up the pace, relieved that it's not her. They fall into step together, walking on the in and out of the waves' foam, making their feet appear and disappear.

"Your turn." She stares. "How did you end up in this weird place?"

"My mom didn't know how to use a tea bag."

"That explains it."

"It's a long story."

"I like long stories."

"My family's from Trinidad. When they went from white to black power, the blacks nationalized my dad's company. He made bitters."

"Bitters? Like they put in drinks?"

"Angostura Bitters. As the label says, 'The bitters are famous throughout the civilized world, because of their delightful flavor and aroma, and as a pleasant and dependable relief of flatulence.' "

"Does your family make anything to relieve bullshit?"

"I'm telling the truth."

"I know," she says. "I knew you were heir to something. You reek of TFB."

"What?"

"Trust-fund baby."

"Jealous?" Chris asks, feeling the jab.

"Sure am."

"Do you want to hear how I ended up in Freeport or not?" Chris asks, changing the subject.

She shakes her head.

"My dad wouldn't reveal the secret bitters recipe. So they put him in jail, supposedly for tax evasion. But even, as he said, when they put him in a cell where at high tide the water washed up to his waist, causing his balls to shrivel like salt peanuts, he refused. As the water washed in, he dreamed of creating his own world, on his own island, where he would be king and there would be no taxes. It would be a free port. He would call it Freeport."

Chris pauses. His face stares back at him from her mirrored glasses, blindly. He wishes he could see her eyes.

"So you make bitters. Kind of ironic. Doesn't fit."

"You mean, like I should be making sweets?"

"No, I mean like you should be making sex toys."

Chris laughs. They continue walking. Multicolored triangular sails of Hobie Cats, Sunfishes, Wind Surfers fly across turquoise ocean. "What about your mom, the tea?"

"My mom was my dad's secretary. She was the only one not afraid to visit him in jail. She was only sixteen. And my dad decided to make her his queen. According to him, he made her, and yours truly, right there between the jail bars. As she was placing little cubes of ripe mango on his tongue."

Robin leans forward, amused. "Did she drop the mango?"

"Probably not, knowing my mother. Anyway, when my dad got out of jail, he married my mom at the airport. She was nine months pregnant. Then they flew to Miami."

A square of sunlight settles on Robin's cheek. He starts to enjoy himself, continues. "Now we get to the tea part," he says, performing. "My mother was so happy to get to Miami because people were all white like her. She ordered a cup of tea at the airport café. The white waiter brought the tea in a tea bag. She had never seen a white waiter or tea in a bag before. She was too shy to ask the waiter what to do with the strange bag. She just ripped it open and poured the leaves in her cup of hot water. The waiter laughed when she got up the nerve to ask him to strain the cup. He brought her a fresh cup, telling her that you have to leave the tea in the bag. So when the sugar came in a little paper bag, she learned from her mistake with the tea. Just dumped the sugar bag into her cup. This time, not only the waiter laughed but all the people around her. And she started to cry."

Robin laughs. "I'm sorry I'm laughing," she says. Chris feels good, imagines licking her teeth.

"After that my mom told my dad to get her the hell out of America because it's so uncivilized they don't even know how to make a cup of tea. They took the next plane to the Bahamas. My mother's water broke as the plane touched down. That woman I was just talking to on the beach, Evalina, Shark's mother, delivered me. I was the first white baby ever born on this island."

Robin claps her hands. Chris bows.

"My mother told me that my dad took me from Evalina's hands right after I came out. They didn't even have time to wipe the gook off. My dad carried me to this beach, held me up to the stars, and told me that this beach was where all the hotels and mansions were going. 'It's all for you, baby Chris,' he said, 'I's gonna build you a city and you're gonna be prince of Freeport.' "

"So you're a prince?"

"And you're a princess."

"Yuck!" she screams, turning around, walking the other way. He grabs her hand.

"Does that line usually work?"

"About ninety percent of the time. You're supposed to fall into my arms."

"Not this damsel in distress," she says, pulling her hand away from his, flexing her arm, showing a tiny muscle.

He flicks her biceps. "Frog. Frog. That's what you are."

"That's better," she says. "I always liked frogs better than princes. My grandfather taught princes. He was tutor to the Russian court. My mother would have to line up in doily dresses and be touched on the head by Rasputin. At the outbreak of the Russian Revolution my grandfather was staying at a suite in the Plaza buying arms for the tsar. He ended up having to wash dishes to pay his bill. My mother and grandmother were smuggled out on a Finnish fishing boat. All they had was a silver spoon. That's how my family ended up in New York City."

"I read that Rasputin's power came from a giant wart on his penis which was in a perfect position to stimulate the clitoris."

"I prefer my penises wartless. Call me bizarre." She laughs and then he laughs. "Even though I'm a frog, I prefer my penises wartless."

They walk past a fifty-foot royal poinciana tree and he remembers everyone laughing at his father when he said he could build a city on this forgotten island. But this didn't stop him from writing to the queen to ask her for land to build Freeport. The queen replied that she had an incurable case of flatulence ever since the Angostura bitters factory closed down, and she would lease him the land on the island of Grand Bahama for ninety-nine years if he built a new bitters factory. She even promised to visit the imaginary city to open the new factory.

"When I was little, Shark and I would play pirates all day long on this beach. There were no hotels, motels, or condos. There was only a small village and mountains of stinking conchs."

"When I was little in New York, I would stare out our window at all the other buildings and pretend they were my friends," she says, sadly. He wants to touch her, comfort her, break through, and he doesn't know why. "Friend," he starts to say.

She catches the look. Shakes her head. "Tell me another story. Tell me one you haven't told all the other tourist women you've walked up this beach."

"Ouch!" Chris says.

"If the shoe fits."

"Queen queen conch."

"What?"

"I'll tell you about the queen queen conch crisis."

"I can't wait."

"It happened when the queen of England decided to visit Freeport. This beach used to be lined with piles of stinking conch shells."

"How did they get there?"

"The villagers would throw the shells on the piles after they cracked the conchs out. The men in the village led by Doctor Conch, who was like the mayor, wanted to leave them alone. As Doctor Conch said, 'With repect, the queen self does have cameo made from queen conch dat she does like better dan she crowns.' The women, led by Miss Maple Proudfoot, the only woman in the village who smoked a pipe, replied, 'With repect to the good doc, I does read plenty white people book and read dat limey royalty weak cause all dems got blue blood instead of red, cause dey does mate with family worse dan Conchy Joe, dat one princess did get all hurt up because some stupid nigger maid spit one of her peas when she was eating peas and rice under the queen mattress.' Maple said, 'If pea can cause all dat, what gonna happen when she does glimpse all dem ugly rotting shells, far less when her nose holes get scratch by the conch pile stank?' "

"You do the accent so well. I love it."

"That's because I used to talk like that. Before I went away to this fucked-up boarding school in Florida, before I made myself talk like a Yankee so the kids wouldn't make fun of me."

"So what happened to the shells?"

"Doctor Conch yelled: 'Dere ain't enough elbow grease in the village to get rid of dem conch anyway. Besides the scientific name for dem conchs is queen conch and the queen self must be name dem dat because she like dem so.' He said, 'A lot of school-bought learning be what ruinating the Bahamas.' "

"Missy Maple," Chris says, imitating a woman's voice, "replied, 'The problem wit dis island is it be run by old men with no learning bout nothing but conch, and gold and silver may tarnish away but good education be here to stay, so we women is not gonna continue to just cook and juck you good-for-noting toeties.' The women in the village cheered. They decided to 'hold back on dere sex favors till something be done with the shells.' "

"You're making this up," Robin says, smiling.

"No I'm not."

"I think it happened once before in ancient Greece."

"I don't know, I don't know about *Lysistrata*, only conch and limbo. Remember."

"And how to pick up tourist girls," she snickers.

"Women," Chris says.

"Touché."

"Turtle."

"Conch," Robin says. "What happened with the conch?"

"Finally the women themselves pushed the piles of conch just below the surface of the water, because, they said, 'playing virgin was paining dem more dan the mens.' "

"Now I know you're making this up."

"Everyone in the village was so excited when the queen arrived. They were dressed up in their wedding-funeral best, innocently yelling 'Rule, Britannia.' Then the wind changed. The conchs gave off such a stink, the queen fainted into my dad's arms. He revived her with smelling salts. She was pissed."

"What did she do?" Robin asks, and Chris can tell from her expression that he has softened her, sucked her in, and he feels good.

"She yelled at my dad that the people in Freeport had worse bouquet d'Afrique than any subjects in her entire empire. She yelled that there was no way he would ever build a city on this smelly island. And from then until independence, everyone in Freeport got a bottle of Limacol on Christmas. Everyone knew it was a present from the queen because it said on the label, 'By Appointment to Her Majesty the Queen of England.' "

Robin claps again. He bows grandly.

"Are you a writer?" Robin asks. "You should be a writer."

"No, I'm a reader," Chris says, feeling ashamed, never knowing what to say when people ask him what he does.

She laughs. And he thinks of his father, thinks how he had the last laugh. Freeport, Angostura company town, foreign hands on the till, where the elite meet and the blacks serve, playground of the Western world, grew despite growing pains, an epidemic of a rare type of color blindness, blinding people to the fact that Freeport was a white town in a black country.

"Chris!" two small black children yell. They drop their boxes full of conch shells and run toward him and Robin.

Chris picks them up. First the girl, then the boy. He kisses them. They are twins, all eyes and teeth, exactly the same size and weight, skinny rubbery arms and legs.

"I'd like you to meet my friends, Roscoe and Gwen. They are the best conch sellers on the beach," he says to Robin.

Robin bows down and shakes their hands.

"Dis you girlfriend?" Roscoe asks Chris, giggling.

"She wants to be," Chris answers.

"I think it's the other way around," Robin says.

"Play hard to get and Gwen will be my girlfriend."

"You wish," Gwen says. Robin smiles. Chris pretends to sulk.

"If you won't be my girlfriend, we won't build a castle," Chris says to Gwen.

"Please," Gwen begs. Her eyes open wide.

Chris sits down on the sand, above where the waves are breaking.

"Let's teach Robin how to make a drip castle," he says, digging a small hole in the sand until he reaches water. Roscoe's and Gwen's small black hands scoop white sand, widening the hole.

"What about me?" Robin asks. Her sunflower yellow one-piece swimsuit shines. Her nipples poke out. Her belly button pokes in.

"You have to sit next to me."

"Yuck," she says to Gwen, sitting next to Chris, her leg touching his leg. He feels a current.

"We have to dig the hole until it's big enough for Roscoe and Gwen to sit in. Then we put the sand into piles around the hole, and finally we cover the piles with drips. Then we have a drip castle."

As Chris watches her hands dig, he sees his mother's hands covered in brown dirt as she dug in the backyard. And he's ten years old again and the blacks had just won the election with the motto "Let your ballot be your bullet," taking over so peacefully that the whites didn't know what hit them. Chris remembers his mother gulped rum every time Radio ZNS reported another island voting black with the chant "Massa Day Done!" and when the results came in for Freeport, she screamed, "Oh my God, but it Trinidad all over again." Chris sees his hands covered in brown dirt as he helped his mother dig, watching as her tears fell and were absorbed in the dirt as she took off her wedding ring with the five diamonds and wrapped it in tinfoil and dropped it into the hole, and covered it up with dirt. His father yelled, "The Angostura family gots too much money for any monkey Bahama government to touch." And then his mother touched his father on the forehead, begging him to get them off the island, and he pushed her away, laughing. That night, the mothball smell of the closet mixed with the smell of starch on her pleated dress as he fell asleep, his head resting on his mother's lap behind the locked door of the upstairs closet, feeling the beads of her rosary stroke his hair as she prayed. He said, "Mama, don't worry, the black people are our friends."

"We white—black peoples never be our friends," she answered.

The next morning, the sun was out and everything was normal, and that evening the new, black prime minister knocked on the door of the Angostura castle and Odillo sent Evalina to tell him to go around back to the servants' entrance. The prime minister banged at the door, yelling, "If you don't learn how to fish or cut bait, you have to get the hell out of my Bahama boat. Freeport will have to bend or break." The prime minister broke down the door and later broke Freeport.

Roscoe and Gwen crawl into the hole. They all take handfuls of sandy water, letting a slow smooth stream run through their fingers like pancake batter. The stream solidifies, each drop turning to sand. They cover the piles of sand with drips. They top off each castle with crooked points, extra slow, one drop at a time, each drop smaller and smaller. Robin doesn't know when to stop the points, and she adds too many drops and her castle tops crumble and tumble.

"The drip castle looks like a Gaudí," Robin says. "He's this architect."

"I know," Chris says, interrupting. "Drip castles look like his church, la Sagrada Familia."

"I spent a week in Barcelona staring at it."

"I was obsessed by it," Chris says, excited. "I bribed the guards and camped out there one night."

And she takes off her glasses and squints, staring at him. He stares back from behind his glasses and he's sure he sees something about her shift slightly and he feels a connection, an intimacy, and he once again wants to flee and clutch at the same time.

She sees this, cuts it off by dropping her glasses back over her eyes. "You only know about conch and limbo. Remember."

"I know how to pick up beautiful, intelligent, tough tourist women," he says, picking up Roscoe, holding him above his head. "Birdy time," Chris says, and Roscoe screams, "Hooray!" stretching out his arms. Chris runs, flying him up the beach.

Robin picks up Gwen and flies her behind them. Chris remembers laughing when his father would pick him up, and he would stretch his arms out and pretend to be a bird. His father would tell him to take a good smell. He would sniff. "What you smell?" his father would ask.

"Conch slop," Chris would answer.

"I smell Yankee dollars, green like grass. A tax-free community stuck fifty miles off the ass of the Yankee dollar-bill land can't lose. Remember dat, little Chris."

"Fly me some more," Chris would beg.

Chris and Robin put the children down.

"How much for your conchs?" Chris asks. Roscoe's and Gwen's faces light up. "Ten dollar," Roscoe says. Chris gives them twenty. Ten each.

"Thanks, Chris," Roscoe says.

"I like you girl friend, she pretty," Gwen says, and then they giggle and run off into the distance. Small black arms outstretched, pretending they're flying.

Chris gives Robin the prettiest conch shell and throws the others into the water. They skip-splash-flash, then disappear.

Robin looks at him, her face a question. She holds the shell to her ear. He looks away at an old man approaching, his brown body spotted with browner age spots, not much more than a paunch connected to bones. He's bent over, as if connected to his Treasure Tracker metal detector. His eyes squint. The aluminum arm of the detector gleams. He sweeps it back and forth, concentrating, listening through the earphones for the sound of treasures below the sand.

"That's Anteater. He once found a ring on the beach. He was so happy he sold it and used the money to buy the metal detector. He hasn't found anything since."

"Any treasure today?" Chris asks.

"Twenty bottle tops, one American penny and a Bahamian quarter," Anteater replies.

Robin's alarm watch beeps. "I've got to go," she says, looking pained. She jogs ahead. Chris follows behind. She stops. He stops and watches. Her hands are covered in white sand as she digs, taking off her diamond earring. She drops it into the hole, covers it up with sand. Then she runs toward a car parked along the beach.

Chris looks at the covered-up hole, at the Anteater, as he sweeps toward him.

He runs after Robin. "Why?" he yells.

She doesn't stop.

"I want to see you again!" The car door slams.

The car pulls away. He hears Anteater scream excitedly. "I found something!"

5

Chris spits in his mask, dips it into sea, sees himself looking at himself with climbing coral, flitting fish, sifting sea-fans superimposed on his image. He washes the spit out with ocean, puts on his mask, sucks the snorkel into his mouth, tasting rubber. He grabs his Hawaiian sling, slips out of the boat, rippling the mirror. Swimming toward a mound of star coral, he thinks of Robin. Starlight, star bright, afraid to wish. He's driven by some alien force. Me caveman, me strong, me kill. He sees a flash, bright with silver white metal. Then it comes into view. A plane, half smashed, its nose grounded, blunted, sticking out from behind brain coral. He surfaces for air quickly, then swims back down. The plane's tail sits straight up, rudder shivering in the current. He swims, peering into the cockpit, through a gash of gnarled metal, at piles of duffel bags. Then a skull. Bone white, empty eye sockets. Chris snaps his eyes shut, swims up fast, pushing the picture out, opening his eyes when his head emerges into sunlight.

He floats, breathing deeply, thinking, Too much coke to fight the flying fatigue on the way from Colombia or the plane was over-loaded or it ran out of gas.

Chris swims back down. A lobster walks backwards—up under the wing. He follows, spots lots of lobster tentacles like oversized in-sect antennae poking out from underneath. Adrenaline builds. The thrill of the hunt. He surfaces, breathes deeply, lungs stretching to capacity. Holding the air, he dives, pulls back the sling, aims, fires. The spear rips through the lobster, clinking as it hits the plane. He reaches under the wing but he can't pull the spear out. The lobster struggles silently, its tail kicking up a cloud of powdery white sand.

Chris races up, his lungs burning. Exhale. Bubbles flow from his mouth, floating, flattening, getting bigger and bigger. They fizz out at the surface. Momentary relief and then the real hollow pain as he fights his way up, racing his air bubbles, bracing against the black. In a near faint, he greedily sucks air. With new strength from new air, he swims back down, pulls the spear with the lobster from under the wing. He glides up, turns the spear upside down, slides the lobster, its tail snapping, into the boat. He shoots until there are no more lobsters.

Breathless, thrilled, the breeze brushing his moist body, he climbs onto the boat. He watches the lobsters crawl around the back of the boat like prehistoric armored cars. The sun dries droplets, leaving him feeling sheathed in salty silk stockings as he pictures his mother's silk stockings, remembers yesterday, pushing his father in his wheelchair through the outdoor market. His father held a box of Angostura Bitters on his lap. He and his father nodded and said hello to people when they saw their faces light up from behind booths, their bodies blocked by colorful, slick, squirming piles of snapper, grouper, angelfish, bonitos, grunts, goggle-eyes, crawfish. He inhaled the strong morning-after sex smell. He couldn't stop thinking of Robin. He had spent another week after she ran away from him on the beach looking for her and he couldn't find her anywhere. He was afraid she had left the island. Scales stuck to his shoes. Conch slop flew. The sound of hammers cracking conch shells and woven baskets full of crab claws clawing and crawling and knives scaling. A fish-faced woman yelled at them, "Two dollar for unicorn fish. If you man's ting dry up like prune, unicorn fish make it harder dan honeymoon." People in the aisles stopped them. His father beamed, as they fussed over him, and gave them each a bottle of bitters.

Then they were surrounded by multisized naked-looking carcasses with pink membranelike skin dripping puddles of blood, covered in vibrating flies. Chris's father said, "Boy, when you mama die she take me heart with she. I plan on everything but she dying first." Chris put his hand clumsily on his father's shoulder, looked away at masses of organs: purplish hearts, red-black livers, sponge-like greenish lungs, bowls of fluffy ground beef, and fat plantain-shaped blood sausages jiggling in the glass cases. Behind the counter of Susalee Meat Inc. sat meaty Susalee in bloodstained white apron cutting thick slices from a fat hunk of fatty meat. She yelled, "For putting the heat back in you old man meat. Buy some of Susalee special treat." Chris's father laughed, choked, coughed; spit dribbled from his mouth. Chris wiped it with his handkerchief. Then from between a carcass and a vat of lard he saw Robin and then he saw Shark and they were together, laughing, and his heart skipped a beat and he wanted to punch the smile off Shark's fuck-ing face and then Shark saw him, and shrugged his shoulders. Shark walked over to him and his father. Robin followed nervously. "You bout to punch another wave, mon?" Shark said, flashing an exasper-ated look, and he grabbed his hand and grabbed Robin's hand and put them together. And Chris felt guilty for being jealous of him. "Chrisy wanna tell you dat he been sulking like love-sick cow, searching up dis island for you since you run off, and dat you have been driving he crazy and he been driving me crazy and will you two stop fucking around and live happy ever after . . . "

"Shut up," Chris said, shocked, putting his hand over Shark's mouth. Shark grabbed Chris's hand from his mouth, took it and twisted it behind his back. Robin stared at him amused. Shark let go. Silence.

"Maria," his father said. "She look like Maria."

"Maria was my mother," Chris said. "This is my father, Odillo."

She crouched down on the ground, touched his father's hand and then held it. Her touch seemed to light him up.

"This is Robin, Dad."

"Marry this one, boy," he said urgently.

He shrugged, rolled his eyes at Robin. She imitated his shrug.

"She won't even go out with me, Dad," Chris said, thinking, She's not going to get away. He stared at Robin, waiting for her re-action. She stared back mischievously. Then smiles ricocheted.

"Chris would like to ask you out. How bout tomorrow, seven o'clock?" Shark said.

"Dey don't come no better dan my Chris, he's an Angostura," his father said.

"If he tells me a story," she said.

Chris stood there, thinking.

"Tell her a fucking story, mon," Shark said.

"Romeo and Juliet," his father said.

"I've never heard that one," Robin teased.

"Juliet was the first cow on the island. The first we'd ever seen. She was so big and black that Shark and I didn't believe Evalina when she said . . . "

"Dat milk does come out from dat pink titty between the cow legs," Shark said.

"Because we knew that milk came from a powder that came in boxes that you mixed with water. And then the four biggest men in the village sort of pushed and pulled Romeo the bull off the boat, and he was just like the cow only bigger and blacker and he had horns. Hanging down between his legs he had a big black sack that scraped the floor when he walked. When the woman in the village saw it they started to bawl and clap."

"Dey yelled, 'Dat is balls, father.' "

"And 'It take a bull from America to shame up all the mens in the Bahamas,' " his father said.

Chris focused on Robin's lips, the color of an overripe tomato, as she smiled. "We have a date," she said to Chris. "Whether you want one or not."

"I want . . . ," Chris said, feeling so happy and relieved.

"Make him plenty babies, gal," his father said, handing her a bottle of bitters.

"I think I'll wait for the second date for that," Robin said.

Then Chris pushed his father in his wheelchair fast and they all laughed hard. "I'm flying you, Dad," Chris said. Robin and Shark walked next to them. Chris felt a curious mix of pride and fear to see the way the men watched Robin walk by. They had an animal look, very sexual in their eyes, and made no attempt to hide it.

A lobster snaps its tails. Chris looks down, counts them. Two big ones, eight average and one baby. He picks up the largest lobster. Oily orange roe clings like moss under its tail. He wants to put her back in the ocean but he knows she will just die, as he tries to stuff the broccoli green gook that's leaking out of her head back inside.

He gives up. Clutching the head in one hand and the tail in the other, he twists the head clockwise, the tail counterclockwise, grits his teeth as he hears a silent scream and then the terrible popping sound like cracking knuckles. The head finally yanks from the tail. He throws the head overboard and puts the tail, still convulsing, confused, into the cooler.

Eleven pops. Eleven agitating tails. He watches the engine churn, bubbling froth like whipping cream from blue-blue sea as he heads for shore. He thinks, When someone is guillotined, they come when the blade chops. And he thinks about spearfishing last week with Shark off Memory Rock, how they found a line of lobsters, thousands, marching single file, head to tail, like a conga line. Every time they speared one, the one behind would move ahead to fill up the gap. They got so many tails the Whaler almost sank and that night they went to SLURP, the Spiny Lobster Undersea Research Project, and all the lobsters marched militarily around and around the edges of the tanks, clinging to one another like cling peaches, a darkened form forming one completed line of connect-the-dots. Finally they stopped after two weeks. Delicious stillness of spindly, spiny lobster legs.

Back at the dock, on his yacht, Marley plays on the radio. He chops onion in time to the music:

> One love? One heart?
> Let's get together and feel all right
> as it was in the beginning.
> One love,
> so shall it be in the end.
> One heart.

Chris hears the engine of a passing boat. The wake chops as the boat bobs, as uniform translucent ovals like fish scales stick and fall off the steel blade. The onion juice cuts into his eyes. He blinks, a tear slips. He feels it struggle against five o'clock shadow, and then it drops into the pile of chopped onion. Disappears. He arranges the pile into a heart shape.

A knock on the door. Chris freezes, pulls off his Speedo, pulls on a pair of old bleached 501's. The jeans are ripped above his left thigh, revealing a slit of tanned skin. He looks at himself in the mirror, tenses his pecs. Doesn't put on a shirt.

He hesitates, opens the door. Robin stretches out her hands, her face covered by a bird-of-paradise flower, its reddish orange sepals rising up like burning, outstretched wings. He takes the plant, takes her in, takes a deep breath. The aluminum foil that surrounds the pot crinkles.

She flicks a tear off his cheek. "Happy to see me?" she asks. She's dressed in an oversized red shirt tied at the waist, sleeves rolled up, and a matching pleated skirt. Her matching, very red lipsticked lips pucker. Chris pictures the imprint of a child's kiss. She smells of earth. His cheek tingles from her touch.

"Onions," he says nervously, placing the plant on the coffee table.

"Not tears of happiness?" she asks sarcastically, kicking off her sandals. Her toenails are painted red.

"Tears of frustration," he says, fighting the urge to kneel at her feet and suck them.

"Poor baby," she says with mock concern. "You live such a hard life." Her eyes sweep over the yacht. She stretches out her arms, long and porcelain tinted. They shake.

"Life's not fair," he says, walking to the bar. She follows him, her fingers caressing the sleek teak, stopping at a row of books, reading the titles.

Then her fingers caress his arm the same way she caressed the teak. He feels his skin spark under her touch. He imagines ripping off her clothes and fucking her till she comes. And then he wouldn't be afraid any longer.

"Drink?" he asks, trying to picture what her face would look like when she comes.

"Anything." She flirts, flitting her eyelashes, leaning over the bar.

Chris squeezes a lime. "One of sour," he says, feeling as if he's caught in the first act of a play. She leans closer. A drop of juice squirts, dangles from his chin. She grins, touches the bead with her thumb and then licks it with her tongue. "Two of sweet." He adds two tablespoons of sugar syrup. "Three of strong," he continues as he pours three shots of rum. "And finally, four of weak." He adds four ice cubes to the silver cocktail shaker and shakes like a pair of shack-shacks. He pours punch into fluted glasses, adds a dash of Angostura Bitters to each. The frothy frigid mixture causes condensation to drip down as a breath of icy smoke drifts up. Their glasses clink. He watches her face as she tastes it, watches the tip of her pink tongue reach, lick her bottom lip.

"It makes sense that you live on a boat," she says, moving to the couch. She crosses her legs.

"How so?" Chris sits on the carpet in front of her.

"You're floating. Fluid. The way you move makes me think of water." She looks at him. "The boat's kind of like a shell. You can pull into it. Escape when things get tough. Like a turtle."

"I'm more like a hermit crab, living in someone else's shell. Not the boat but Freeport." He takes a sip of his drink, thinking she's the one always escaping, running away, and he wants to ask her about it but he can't.

"But you've been part of this place from the beginning."

"Freeport's got a black Virgin, a black Santa and a black Ronald McDonald. I'm a white elephant, the past they want to forget. This boat is gassed up and ready to go."

"Where?" she asks.

"I don't know. Leaving would be surrender."

And then a minute passes without a word. She stares at him as if she's trying to look into him, break through the shell. He gets up and walks to the galley.

"Help?" she asks, walking over and standing next to him.

He turns on the tap, washes the vegetables.

"Decapitate this broccoli," he says, handing her the bunch. She touches the skull and crossbones tattooed to his wrist.

"You a pirate?" she mocks.

"Yo-ho, yo-ho, yo-ho, it's off to the open sea. A hurly-burly pirate, a pirate's life for me," he sings.

She smiles fully. Red lips outline white teeth. "I love tattoos but I hate needles," she says, snapping the head off the broccoli. "I love broccoli. When I was little, I would pretend I was a giant eating trees." She hands him the stems. "What next?"

He gives her the mushrooms, carrots and zucchini. "Chop them into bite-size pieces," Chris says, cutting the stems of the broccoli into thin slivers.

He takes the lobster tails out of the fridge. "I speared them my-self," Chris says, dripping peanut oil and three drops of sesame oil into the wok, then placing it on the burner to get hot. "There used to be a lot more lobsters than there are now." He pushes the lobster tail flat on a flat board, places a knife against it. Pounds the knife with a hammer, splitting it open.

"What happened?" She keeps chopping.

"Overfished or fished out of season. They call them summer crabs when you catch them out of season. Things are getting better now that people fish for square groupers."

"What?"

"Drugs. Pot, coke." Chris smashes another tail open.

"People push drugs here worse than in New York."

"This island has become an overgrown drugstore."

"Why Freeport?"

"Location. The Bahamas has always been like America's border town. Supplying whatever. Guns during the Civil War, rum during Prohibition. Now drugs."

"You take drugs?" she asks, looking away from him, playing with the vegetables on the cutting board.

Chris pulls the translucent lobster flesh from the tails. He shrugs his shoulders. "Recreationally," he lies, thinking, I'll stop, and then thinking, I'm full of shit.

"What about you?" he asks.

"I went through that. Never again," she says firmly. "Art is kinda like my drug."

Chris cuts slivers of ginger. He rolls the wok, spreading oil on the sides. Then he drops in the colored piles. Stirs and fries, adding dashes of soy sauce, sprinkling sugar, sherry, grinding pepper. The wok cries, ingredients explode, spitting up oil and fragrant smoke. The sound of storm hitting sidewalk.

"What about Shark?" she asks.

"What about him?"

"He deals, right?"

"How do you know?"

"This is a small island. How do you feel about it?"

"I try not to feel about it," Chris says, picturing the skull in the submerged plane, hoping that Shark's really getting out, opening the club, and not just bullshitting him.

"I like him so much," Robin says.

"I love him," Chris says.

"Are you two lovers?"

"No," Chris says, frowning.

"You two act like some old married couple," she says. "You don't want to sleep with him?"

"I want to sleep with you."

"Really?" she asks, looking directly at him. His heart beats hard. He looks away.

"You cook?" he asks, changing the subject, adding a pinch of salt to the wok, tossing quickly and taking it off the burner.

"Scrambled eggs and tuna salad. I lived off salad bars from Korean markets. They're on every corner in New York. They're open all the time."

"That sounds lonely."

"I had no time to be lonely. Because of my art. I even made art out of food."

"Like what?"

"Promise you won't laugh."

"Promise."

"I sculpted a five-hundred-pound cube of chocolate and a five-hundred-pound cube of lard with my mouth."

"You did what?" Chris says, shaking his head, trying not to smile.

"I bit the chocolate and the fat."

"You ate it."

"No, I spat it out," she says seriously. "I made lipstick out of the lard I spat out. It was my first one-person show."

"You're not fucking with me, right?"

"I even have some of the lipstick on," she says, licking her lips.

"O.K.," Chris says, amazed. "Let me get this straight. You take this hunk of chocolate and start gnawing on it?"

"Right. The name of the piece was *Gnaw?*"

"Right," he says sarcastically.

"It's simple. I built a cube shape and melted the chocolate and poured it in. I did the same with the lard, except I just packed it in. Then I bit away."

"And spat away."

"Into a bucket. I mixed the lard with pigment to make the lipstick. I recast the spat-out chocolate into heart-shaped candy packages."

"Take me through the show," Chris says, shutting his eyes. "Talk me through it, as if we are there."

"You walk through the door. The gallery: white walls, wood floor. It's empty except for two marble pedestals. On the first pedestal there's a cube of chocolate about five feet square. You can see rows of teeth marks on the surface of the chocolate cube. It's brown, looks heavy, like shit or bark. On the other pedestal is a cube the same size. The opposite. It's white and fluffy. You can see chin, nose and mouth marks. At the back of the gallery, in a separate room, there's a slick display case. Like in an expensive department store. It's filled with forty-five perfect heart-shaped packages and four hundred lipsticks."

"Wow!" Chris says, opening his eyes, squinting. "It's fucking wild!" And he sees the apprehension on her face soften as her eyes light up. "I want to bite it too, that big clump of chocolate shit. I want to dive head first into the fat. I'd like to fuck the fat while I eat the chocolate."

"While somebody sticks a lipstick up your ass." She laughs.

"I'm serious," he says.

"I know you are," she says. "You're saying what the critics said, 'simultaneously scatological and erotic.' "

"And innocent. Infantile. I can't help but picture a child, mouth smeared with food, ass smeared with shit."

"One little kid screamed like a maniac and attacked the chocolate block. First kissing, then kicking, then hitting, then biting."

"Yeah, there's something violent going on. Something animalistic. All that biting, devouring. Like that Blob movie, the Blob eating everything, getting bigger. Not being able to stop. It's so fucking compulsive. So fucking fetishistic. So fucking repetitious. Like fucking till your dick is so sore it hurts. Like eating till you want to puke."

"My lips blistered and swelled up from biting the chocolate. I almost puked from biting the fat."

"Like a Roman orgy. Pukatoriums."

"Like actually puking. I spat it all out."

"Bulimia," he says, excited.

"I think bulimia is the eating disorder that connotes the most. We're a bulimic society—twenty percent of all American high school girls are bulimic. We can't get enough of that fast fix, and then we throw it away," she says. "After the show, people started telling me about their eating problems. Then they'd be telling me about their childhood problems. Like I was some sort of shrink."

"That's what packaging is; it's all for immediate satisfaction, then discarded. That's why you made heart-shaped packages from the spit-out chocolate?"

"Right," she says. "I use bulimia like this metaphor for this neurotic, insatiable consumer society we live in." And something in her seems to slip. He sees it on her face, the way she looks at him, her posture. He has penetrated something.

"What?" he asks.

She starts to say something, stops.

"Speak," he urges.

"It's not fair you look the way you do and have a brain."

"Ditto," he says, feeling proud of himself. He picks up the tray and walks to the back of the boat. She follows. He motions with his eyes for her to climb the ladder to the flying bridge. His eyes slip up her long, smooth, tanned legs, under her red skirt, and then stop at white panties with red hearts as she climbs. He takes a deep breath, staring at her attractive, luxurious ass. He wants to bite it.

She reaches the top. He passes her the tray, then follows.

She stands with the tray in her hands staring at the aqua blanket set up with Baccarat wine glasses, silver cutlery, white candles and red hibiscuses. It looks like a pool against the white fiberglass. A bottle of white wine sits bathed in ice. Silver black sky melts into silver black water. There are so many stars. And an almost full moon.

She looks as if she can't believe it's real, and then she looks at him the same way. A sad expression passes over her face. She sees him see it, forces a thin smile. She sits on the floor, puts down the tray. He sits across from her.

Moonlight swims in her thick shoulder-length blue-black hair. It's so perfect it looks fake. He strikes a match. She cups her hands around the candles as he lights them. He looks at her long fingers. The half-moons on her nails shine like the inside of an abalone shell. Lips pucker. She blows out the match as it starts to burn his fingertips. White smoke dances.

She touches her earrings, four frosted blue teardrops of glass. One in her left ear and three in her right.

"Your earrings look like bits of ocean, the way it looks off the continental shelf." He opens the bottle of wine.

"I made them out of beach glass. That's how I made money before I could sell my art. I made earrings."

"I used to collect blue beach glass. It's the hardest to find. I think it only came from milk of magnesia and Vicks bottles. I'll give you my collection." He fills their glasses.

"I'll make you an earring."

"Will you pierce it too?"

"Sure," she says, touching a bright red hibiscus and then sticking it behind her left ear. "I don't mind sticking needles in other people, I just don't like them stuck into me."

"Don't worry," he says, "I'm a masochist too."

"What do you mean, 'too'?"

"Come on, all that chewing and spitting. Bruised lips. Almost vomiting."

"You have to suffer for your art," she says smiling, picking up a flower and sticking it behind his ear.

He laughs.

"What?" she asks.

"I can't help but think how weird it is. Your *Gnaw* sculpture. And that the second time we met I was puking."

"To fate," she says.

"To whatever it brings." He clinks her glass.

"Did you know flowers are genitals?" she flirts.

"What?" Chris asks, startled, and then turned on.

"The only sex organs people can deal with belong to plants."

She sips her wine. Tongue licking glass.

"But we pick them and they die," he says, putting his napkin on his lap. Why did I say that? he thinks, looking at her. She looks sad, touches the hibiscus again. And he thinks about her and her mother on this crazy island, going to that crazy cancer clinic, and how the people who have come here for treatment have all gone home wearing body bags. They all think they're gonna be the one to beat it. Gobs of hopeless hope. "How's your mom doing?"

"O.K.," she says, stabbing a piece of broccoli. And a look of despair settles on her face as she chews slowly. And he feels so sad for her and he wants to help her, wants to tell her he wants to help her and her mother. He feels the metal fork touch his tongue, looks at her brown-black eyes and goes blank. They stare at each other stiffly. He feels broccoli between his teeth, feels panic. He doesn't know why. They eat in silence. She looks at him and then down at her food like a fish hitting a piece of bait and then retreating.

"I wish we were like hermit crabs," she says, looking away.

He swallows, feels the food slide slowly down his throat, wishes he could just take off his clothes and show the outside.

"Why?" he asks.

"I could crawl into your shell and you could crawl into mine and then we wouldn't have to go through this awkward bullshit."

"Like your *Gnaw?* I wish we could fuck facade. Scrape off the cosmetics. The packaging. Get inside."

"The fat cube cracked halfway through the show and a lot of

white liquidy stuff oozed out," she says. "So what's inside you?" she asks, her look flashes from joking to very serious.

He struggles, as if with a lid on a jar that won't open. He thinks, What the fuck does it matter, anyway? But it does. "I'm scared," he forces out. And with this he feels relief, feels that he no longer has to perform for her.

"Me too," she says, tenderly.

And he wants to touch her. But he's afraid if he touches her, she will flicker, fade and then disappear.

"Christopher," she says softly. She fights to say something and then stops and says, "Thank you."

"What for?" he asks.

"For this beautiful meal. For accepting my art. For not dismissing me as some kind of weirdo artist like everyone else."

"It's your art that makes you so fucking great," he says.

"It's so great to have someone to talk with," she says.

"You make me think. Do you know what it's like to talk about conch all the time?"

She stands up. "I have a surprise for you. Wait." She climbs down the steps.

And Chris sits, waiting, wondering what it's gonna be as he looks up at the stars, starlight, star bright. He makes a wish.

And then she's back on the flying deck. She sits down next to him, her smooth legs brushing against his hairy legs. She hands him a manila envelope.

"I love surprises," he says, bending the little clasp, and then ripping the tongue of the envelope. He slides out the photograph, stares at himself and Shark and her smiling back at him, surrounded by gleaming reds and yellows and blues and purples and greens. The she hands him a lipstick. It's labeled "Gnaw."

"You made this," he says, "from the fat you spat out." She shakes her head. And he feels so happy. He opens the lipstick, screws. A perfect tube of blood red sticks out. "Put some on me," he says, handing it to her. Their hands touch. Her hand trembles. His lips tremble. And he's amazed that she made the lipstick, that it was in her mouth. And as the lipstick touches, he feels blood rush to his midsection. Hard. And it smells of woman as she spreads it on his lips.

He looks at her lips as she looks at his lips. And he pictures two blood red hearts coming together and her lips start to tremble as he leans forward slowly, fighting gravity, the ripe earth, her smell, fresh, grows stronger and then her breath, warm, wet, and his lips quiver as they touch hers.

They stay still, frozen delight, lips upon lips, soft upon soft. Mouths open shyly, just a slit, then wider, wet tongues exit, the tips of the tongues meet, the electrical circuit is connected. Lubricated with saliva, they explore, separate, then together, tasting each other.

And he's so lost in the feeling he forgets to breathe. Her eyes close. Robin's long eyelashes brush against his cheeks like the soft red stamens of little powder-puff flowers he used to rub on his face as a child. He inhales, reaches up, caresses her hair, touches the tips lightly with the tips of his fingers. Then. Then he slowly, lightly, reaches his hand up along her neck, her scalp.

She jerks up wildly, electric shock, a scream, her scream, her head, no, her hair, is tilting, coming away with his hand instead of staying on her head. And then on her plate of leftover stir-fried lobster, all too fast. She's running down the stairs with a head full of hair in her hand and a shiny bulb on her shoulders. He rewinds the movie, the head inserted back on to the tail, the brain, the eggs . . . He can't breathe. His stomach tying itself into knots.

He walks down the stairs. Sobs, muffled through the bathroom door. And he thinks, Robin, please don't cry, don't cry. Not knowing what but knowing he wants to do something, he pushes open the door.

She's on the floor, folded into herself. Her whole body shuddering as the grief overflows. The toilet is open. The wig clogs the bowl. The gold-plated shiny sign above: "Don't put anything into the head unless you have eaten it first."

He stares at the wig paralyzed, remembers being picked up by his hair. His mother's fuming face, words slurring, screaming. Rum smell. "Where you been? You supposed to be in by dark. You animal." He backed against the wall. "Just like your father. Look at you hair. It filthy. Fill up with prickers. Both of you. Monkeys!" And then the sound of snapping steel, the sharp stinging blade of the scissors as it sliced and pulled. He stood paralyzed as the hair dropped, and then it stopped and she reached down and touched the hair lying on the floor. The words convulsed from deep inside him, "I'm sorry. Please don't cry. Don't cry." Then she hugged him and he felt the words "I love you, my Specialman" brush against his ears, and they came from her. And he shakes his head, trying to shake the memories out, feeling ashamed about thinking them when Robin's the one in pain, when she needs him. But he's afraid to look at her, as if she's an open pit and he would fall into her, and he can't stand it. A voice yells inside his head, Don't feel! He just stands there. She stares up at him, her eyes demanding.

He fights, gets down on the floor and touches her on the shoulder, and she says, "No," stabbing at him. He touches her again. She moves sideways, slowly, erratically. Slightly beyond his reach. Just beyond his fingertips. And he finally grabs her. She pushes away but he holds on. She feels like rigid metal.

She looks at him awkwardly. He looks into her red, tear-stained eyes. "I don't . . . ," she says, struggling for control. "I'm sick. Sick of it. Pity. For just one night I wanted to be treated like normal. Like I didn't have cancer." She takes a deep breathe. "One perfect night . . . "

He freezes. Like being attacked in a dream, unable to scream. A blunt stab in the chest. He's sinking. He forces himself forward, his face closer and closer. Surface. Her head. He kisses her bald scalp. Again and again. All over. Bloody lipstick smudges. And then his tongue is out and he's licking her scalp like a lollipop, like a kitten licking cream.

He feels her shudder. He starts to cry. Something happens in his throat and he can talk. He whispers, "I'm crying not because I feel sorry for you but because I feel sorry for myself."

6

"Shark, bend your head forward," Robin says. Shark bends. "More," Robin says. She takes a few steps back, her feet sinking into the sand. Chris listens to the suck, roll and collapse of the waves, studies her as she studies Shark. A white turban like a giant squirt of whipped cream covers where her hair should be. Tiny white bikini accentuates curves and sun-glazed skin the color of blond wood. She looks so strong and sexy and healthy. Chris shakes his head, refusing to believe that she's sick. And then he thinks about the last three weeks, about picking her up each morning at nine, pretending that everything was fine, driving, fantasizing that they were going out for Bloody Marys and croissants. Instead, they drove to the cancer clinic to pull the blood sample.

"Good. Now put your hand underneath your left breast. Good. Stop. Don't move," Robin says to Shark. Shark looks like a ballet dancer frozen in midstep. His muscles stretch against sweat-shined black skin, his ass and genitals stretch against sunshined black Speedo.

Robin grabs Chris's hand, pulls him over to Shark. "Get down on the sand, below Shark, at his feet, on your knees."

Shark laughs. "Dats where you belong homes, at my feet."

"You got that upside down," Chris says, getting down on his knees, feeling the warm sand, squinting against the sun bouncing off the aquamarine waves.

She stares at him intently. Chris feels her eyes on his midsection. He wants to cover his crotch. "What are you looking for?" he asks.

"Flaws," Robin says, walking a few feet away. "Try lying down."

Chris lies on his side, his head resting on his arm, his other arm over his stomach.

"No, that's not right either," she says, brow furrowed in concentration.

"Chrisy should lay face down," Shark says. "Dat's his best position."

"Your best position is your head up your ass."

"Fetal position. Get in the fetal position," Robin says pacing, ignoring them. Chris curls up.

"Great," she says, stopping, grabbing her pad, sitting on the sand and then sketching.

Chris takes a deep breath, drifts back to earlier that morning, sitting in the cancer clinic waiting room. Waiting. Mouth-breathing antiseptic air so as not to smell. Robin sat next to him. He gazed around the room. It looked like a convention of car salesmen mixed with a Tupperware party. The walls were laden with a mess of letters and plaques and paintings and poems presented to the cancer doctor, "To Dr. Johnson, in Grateful Appreciation."

He listened to the conversations buzzing around. A man chewing on a toothpick said to another man, "Well, you think you got it bad. My first wife died of breast cancer and then I married another one and six months later she got it too. Talk about double whammy."

Chris whispered into Robin's ear. "If I had to look at that man chewing on a toothpick for the rest of my life, I'd get cancer too." She fought the smile trying to spread on her face.

Then there was a hush in the room. Eyes stared with amazement at the man who entered. Chris looked from Robin's hoping eyes to Dr. Johnson's tiny darting eyes, to his face covered in dirty brown beard, to his airport–Hare Krishna smile, to his fat cigar, to his hanging stomach. Chris didn't know whether he wanted to kiss him or hit him.

A young man, body of bones slathered with repugnant brown

spots like graffiti on a once beautiful building, walked in supported by a muscular black man dressed in jogging shorts. They sat away from the others.

A mousy woman in a sundress covered in cat pattern, next to Robin, mouthed "AIDS" as if it were a dirty word. Robin ignored her.

"Doctor Bryant can cure it," the woman said. "He found out AIDS come from the lubricants they use. Doctor Bryant did tests. He stuck some up rats' asses. They got AIDS. They refused to publish it. It's part of the AMA conspiracy. Cancer and AIDS is big money. They don't want to find a cure."

"Mon, I never know it so hard to be a statue," Shark says.

"Yeah," Chris says, moving. "I hope you're almost finished."

"No!" Robin says, staring from Chris to Shark. "Don't move. Statues don't move." And that's how he feels when he's with her, like a statue, a male fertility statue, erect phallus half the size of its body, hard as stone, frozen in full passion, unable to move. And every time he tries to make a move he feels a bulb of petrifying, softening fear swell up from so deep inside he didn't even know he went that deep. And when he's away from her, he's still with her, and he tries to get her out, jacking off two-three-four times, using lard as lubrication, hard till he's sore and exhausted and can't do it again and then he can sleep. And he thinks about last night, how he couldn't stand it, coking out, staring naked into the full-length mirror, into his own eyes, seeing her eyes, seeing her inside him, seeing her reflected in the mirror. And his dick stood up, so hot he thought it would spontaneously combust, and then he was fucking the cool mirror, a sheet of ice, his dick sliding, seeing her in him. Come spattered and dripped against the fogged, smudged mirror like bird droppings.

And he remembers three weeks ago, back on the yacht, in the bathroom, her wig clogging the toilet bowl. He licked her bald head and then under her eyes. Tongue touching-tasting-swallowing salty tears. Then her earrings—then her ear lobe. He licked around it, in the crack between her ear and her scalp, then the ear itself. His tongue penetrated her ear hole. A warm feeling bubbled through him, and the heat built as she started to kiss him back and it got hotter and hotter. Boiled. And he felt himself throbbing, lost in liquid kiss, and he wanted her so bad, but he was so afraid, afraid because she might be like all the others and would disappear after, but he couldn't stop, didn't want to, his mouth tasting the skin of her neck, licking down as his finger touched her face, her lips, his heart pounded so hard he thought his chest would rip open. He reached for her breast, her heart. She held his hand, stopping it, her eyes opening. "No." And then he felt such relief. He just held her. She fell asleep in his arms on the bathroom floor and his arms got cramp from holding her and his dick got cramp from wanting her. He just looked down at her in his arms.

Chris feels the sun burning. Sweat coats him like paste. His muscles start to twitch. "I'm gonna go on strike," he says.

She acts exasperated, shuts her pad, unfolds her long legs. Stands. "O.K.," she says. "That's it."

Chris sits up as Shark straightens up, then sits down. "I wanna see the drawing," Shark says.

"Me too," Chris says.

"It's not a drawing. It's only a study. For a sculpture." She hugs the pad to her chest. "You may never see it."

She sits down on the sand in front of them, the tips of her fingers covered in charcoal ash. Thinking of Ash Wednesday ash, Chris hears, "Remember that you are dust."

"I still want to see it," Chris says. "Me too," Shark says.

"Tough," she says, putting the pad down, pressing her middle finger into Chris's bellybutton. Sweat runs out. Her touch follows the sweat. His stomach muscles quiver. He shivers, swallows. Her fingers stop at the top of his Speedo. He wants to jam her hand down his pants. Instead, he pushes his finger into her stomach, finding her belly button, poking. She giggles, falling back onto the sand.

"None of dat, children. You gonna embarrass me," Shark says, and he smiles, but a lonely look crosses his face and Robin sees this and she opens her arms and says, "Come here." He looks shy as she leans forward and hugs him. Chris feels jealous and then feels guilty for feeling jealous. He leans forward and wraps his arms around

Robin, around Shark. They feel so warm and good and Chris feels so good that he took care of Shark, gave him money, and he thinks how the Studio 69 is opening tomorrow with an Independence Day party, and he thinks how hard Shark worked, and he's proud and envious of him. They let go of one another reluctantly.

A sweat drop drips from below Chris's breast, down. The droplet drips into his navel, where a pool of sweat is accumulating. He thinks how when he was young his navel stuck out like the native boys', like a dried black-eyed pea, and how it felt like a boil. His mother would tell him that if it didn't stay in, he would have to get the operation that turned outies to innies. "How come all the black kids don't need an operation?" he asked her. "Because you're different," she replied. "You an inside child, not an outside child. You're white."

"Do you like my navel?" he asks Robin.

"I'm terribly attached to your navel," she says sarcastically.

He flashes a look of mock seduction.

"Don't look at me that way."

"What way?"

"Like a safe-sex ad," she says, trying to look pissed off.

Shark laughs. "Chris and I gots the same navel. Only mine's black and his white."

"I made a navel sculpture once. I cast seven hundred and eighty-two people's belly buttons. I put Vaseline on their skin and then filled their navels with fast-drying plaster."

"So you got dem insided out," Shark says.

"They all looked so different inside out. Some rounded like hills and some pointed like mountains. I put skin-colored latex on the plaster and then cast a negative, so they were outside in and looked like navels. I stuck them all together in a big square. They looked like a giant cracker."

"So what did it mean?" Chris asks.

"It means she crazy as crazy-self," Sharks says.

"So you tell me," Robin asks, challenging Chris.

"You don't want to make it easy for me?"

"You've had it easy enough."

"He sure did," Shark says.

"O.K. Belly button. Mother and child. The point of separation. The point of connection. A birth scar," Chris says. "And also gaining and losing identity," he says.

She gives him a strange look.

"What?" he asks.

"How come you're not an artist? Or a writer? You could write about art."

"I don't know," he says embarrassed, thinking, How come I'm not anything? "I don't know what I should do."

"Then do lots of things. You're smart. You can do anything. Maybe that's the problem. You have too many options."

"What problem? Chris ain't got no problem," Shark says to Robin. "He's white and he got money."

Chris feels the burn, feels useless, feels a flash of jealousy that Shark has the 69, that he's doing something, moving away, may not need him anymore.

Robin looks away, grabs a bag, takes out a navel orange, starts to peel it. "Why are the oranges here green?" she asks, changing the subject.

"Because it's not cold enough to turn them orange," Chris says.

"Then they should be called greens," Robin says.

"Then what would you call greens?" Chris asks, sniffing, breathing in the orange smell.

"Vegetables," Shark says.

"Why do you put salt on your orange?" Robin asks Chris, separating the orange into three, giving him and Shark a piece. Shark puts the whole thing into his mouth sideways, pink lips surround orange lips until he bites down. Juice squirts and drips.

"It makes it sweeter," Chris says, walking and dipping his piece of orange into the ocean. He sits back down, holds it above his head, squeezes, lets the juices flow and then drip into his mouth.

"No, it make it saltier," Shark says, chewing and swallowing.

"I do it for the same reason I wear socks to sleep."

"Explain that leap of logic," Robin says, eating her orange one peg at a time until all she has left is the navel. She holds it on her palm. It looks like a tiny orange, the size of an egg yolk. Chris stares at it.

"Because I'm just like my mother. For some reason I like to do whatever she did," Chris says, picturing his mother, her face frowning in concentration, peeling oranges. The sharp silver knife going around and around and the peel coming away in a uniform strip, one long curlicue. She would take the peel and wrap it back around the orange and put it in the fridge and then go on to the next one.

"My mother used to save all the navels from the navel oranges. When she had about a hundred, she would come into my room in the middle of the night, always on a night when Shark was sleeping over. She would bring the navels on a silver tray in three Lalique bowls and wake us, and say . . ."

"Happy navel night," Shark says.

"And we would rest the tray on our knees and eat the navels together. Pick each one up with our fingers, salt them and then plop them into our mouths."

"Your mother sounds wonderful. And strange," Robin says, holding her palm open, presenting the navel to him. It looks like a big orange eye.

"She was wonderfully strange," Chris says, his tongue touching the navel, then her palm, then sucking it into his mouth. He bites down. Blood rushes to his dick.

Shark looks at him tenderly, gets up, says, "Mon, I gotta go. A nigger's work never done. Got to put the final touches on the 69."

Chris stands up, grabs Robin's hands, pulls her up. "Later," Chris says, shaking Shark's hand. Robin pecks him on the cheek.

"See you two at the opening," Shark says.

Chris puts his arm around Robin and watches Shark walk away and it's like his life is split in two, one side with Robin and the cancer and the other side with Shark and the coke. And he thinks of the last three weeks, sees himself driving desperately late at night to meet Shark, to get high. And they would snort and they would work on the club, and he would try to keep up with Shark and Shark would try to tell him he shouldn't be doing nigger work. He would snort and work till his muscles and brain got numb, till he could no longer feel. And Chris sees him the night before last interviewing the bartenders, the waitresses. And Chris thinks Shark never looked happier.

Chris shakes his head, grabs Robin's sketch pad, yells, "I'm going to look at the drawing." He runs, feeling the sun-warmed salt water splash against his shins, piercing the flat stream of pale green ocean—the color of seedless green grapes. He hears the snap and slap of his feet and Robin's feet close behind. She chases him among the riblike ridges of sandbar. And her voice sings out, "Stop!" and he's a child again, playing tag with his mother, slowing down so she can catch him and hug him and tickle him. He felt her from behind, the splash from her splash in the shallow water as she yelled, "Stop!" Her cool hands tugged his salty sunburned shoulders as he felt the sharp needles pierce deeply into the bottom of his foot. He fell backwards, fell into her, screaming as she laughed, thinking he was playing. He brought his foot up and out of the water along with a purple-black ball of sea urchin. Needles writhing in the sunlight.

Then the shock on his mother's face as she grabbed his foot and tried to pull the urchin out by squeezing a handful of its longest spines. He swallowed the scream. These spines broke off, leaving the urchin stuck into his foot. She got down on her knees and took off her scarf, wrapping it around her hand. He squinted, seeing the tendrils of her brown-black hair fall in front of her face, light up red-orange. He saw her lips pull and felt his teeth clench as the spines broke under his skin. She yanked the urchin off. And then back at home, the church-wax smell as the thick white hurricane candle flickered. She dripped the burning wax onto the sole of his foot, her voice soothing as she said, "Cry if you want to." But he was brave for her, holding his breath as the hot drops dripped, exhaling. She gently touched an ice cube to the heat and it felt like the frigid blue of a glacier.

Chris slows down and Robin touches him from behind. He stops. Her arms reach around him, her body silky and warm against his. He remembers the wax turning from hot to cold, from clear to white, from liquid to solid. And finally the bottom of his foot was completely covered in wax, like another thick layer of skin. His mother peeled it away slowly in one thick shell and he felt little pricks like hair being plucked as the broken needles came away with the wax.

He feels Robin's chest heave in and out against his back as she grabs the pad. They catch their breath together.

"You really want to see it?" she asks coyly.

"See what?"

"You missed your chance."

"Please!" he begs dramatically, falling to his knees, grabbing her legs.

She hands him the pad, walks away.

"I don't want to look at it unless you really want me to."

She turns. "I just can't watch."

He sits down on the sand, opens the sketch pad. He stares at himself, at Shark. Naked. Shark has one ripe beautiful female breast which he's sucking, suckling, nursing himself. Chris looks at himself at Shark's feet. A pornographically large Jeff Stryker cock between his legs. He's giving himself a blow job. He tries to look at her, tries to say something. Can't. He continues to stare at the pad, transfixed. He feels shocked, invaded, dislocated, turned on, happy, sad. The drawing is surprisingly tender, rather than obscene. It bleeds. It makes him want to hug and fuck her at the same time.

"Why don't you ask?" she urges gently.

"What?" He clears his throat.

"What it means."

"Because I know," he says.

"Then tell me."

"I want . . ." He takes a deep breath, looking at the waves flick sunlight. "Can't . . .," he stutters.

"Separate yourself and Shark from it."

Chris looks at the drawing. "The two figures seem alone, yet there's an intimacy. They are joined together. By their positioning, by both being engaged in auto-erotic activity. I guess we're, they're, eating themselves. Destroying themselves. Draining their own body fluids."

"The figures could be feeding upon themselves in a process of renewal. It's their choice."

"You're so subtle," he says, still looking at the picture.

"And beautiful," she says sarcastically.

He forces himself to look away from the drawing, to look at her, at her face. Eyes glittering. "You are beautiful."

"You must think bowling balls are beautiful."

His muscles relax. He shakes his arms and then his legs. "Don't say that." He wants to kiss her. "I love your head. I love watching the hair grow back in."

She touches him on the cheek. "You're making me better," she says, hugging him. He feels the sun, the cool breeze. Hot and cold. Excitement and fear. They breathe together. He hugs her back, tighter and tighter. His pulse racing. "You're making me . . . feel." He fights to bring his lips toward hers. A fraction at a time. Their lips touch. Her alarm watch beeps, once, twice, three times.

He throbs, his hands clenching sand. Fuck.

She looks away. Unzipping her bag, she takes out the syringe, the serum, a cotton ball and then opens the alcohol bottle. Placing the cotton on top of the bottle, she pours. Sterility smell. She pulls the plastic tip off the syringe. The needle like a tiny spear reflects a silver sliver of sun. She pushes it into the serum, puncturing the sterile cover. The needle sucks as she pulls back the plunger, slowly, engorging, red liquid like red-red wine. She measures. Notch after notch. The black plunger slips. Then she pushes. Slight. A red dot lights up on top of the needle.

"You're sure it doesn't hurt?" he asks her every time.

Her smile drains. "It's only a little prick, you big prick," she says, placing the cotton on her skin.

"Scream, if you want," he says, gritting his teeth, gripping his hands together. Robin plunges the needle into her thigh. "Don't look so sad. The serum is killing the cancer." She pulls the needle out. Chris exhales.

"I have a surprise for you," he says, grabbing her hand and leading her off the beach down a path through the bush.

Everything drips: The light drips through the canopy of leaves above their head, the stream that the path follows drips water over the rocks. The trees are dripping with dripping air plants shaped like pineapples, corkscrews and mossy old men's beards. He picks a red-orange, ball-shaped cluster of small flowers. "The flower is called ixora, flame-of-the-woods." He hands it to her, stops walking.

"How do you know so much?"

"Shut your eyes," he says, "and stick out your tongue."

"The surprise?"

"A little one, not the big one."

He plucks a tiny red flower from the spherical head and pulls the stamen of the flower out through the stem. His hands shake. Her eyelids shake. Her tongue shakes. When the stamen reaches the end of the stem, a tiny drop of liquid collects and he places the drop of nectar on the tip of her pink tongue.

"Mmmm," she says.

They continue to walk up the path in silence.

"Thirsty?" he asks.

She nods.

He makes monkey noises, squeezes his legs and arms around the trunk of the tallest coconut palm. He pulls up with his arms, pushes up with his feet. One inch at a time, he climbs the shaft. He likes the feel of his muscles straining against the hard, smooth, warm wood. Sweat forms on his chest, between his legs. Lubrication. He uses it to slide up faster. Breathing heavily. And finally he's ten feet up and grabbing the palm fronds as handles. They hiss in the breeze.

"Tarzan," she yells.

"Jane," he yells, turning a coconut around and around until the green stem frays and then gives way. He holds the green coconut, heavy in his hand.

"Bombs away!" he yells, dropping it. He slides down the trunk. She claps when his feet touch ground. He bows, picks up the coconut and shakes it. Then he holds the nut over his head and smashes it against a sharp rock. A cracking sound and then water is dripping out.

"Ladies first," he says, holding the coconut above her head.

"No, you first."

"But I insist."

"You Tarzan, me Jane."

"You crazy, me sane."

She opens her mouth. He pours the coconut water into it. She swallows. He swallows. A trickle of water drips down the side of her mouth onto her chin and neck. She giggles, wipes her mouth. "It's delicious. So subtle."

"Like you," he says, drinking from the coconut, then shutting his mouth, letting the water flow over his face, his neck, his chest.

Her eyes flit over his wet, tanned skin.

And he feels a stab of fear again as she picks a small yellow-red banana, peels it. She holds it up to him. He opens his mouth slowly, sucking it. He envies the banana. "In *Art in America* they wrote that the rows of teeth marks on my chocolate piece evoked primal fears of the vagina dentata."

Then he bites down, swallows, laughs, choking. "Vagina with teeth!" he yells, running up a slight ridge. She follows, laughing.

A bird sings. Chris sings,

> Yellow Bird, up high in banana tree
> Yellow Bird, you sit all alone like me
> Let them fly away, in the sky away
> They'll come back and soon
> Fly from night till noon
> Black and yellow you—
> Like banana too—
> They might pick you some day.

"I can hear the ocean," she says.

"Just a few more steps," he says, putting his hands over her eyes. He stops her at the top of the rise. "My gift to you," he says, thinking, At least I can give her this, moving his hands away slowly. "Paradise."

She opens her eyes, gasps.

The setting sun, a burning orange sphere, paints the perfect half-moon of bay beach, pink like cotton candy, like pale flamingos, as they watch together.

"Look for the emerald drop."

"What?"

"The green flash the instant the sun sinks into the sea."

The sky turns orange as the sun turns yellow, melting slowly into ocean; the lower it goes, the more it glows. Their skin turns the same color as the sunset.

"Now!" Chris yells as the top tip of the sun disappears, and then the green flash.

"I saw it," she screams.

"I did too," he says, hugging her, picking her up in his arms.

"It's caused by the yellow-orange light reflecting off the blue ocean," he says as he puts her down, and they continue walking and the sand is warm, and soft and smooth as confectioner's sugar under their feet.

"You haven't seen the surprise yet," he says. "Come on." He runs, pulling her after him. They stop at a tall chain-link fence with barbed wire on top. A sign on the fence says:

WARNING! WARNING! WARNING!
ELECTRIFIED FENCE
TRESPASSERS WILL BE PROSECUTED

He uses one of the keys hanging around his neck to unlock a gate in the fence.

She looks puzzled. He leads her out onto a dock that forms the side of a large pen, a netted-off section of the bay. They sit on the dock, hang their legs into the water.

"What is . . . ?" she starts to ask, and then three dolphins leap in unison out of the black water high into the air and crash down on their sides. Slapping. Cool, silver white splash water soaks them. Robin screams with delight.

"I'd like you to meet Rocky, Sunset Sam and Aphrodite," Chris says, laughing.

The dolphins swim over to where Chris and Robin are sitting.

Robin laughs. They stick their heads out of the water.

"Pleased to meet you," she says, her whole face a smile. "They're smiling."

"Like clowns," he says, "smiling on the outside, crying on the inside. That's why Shark and I set all the others free. Five of them. They captured the first group about ten years ago. They kept them in the waterway by the hotel. Shark and I were obsessed. We spent all our time hanging around them, floating on inner tubes in the pen, putting on tanks and spending time underwater with them. We helped Rick, their trainer. He trained them for this 'humans swim with dolphins' thing."

Chris hangs his arms over the side of the pen. He pets them. They feel soft and smooth like balloons filled with warm water, like cocktail olives. Their blowholes open and close like grey, toothless mouths. And he takes Robin's hand and touches Aphrodite with it. She shuts her eyes, savoring the feel.

"The dolphins trained me and Shark, cast a spell on us, made us set them free. We used tanks, at night, cut the fence right under the drunk guard."

"My hero, my prince, my frog," she says, grabbing his hand. "Weren't you scared?"

"I knew if I got caught my family would fix it."

"What about these three?"

"They're from Mexico, where the water is murky. They're disoriented in the clear water here. They wouldn't leave. Then insurance closed all the 'swim with dolphin' programs. The male dolphins kept trying to screw the women swimming with them. They got warped from being in captivity. Programs became known as dolphin rape experiences."

"What are they gonna do with them?"

"The same guy, Rick, who trained the original dolphins we freed, is now an anticaptivity activist. He's untraining them before they fly them back to Mexico to return them to the wild. I'm helping him rehabilitate them."

"That's great," she says.

He stands up straight. "Time for a swim." He flicks his head back, pushes his hair back. She stands up and walks toward him. She grabs his hand, kisses his wrist, kisses the pirate-skull tattoo. She shuts her eyes. He looks at her lips, the red color of the wax covering of Edam cheese. He kisses them. Her arms encircle him as his arms encircle her. He can't tell where he stops and she begins. And he feels scared and exhilarated and he shuts his eyes as she slides his Speedo down slowly, one inch at a time. He opens his eyes. His Speedo drops on the dock. He stumbles as he steps out. She steps back. He stares at her tight mouth and not so innocent eyes. He rubs himself, animal-like. Biceps, triceps, chest writhing. Brown all over. He's proud of his body. He puts his hands on his hips. She stares back, taking him all in. Hesitation mixed with desire. Her artist eyes on his crotch. Causing it to curl up and out. Slow and not so subtle, above curling hair, straight and hard and red.

Then he panics, dives into the dolphin pen. Splash absorbing nakedness. He stays still in the water, floats, looks at his dissolving dick floating separate from his body. He pictures a Medusa jellyfish lying on the bottom, tentacles floating upward, waiting to sting. What the fuck is wrong with me, he thinks, as the dolphins glide up and he pets them as they fight for attention, like puppies. He grabs the back fin of Aphrodite, unable to look at Robin on the dock. She tows him around the pen, making clicking and crackling sounds, and the water feels full of electrical charges as it rushes against him. Aphrodite dives, pulling him under—down—down—down. He lets go, floats up, forces himself to swim to the dock, to where Robin's sitting. She grabs his hands. He puts his arms around her legs, dangling in the water, holding himself up, looking up at her.

"Why don't you come in?" he asks, letting go of her legs. He swims away. Watches. She hesitates, takes off her white turban, leaves on her white bikini, which looks like white tan lines in the moonlight. She jumps into the water, swims over to him. They caress the dolphins together. It's like they're on another planet, communicating with alien life. She grabs on to Rocky's fin and he tows her around and around.

"Incredible," she says as she dog-paddles over to a buoy that's floating in the pen. She holds on. He follows her. She kisses him, salty and fresh on the mouth. Blood shoots to his midsection and he swims away. Down. Watches her and the dolphins swimming above in the moonlight.

He swims up behind her, wraps his arm around her shoulders and his legs around her thighs, scissoring her, bringing it hard against her, straining against her bathing suit. He holds her and the buoy, brings his mouth to her head, her ear. He wants her so bad, and he's so afraid he can't. He shuts his eyes, forces himself to speak. He whispers, "The first time I ever came I was around twelve. One night Shark and I snuck out and swam naked with the dolphins and I grabbed on to one and it pulled me faster and faster. The vibrations of the water felt so great and it was like something was being pulled out of me and I exploded and I couldn't believe how fantastic it felt. I didn't know what happened. Like I lost something but at the same time I gained something that was so much greater." He takes a deep breath. "Now, with you."

"Yes," she gasps.

They swim in to shore, lie on the hard sand, where the waves are hitting the beach. He feels the surge of warm water touch his toes, his knees, his thighs. Then higher, each wave between his legs, his cheeks, the crack of his ass. Then retreating. Then white foam and the spray on the back of his neck and the sound of bubbles popping. He touches her. Her scalp the same texture as the dolphins' skin. Her cheek soft as a pink poui petal. Then her lips on his eyes and nose and on his mouth. Liquid kiss. As a wave sucks out, he sucks her mouth in, slides around the silkiness with his tongue, tasting and probing, so salty, and he imagines he's kissing the ocean as a wave rolls in, as her tongue slips into his mouth. And he rolls on top of her, unclips her top, pushes it up. And her nipples hard and alive, and then his mouth is on them, licking and sucking, and he pictures Shark sucking his own breast. She pulls off her bikini bottom. He spreads his legs on either side of her body. Sliding down. Slowly. So much. To taste. He feels his hardness against her softness, pushing, and then the smooth sand between his legs, and her smooth hands stroking all over. And his tongue penetrates her belly button. Faint sea sound in her stomach. He feels the rise and fall of her belly as the waves rise and fall. Greedy, he slips down further. His eyes shut. And his mouth is between her legs, and it feels so good, bald like a little girl's. She strokes his head, his hair. And he wraps his arms around her legs and buries his face in between them. He feels so engulfed, heavy, filled with pleasure, that he wants to cry out. And it's like he's swimming in all the earth's juices as a wave rolls over his entire body, pushes him in. Then pulling him out. So he has to grip with his tongue and arms. And he can't stand it anymore and he wants to be swimming inside her, and she pulls his hair lightly. He gulps his way back up. His mouth is on her mouth, breathing her in as he anticipates the feeling of it inside her. As she spreads her legs as a wave washes, he goes in with the flow and then she clenches down, feels rigid, frozen, and he doesn't know why and then she pushes him off.

It aches, the pain throbbing, and he can't figure out what's wrong. He wants her so bad and he's too afraid to ask her what's wrong. He just blanks it all out, floating in the surf, letting the waves pull him in and out. He tries not to breathe, hears his mother saying, "Don't breathe hot air on me." He rests his hand on the sand, lets it rub against the ocean's bottom as he flows with the waves and he imagines the ocean is a heart and his hand is marking its beat. He tries not to think about Robin, about what he did wrong, about what she wants, about how it felt so right to him and he feels a touch and he ignores it, then again, and he turns over. It's her and she says, "We have to talk." He wishes he were somewhere far away.

The salt burns his eyes as he tries to read her eyes. He stands up and she's wrapped in a towel and she dries him with another towel. His body, and then he shuts his eyes as she dries his hair. She lays the towel on the sand. And she sits down. He sits down next to her. Shivers. He covers himself with his arms, hugs his knees, and he looks away and says, "I'm sorry." She puts her finger on his lips, stopping the "sorry."

She pushes his hair off his face, looks at him gravely. He stares back. She shuts her eyes, shakes her head. "It's not mine anymore. Not my body," she says, touching her chest. "I felt great. And I go for a checkup and they tell me I'm dying. My cells are freaking out . . . there isn't any pain . . . my body is eating itself. Then chemo and I'm a white rat trapped in a maze of poisons to attack the poison taking over my body. I feel so bad I want to die. I'm vomiting and my hair falls out and my pee turns bright purple and it hurts. I felt you were touching the poison, going into the poison. And I want you so bad . . . waited . . . and I thought maybe you didn't want . . . the cancer."

Chris takes a deep breath. His heart is beating in his mouth. "I . . . It was so hard to show, to try. Thought maybe I couldn't. And when you pushed me off I felt . . ."

"I just want to hold you. Please?" And he hugs her.

"What's wrong with me?" he whispers.

"Nothing," she says, and she hugs him back. They hold one another and he listens to the waves and he synchronizes his breath with hers, breathing in with her and out with her, over and over, and he feels her breath get faster and his breath gets faster and then the heat is back and he doesn't know if he started kissing her or if she started kissing him. And he's on top of her, and she has him in her hands, pulling him, guiding him in, and then the wetness between her legs. He feels Robin wriggling and she pushes as if she's trying to get it in from below. And he grabs her smooth head and he sees a flash of his mother in her white bathing cap. And he tries to get the picture out as he thinks, Why the fuck am I thinking about her now? but he can't stop it and he's diving, swimming between his mother's legs. Back and forth. He's having so much fun. And she said, "Stop!" and he didn't and as he was swimming through, she clamped her legs together hard, around his neck, knocking the wind out of him, and she squeezed, holding them shut, and he grabbed her legs and pulled and his nails scratched. Then he was above water, spitting out water and gasping for breath. And he feels fear and he tries desperately to ignore the feeling, and he thinks how he ignored his mother as she was dying and he's so afraid of failing again with Robin. He jams his head beneath her arm and next to her breast and it's so good, so calm, so warm and dark and smells so nice that he feels the fear drain as he thrusts into her. Then panic shoots. He's enveloped in a wave of terror. He starts to sink and shrink. Oh please, don't desert me! Get hard! Think, fantasize, anything, dick, don't fuck me, oh fuck! Breathe-breathe-breathe, he tells himself. He understands what she meant when she said it was like her body didn't belong to her anymore and he wills it to react but it doesn't, defiant, lying soft, and he hates it. He clings to her to stop himself from shrinking. He feels himself scraped raw with sandpaper and feels her underneath like a cold slab of meat. The ocean slurs. And he thinks, No! And she says, "Don't worry, Chris, it's all right, it's not your fault." He drowns in the shame.

7

Chris concentrates on the road. Heat spots puddle the jet black tar. As he gets near, they disappear. The air blurs. He thinks of last night on the beach with Robin as he pictures his dick, soft, so soft and tiny, just lying there. He drives faster, as if escaping from it.

Cars line the sides of the road as he approaches Independence Park. He slows down, then is stopped by a crowd blocking his way. Most of the men have jerri-curls or cut-up Afros, mirrored sunglasses, and slick polyester shirts, with thick gold chains hanging fist-size gold pendants of dollar signs, Mercedes insignia and coke spoons. Young women, hair platted in intricate braids, wear Calvins, carry gold or silver handbags matching gold and silver high-heeled shoes. Fancy-hatted old women in boxy bright-flowered dresses hold the little hands of little children.

Chris parks, gets out of the car, smells greasy conch air, hears the cry from Bowleg's Native Food Emporium booth: "We gots scorched conch, stew conch, conch salad too; conch fritter, crack conch, just to name a few." He joins the flow of people, hears the twack-twack-twack of machete hitting coconut at Mr. Nut's Coconut booth where Mister Nut himself yells, "Try a nut and you will see how juicy someone's nuts can be."

Then a mechanical sound overhead. People look up, push forward. The helicopter lands, blade spinning, then coughing and stopping. The prime minister steps out. His T-shirt says "Black by Popular Demand." There's a hush and then people scream and clap. Children jump up and down. The little prime minister, dwarfed by a wall of bulging bodyguards and his tall red-skinned wife, walks up to the stage, decorated in crepe paper the color of the Bahamian flag, black, gold and turquoise. The crowd explodes. He smiles, pulls out a small Bahamian flag and waves it.

"What I tell younna thirteen years ago?" he screams, his left eye staring straight ahead, his right scanning the audience.

Chris looks at the PM's wife and it's as if she's pulling a Michael Jackson. She's black, she's white. Rumor has it that she bathes in vats of Porcelana. Chris watches the prime minister's short, blood-sausage arms as he fists the air, shouting again, "What I tell younna thirteen years ago?"

The crowd erupts with the cry, "Massa day done!" The Royal Bahamian Police Band plays:

> Massa day done
> Bacchanal begun
> So what to do on a night like this?
> Independence sweet
> You can't resist
> Feeling hot hot hot
> Hot hot hot!

Chris pushes his way back through the bodies now swaying in unison. Waists flow with the music, arms held high in the air. The prime minister dances, one hand on his stomach and one arm out to the side. He shakes his waist. The crowd matches his movement as if they're all his dance partner.

The music stops. People cheer. "Who lead you to freedom?" the PM asks. The microphone whistles.

"You! Little Moses! Moses!" the crowd yells.

"I take you out the desert and makes dis Bahama land into land of milk and honey. We's talking chocolate milk! Younna got car and plenty moneys. Praise the Lord! And we country do so good dat the Yankees jealous-mad. Because we black, a black country. Dey wants to make us slaves again. America, stay out of we business or we'll lick you with bottle, stone and old razor. Massa day done!"

"Yankee, go home!" the crowd chants. Chris pushes, walks back to his car. He's covered in sweat. A Cessna flies low overhead, its door open. Heads stretch skyward as a cloud of paper floats down, fluttering white against a cloudless blue-chiffon sky. Black hands reach as the plane makes another pass. Everyone chases paper pieces falling-blowing in the wind. Chris gets into his car. One lands, sticks to his windshield. He reaches out through the open window—grabs it. It's a pamphlet. He reads "DEA—GO HOME!" signed "The Cartel." Attached to the back of the leaflet, a hundred-dollar bill.

Chris drives away, heading east towards the Studio 69, towards the setting sun. Fire orange sky. He swerves at a fork onto a dirt road, into mangrove, driving faster and faster. Swamp. He sniffs— sharp, sticky. Ripe Brie. Brackish backwater breath. A latticework of shadows, mangrove banyans in thick tangles, fracture the light, touch the car like many beggars' hands or legs. And he thinks that these plants are responsible for the Bahamas and therefore responsible for his fucked-up life. They were the first, their green pods like floating periscopes checking out lean ridges of shallow sea—finally sucking onto Pleistocene sand dunes like sucking spareribs, spreading roots over ocean floor, squeezing dry land from water. Liquidation to solidification.

He remembers himself and Shark at Independence Day twelve years ago, when he was thirteen. They were licking mango snowballs as they lowered the Union Jack, raised the Bahamian flag. People cried as they sang "God Save the Queen" and then the new national anthem with pride, "Lift Up Your Head to the Rising Sun, Bahama Land." The prime minister beamed, his hard black body shining in the sun as he saluted the queen of England, who looked matronly, pasty and old. And he pictures the young black man, hair coming out of his nostrils as he pointed his little Bahamian flag at him and spit and said, "We's gonna get all you white fucks off dis island. Freeport black-people country now. Dis time not like before time."

"I was on this island before there was even a Freeport," Chris shouted. "I fucking belong here!"

Shark sucked his teeth, asked the man, "Who you is? When you sorry self wash over from Nassau? A year ago? Two year ago? We is Freeport," he said, putting his arm around Chris. The man spat again and walked away.

Then Chris passes through Boiling Rock, the village where he and Shark would come as children to fish with Doctor Conch, where they would catch jewfish seven feet long with heads the size of a very pregnant woman's belly. He pictures the hook as huge as his hand and the line as thick as his finger and remembers how, when the jewfish hit the turbot bait, it would take two men to hold the line, and sometimes they would tie it to the boat, letting the jewfish pull them around until it drowned. Chris hardly recognizes Boiling Rock village anymore or the villagers sporting Rolex watches, Gucci purses and the latest hairdos from the newly opened Betty Beauty Parlor. All the houses have split at their seams, with cement extensions dwarfing the old frame houses they're attached to, like gigantic artificial limbs. The church has a new steeple. Even the stray dogs have grown fat; where ribs used to stick out, paunches now cover, thanks to the regular snowfalls.

Chris arrives at a clearing in the brush. Parks as dogs bark. His Jag joins the ranks of other cars, including a black overstretched limo, a purple Porsche, a raspberry red Rolls-Royce. He walks on wobbly wood pilings, slapping the air around his ears, trying to silence the distressing hiss. Standing in front of a rusting warehouse, two over-steroided black men in fatigues, like matching bookends, block the door.

"What's up, Rambo?" Chris asks. "You looking weak, Ali."

"Oh, dat you, Mister Bitters," answers Rambo, swinging the door open. "Welcome to the grand opening of Shark's Studio 69."

Chris is sucked into heat-slamming beat, dark and then fuzzy. He breathes. Fatty hot air. Irresistible. The pressure. The rush. Demands. He doesn't fight it. Feels it. The rank rhythm of Africa, captured and whipped into submission, now released, more potent through fermentation. Heat flows from frenzied flesh, torsos and trunks, heads and tails. Chris's eyes adjust to the dark. He focuses. Makes out bodies, seeing every shade from chalk white to absolute black. And no one cares. Whole trains, like snakes, jam together back and forth, slaves to the ejaculating beat of the drum. An amazing assortment: tough tattooed sailors; decadent gin-tonic drinking, butterfly catching, bird watching quasi aristocrats from Windamere and Lyford Cay; alligator-skinned old men groping the bubble butts of beautiful shirtless boys; emaciated models, just bones and cheekbones; black butterball Bahamian politicians with multimillion-dollar Swiss bank account smiles; Colombian, Bolivian and Cuban American drug runners; an alphabet soup of bought DEA, FBI and CIA agents; drag queens with too-firm breasts and surprising cocks that swing out from under miniskirts during not so dainty pirouettes; vacant-faced whores with oversized asses dancing like robots in slow motion, swishing cumbersome tails, moving mimelike, like the mating dance of curly-tailed lizards.

Chris's body responds on automatic, moving to the music. Dancing. He's swimming in the people, flowing with the music, as light as ballet dancers, as heavy as Sumo wrestlers, as chewy as Gummy Bears, as blue as blue eyes behind fake-blue contact lenses. He gets drenched in sweat, his own and from rubbing up against other people. Like splashing naked in the water. He peels off his saturated shirt. Sopping, he tenses his muscles, watches them bounce and stand up hard. It feels good. He watches the flesh of other bodies. So much skin. Male members and female fruits bounce to the beat of the drum, rising louder and louder. Pumps hard. Sweat greases the floor. In the dark corners, under tables, orgasmic screams sting above the melody,

> Like the sweet soca music
> And the beat of a drumstick
> Someting moving in you pants
> Whenever we dance

I feelin it
I feelin it.

Hands adhere to his ass. He pushes back up against them like dou-ble-stick tape. He turns, looks at Cleo and takes a deep breath as she takes his breath away as he takes her in. His eyes slide around absolutely suckling curves. Her skin burning black. Eyes like sunspots. Burning and black, surrounded by silver glitter matching her skintight silver lamé body stocking.

"What's up, Cleopatra?" he yells over the music.

"I'm sure you is, white blood," she screams, looking at his mid-section, licking her lips. "If not, we best fix dat," she hisses into his ear as she winds on him, teasing him to the beat of the drums, the pump of the horns, rotating her waist around in circles and in and out at the same time. As if her midsection has become detached, attached itself to his. And he feels blood rush. She moans, "Oh yes, we have bananas."

Chris thinks, Thanks a lot, dick, just when I don't need you, and last night with Robin hits again. He craves coke.

"Chris, like you got bootoo in you pants or you just happy to see me? You find saltfish you want to bang?" Cleo's breath hot in his ear.

And he just holds on to her ample ass, feels the dimples on it, as if it's smiling at the world. He closes his eyes, pushes last night out of his head, feels her bumbum jamming, ramming on him pur-posely as he falls into the cement mixer, feels his sweat and her sweat. The band plays,

Baby, something in you pocket
I feelin it, I feelin it
Baby, it shape like a rocket
Feelin it, Feelin it.

"I needs to powder my nose," Cleopatra says, her hand pushing into the crack of his ass.

"I don't got . . . ," Chris says.

"If you find Snow White, I'd love to love you, baby," she says, pulling away as the band plays,

> Squeeeze me tight
> Hold me darlin
> All through the night
> Keep on rammin,
> Too much sex never kill a man yet.

He slips away from her, extracts himself, works his way through the crowd to the back of the club, climbs the steps, bangs on the door with a painting of a shark, marked PRIVATE. A slot on the door slides, bloodshot eyes stare, checking him out. The door sweeps open.

"How's it going, Tweed?" Chris asks, laying his hand flat on his flat eraser head, which seems to have stretched even higher since the last time he saw him on the beach.

"I'm cool as ice and twice as nice. Tweed's my name and smugglin, not snugglin, my game."

"Shark told me he's not dealing anymore."

Harry laughs, picks up the phone, says, "Shark, Chris here."

"What happened to all your girls?" Chris asks as Tweed leads him through the back door to another, larger room.

"I's like Clark Gable, always able, my body may be small but where it counts I tall, but dem gals ain't coming no more. Not like before. I found one last week so ugly, she can't get it for free. But the ting what is, she ain't give me no ting. I end up with pocket full of empty." He leaves.

Chris waits for Shark, staring at the burgundy flock whorehouse wallpaper, burgundy velvet curtains, mirrors and more mirrors, reflecting paintings and more paintings of fat pink nudes on black velvet, and a life-size statue of Michael Jackson naked with the word LOVE discreetly covering his nonexistent genitals. Chris cups his own midsection, shakes his head. The music from the outside bangs, muffled against the walls of the room, as if it's trying to break in. His sweat dries. He puts on his shirt, sits at the bar, grabs a bottle of Añejo and takes a long pull. Then another and another, turns all warm inside. He hears something, looks up, sees Shark staring at him. His eyes blaze. He slings an arm around Chris, gives him a masculine thump on the back, then sits next to him at the bar.

"Ain't the office great?" Shark asks. "All the shit get here yesterday."

Chris doesn't answer, just stares at him. Shark is covered in a jewelry store, dripping in gold, thick chains from his thick neck, a globe-size pendant of Africa, and a ring on every finger, and a diamond in his right ear, the stud ear.

"What wrong wit you?" Shark asks. "Art pussy got you tongue or what?"

"You don't deal anymore? Right?"

Shark shakes his head. "The Lord is my shepherd, I takes what I want. Dis nation on the take and I's taking." The muscles in his neck twitch as he grabs the rum bottle, takes a swig. "Cool out, mon," he says handing Chris the rum bottle.

"Fuck you, Shark," Chris says without emotion. He gulps some rum, feels it hit his head. "I fucking believed you. I gave you money cause I believed you. That you would get out. You fucking lied to me."

"Fuck dat shit," Shark says, standing up pacing. "Green turns your black ass white. You see my new Rolex watch. Dat's fucking freedom," Shark says frowning, breathing rapidly, waving his big hands. "I gots respect now and I's a big man. All the boys wants to grow up an be just like me and all the girls gots crush on me. Mon, I get more love letters from gals dan Prince. Dat's what I is, the prince of the Bahamas, the great black hope. I need more money. Nough money dat I never have to be a nigger again," Shark says, his voice getting louder and louder. "You white and you gots money." He walks to the closet, pulls out a box of Tide. "You don't understand."

"I'm sick of that shit. That I don't understand because I'm rich and white." Chris sighs in frustration. Shark hands him the box. He sits back down, leans toward Chris, watching expectantly. "What the fuck is this?" Chris asks, confused.

"Open it," Shark says. His foot shakes up and down.

Chris opens the box, smells soap powder, sees green. He pulls out a stack of hundred-dollar bills. The box is jammed full of money.

"Dat be all the moneys you lend me. The money for the *Black Thunder* plus the 69 money plus interest," Shark says, his eyes hot.

Chris raises his eyebrows, shrugs, puts the stack of money back into the box. "I don't want this. I don't care about this." He shakes his head, hands the box to Shark. "I got money and it's no fucking help. I don't want any fucking money," Chris says, hurt, shaking his head.

"What you want?" Shark asks, his voice cracking. He rubs his forehead.

"I want you to fucking tell me the truth."

"Mon, if there was no dealers, how you think you'd fill your face with coke? Using ain't no different dan dealing. Too fucking hypocrite." Shark shoves the box of money at him. "Just take the money. Dat way you don't have to feel guilty."

"Fuck you, you fucking liar," Chris says, flinging the box across the room. It slams against a nude. Money spills out.

A stillness envelops them. The only sound is their breathing. They stare at one another as if they're waiting for something.

"What you want?" Shark asks again, over and over, shaking his head.

"I want you safe. I want you alive," Chris says. "I want you to fucking tell me the truth."

"Truth," Shark says, his chin resting on his hand. Chris continues to stare at him and he looks like such a confused little boy, and there's such sorrow showing in his eyes. It hurts. Chris fights the urge to hug him.

"The cartel tell me dey want to use the club as a washing machine. Tell me dey want me to work for dem. I tell dem to eat my fuck. El Hombre, the main man, say, 'I could have you dick cut off and stick up you ass with one phone call or I could do it myself.' Dat's an offer I can't refuse." He takes a deep breath. "Dat's why I want you to take the money, I don't want you involved in dis shit."

"Can't you do anything?"

"I can do what dey say and hopefully live happy ever after. Dey own the fucking Bahamas."

"I'm scared for you."

"You the onliest person ever give me a break," Shark says. "You the only one I got. Don't worry."

"What about your mother?" Chris asks, picturing Tantie on the beach the other day, thinking how happy she looked when he told her Shark wasn't gonna deal anymore.

"She gone crazy too bad," Shark says, sitting upright. "She only scream Bible."

"Don't fuck with people who love you," Chris says softly.

Shark looks concerned. "So you having love problem? What happening with you and Robin?" Shark leans toward him, as if he wants to touch him. His eyes search. "Fuck her yet?"

"She . . . but . . . ," Chris says, folding his arms, unable to meet Shark's insistent gaze, wondering how he knows. He takes a deep breath. "Well . . ." He shuts his eyes, rubs his neck.

"It only Shark here," he says.

Chris forces the words out. "She's dying and I can't . . ." He takes a huge swig of rum.

Shark is silent for a few seconds. "We's all dying. From the time you born you dying . . . ," Shark says, his eyes not wavering from Chris's. "Don't punch waves."

Chris looks away, over Shark's shoulder, caresses the rum bottle. His throat constricts. He forces a deep breath, feels sweat trickle down and dry under his arms. His heart beats, pulses on his left temple. He forces it out. "I can't deal . . . I feel useless, worthless. Nothing. Not enough anymore. And my fucking mother. I can't stop thinking about her . . . And my dick. I mean it doesn't work . . . with her . . . Robin. My dick. It didn't work."

"Cool out," Shark says, laying his hand on Chris's hand on the bar. "Relax. Breathe," Shark says, looking at him tenderly. He feels his warm palm, the cold gold of the rings.

"Don't. Don't preoccupy bout you momma. She dead. You can't help she. She can't help you. And don't worry Robin sick. Let you

brain have a talk with you dick. Say, 'Dick, why you fucking with
me? Why you don't want dis gal?' It will tell you. And den you tell
her. And if you's tired doing noting, just do someting. Do someting
bout it." He moves his hand away, getting up from the bar. He
walks over to his desk, takes out a little vial, bites the cap off, pours
the rocks onto his hand, walks back over.

Chris stares at the base, tiny, translucent white and harmless-
looking on Shark's brown palm. He tries to ignore it, to blank it out.
He swallows.

"Dis here fix you, fix everyting," Shark says, putting the rock into
a glass pipe, leaning his head back and lighting. White smoke flows.

Chris smells the smoke, feels his brain start to dribble. He fights
his brain, picturing his hands inside squeezing the drops dry. But he
needs to get away, farther than the rum can take him.

"I'm not going to smoke crack. I'm not going to take another
swim in the shark pit." He grits his teeth, sees his seven-year-old
body, brittle arms and legs, shaking as he looked down into the pen
at the hotel where they kept a six-foot hammerhead shark as a
tourist attraction.

"How was I to know dat shark would bite you sucked mango
seed of a body? Dat he never eat a white meat yet. Basing ain't no
different from snorting. It just more concentrate. Like the differ-
ence between beating off and fucking."

"It's supposed to fuck you," Chris says, nervous, craving the high.
Shark's eyes taunt, and the look takes him back and he's a child
again.

"Les go for a swim, mon," Shark taunts. "Don't be dread, Chris?"

"Fuck no!" He inflated his chest.

"You scared of you own pink backside," Shark mocks, jumping
into the pen. "Chris is a scared whitey," Shark chanted as the hammerhead ignored him, swam away from him.

"Fuck that noise!" Chris yelled, his heart beating in his mouth.
He jumped.

"Quit dreaming," Shark says. He flinches. Shark holds the pipe
out to him.

The pipe taunts. It says: Escape. Just one hit, numb it, numb it, just for the moment, think about the moment, you can stop, you know you can stop, you control it, it doesn't control you, and that's the fucking answer, just one hit and then you'll be set, swimming in the high, head like a blimp floating, soaring. And Robin won't die, the treatment is working, doesn't she say she's feeling much better, but they all fucking die and he imagines putting her in a plastic bag, a slab of cold meat. He imagines the earth spreading its ass to suck her into its bowels. A garbage disposal. No Vaseline needed. She grips two asshole hairs, him and the cancer quack. Defeat without even one thrust. Chris sees the black fin cutting the water like a knife, heading straight for him as he turned and swam as fast as he could to the side of the pen and exhaled as he fought to pull his body over. Then he felt a tug and a sandpaper feeling. The water around him beat. He screamed.

Chris's heart beats in his mouth as he takes the pipe from Shark, tries to keep his hands from shaking as he puts the pipe to his lips, tilts his head back and inhales. The smoke tastes like the insect repellent. The nugget sputters.

He waits expectantly, looking at Shark, a satisfied smirk on his face like the smirk on his face when he got his nickname and trophy from the Boiling Rock Women's Association, presented by Miss Maple Proudfoot, where he made a speech, saying, "Me best friend Chris fall in the pen and the shark grab he. I didn't want to lose he to no stupid black shark so I dives in and pull he out the shark mouth."

And then. Rush. Rush. Rush. Rush. A thousand icy, delicious, crisp orgasms . . . of continuous explosion, white crystal fireworks breaking the pleasure barrier . . . heightening . . . almost too much pleasure . . . heart pounding . . . brain cells swollen with it . . . pronounced . . . time stops . . .

Hit after hit after hit. Chris is drinking it in, drinking in the feeling, satisfying the craving, the relief, the satisfaction, and he can finally breathe secure, can handle anything. And then he gets it, it comes all by itself. He smiles to himself. He gets a hard-on.

"What you smiling at, mon?" Shark asks.

"I got a coke-on."

"You and me both. I's hard as rock stone. Dis like old times, aye mon, you and me sitting around horny. How you spell relief? P-U-S-S-Y. It like when you fall off horse. You gots to get right back on and ride again. And when you know it work, you relax and it gonna work with Robin. If not, you's got to drink some cock-hard tea that Pa Beah make and den it may never come down and you have to use it to hang towel." Shark winks at Chris. He walks over and presses the intercom on his desk. "Tweed, send up Cleo and Pam."

And Chris thinks, I should leave, as he tries to get up and Shark walks over, hands him the coke. Reflex action, he sucks, breathes it in. As long as the coke's there he'll be there. Fuck it. Fuck life, his brain tells him.

The door opens. Music blares in, as if pushing them in. "Dis be Pam. And you knows Cleo."

Chris shakes Pam's hand. She's chewing gum. He looks at the peroxide hair, at the black roots, at the buttermilk-colored face, the red racing stripe painted on cheekbones. She winks at him. "Nice to meet you," she says.

"I met you one night at the Tipsy Turtle," Chris says. Shark lights the pipe. Chris fights the urge to grab it out of his hand and suck.

"You do look familar," Pam says naughtily.

Chris wonders if she is playing with him as she walks over and puts her arm around Shark's shoulder. Cleo walks up to Chris and asks, "How dat bootoo in you pants?" Then she touches his crotch and kisses him, forcing his mouth open with her tongue, and Chris kisses her back and it's like sucking the purple flesh of a coco plum for juice, tastes dry and sweet.

He pulls away and Shark and Pam are sitting on the pink fur couch, basing, passing the pipe back and forth. And Cleo rushes over and sits next to Shark and grabs the pipe from Pam and smokes. Chris stands watching and Shark says, "Come on, mon. What wrong with you?" Then Chris sits on the couch next to Cleo and she hands him the pipe and he inhales, more and more, feels so high that he isn't himself, not in himself, like there's this body and then there's him and like the body is this heavy baggage that he has to carry around to satisfy. And there it is, the satisfaction. Cleo's eyes so bright, he pictures meltdown. Chris looks at Shark and Pam and they are all wrapped up, blue-black on and in pink-shrimp white, and Cleo squeezes him hard between the legs, saying, "What wrong with you?"

And his brain, racing from the crack, says, "What the fuck does it matter?" as he focuses on the silver glitter around Cleo's eyes, focuses on her Maraschino-cherry-colored lips. She looks like a Caribbean queen. As rich and sweet as chocolate mousse. And his lips stick to hers like a goose barnacle to a dock. She unbuttons his shirt and unzips his pants and it's in her hand and then she lets go, pulls away. He looks over at Shark, flat on his back, on the imitation zebra-skin rug in front of the couch, and he has spread coke all over his hard stomach and hard dick, like white pollen on a black flower and Pam is snorting, her nose on his stomach, and then on his pulsating black dick. Her sharp white hair sticks into the air. His big black balls hang heavy. Cleo is naked now and she walks over and starts snorting up all the leftover coke off Shark. Her coked-up mouth meet's Pam's coked-up mouth and they are kissing and caressing, and then they are between each other's legs, eating each other. Chris stands there watching and he's so high. Shark smiles, bright white teeth, says, "Come."

Shark pulls Cleo off of Pam and she lies flat on her back and Shark picks up the bag of coke, pours white on her nipples and between her legs, like whipped cream on a hot fudge sundae.

Chris pulls off his clothes and walks over and gets down on the floor and licks and he imagines he's in a storm in the ocean, licking whitecaps off black waves, and her blackness tastes soft and numb. So delicious. And he's all over her, sucking and licking and snorting, her and the coke. His noises, like the noise the grunt snapper makes after it's caught, are echoed by Pam and by Shark, and Cleo giggles as he works his way down, snorting-licking her outie belly button like a black-eyed pea, and then his face is between Cleo's legs, and he opens his eyes and looks at the white on the pink between the black and then at Shark next to him, his black head between white legs, and he remembers when he and Shark were kids, walking on the beach, and they saw one of those sucker things, some kind of anemone, and they crouched around it, staring. It was all buried except for its mouth, like a rounded pussy, with a flower pattern printed in loose, fleshy warts. "Poke the ting!" Shark said. "No way. I don't want it to squirt on me," Chris answered.

So Shark picked up a sand dollar and stuck it right in the center of the pink hole of the flower. The animal ejaculated a tiny jet straight up, pushing itself into the sand. The flower shrinking, disappearing. The two of them immediately began digging, throwing wet sand between their legs until they had a hole three feet deep and had given up trying to find out where the animal had disappeared to. And they kept trying, deflowering all the anemones, and never did find any of them.

And Chris thinks about all the women they stuck it in and how they all disappear and he thinks of Robin and pictures her dissolving, shrinking before his eyes, and how he can't do anything about it, and Shark moans and it feels like Shark is yelling at him to "poke it!" He sticks it into Cleo, afraid he might not find it, afraid he will dissolve and turn soft, as if she were an anemone, as if he were entering alien territory, and he wishes she would take him in her hand and guide him in but she doesn't. But he finds it and he's sure he feels it squirt when he sticks it in.

There's nothing subtle, nothing slow. He and Shark are on top and the women are on the bottom, next to each other, and they are hammering it, going as fast as they can, slapping jackhammers.

Then the women are on top and they are riding away, and it's Pam in white on black and they're in the lead and right behind them, gaining, is Cleopatra in black on white. And he's a child again, riding his plastic horse connected to four posts by springs, back and forth. He would talk to it and sneak out of bed and ride it all night long, singing, "Nobody loves me, nobody loves me." The springs would go squeak, squeak, squeak.

Chris looks up at Cleo, frenzied, galloping. Slap, slap, slap. He closes his eyes and he's on the horse again, frenzied, galloping, going places in his mind. He looks up at Cleo again and she has no head. That's how it looks as she presses her chin into her shoulder.

And when she tilts her head back and looks up, it's like a turtle's head when it withdraws halfway into its shell to die. And he feels how she looks, dead and headless. She keeps going on top, and he keeps going in his mind on the bottom, forcing the fantasy, wanting to come, wanting the release, and he can see and feel her coming, one after another, even though she makes no noise. He can see in her eyes that she doesn't even know that he's there. He keeps going, willing it to end, begging it to end. Like a baby turtle struggling to a never seen sea. Where is she? he thinks. He can't even feel her, as if he's covered in ten rubbers, like that sticky Stud stuff he used to spray on before he trained himself to hold it. And Shark screams, "Ah, oh, oh, ohhhh!" And he feels jealous and he looks up at the ceiling mirror as Shark pulls out and he sees it, between his legs, like a bitten black Twinkie dripping white cream. Chris clenches down, tries, but he's lost, lost in her, his ship lost at sea, trapped. And he thinks, she's doing this for the coke. And what am I doing it for? And I might as well be fucking one of those blown-up dolls. And pop, he fakes it, lets out a hiss of relief, like air escaping a tire.

He wonders how to get out from under as she pulls away, and he slips out and he stays hard and he thinks how fucking sly the white lady is, giving you a hard-on for no reason and then not letting you lose it, not ever going away, and she is never satisfied and as she makes you feel more confident, better able to deal, all the while she's taking charge as she makes you gradually lose control.

He looks at Shark's dripping dick, like a sea cucumber, his come sticking to it in threads. He looks at the drops of come, white on Pam's white belly, like pearls, and he thinks of the pearl fish that uses its knifelike tail to cut into the asshole of the sea cucumber, where they live munching away at the sea cucumber's guts as fast as they can grow them back, until the sea cucumbers ejaculates its insides, making the pearl fish's home and food its coffin.

The pipe is lit again. Chris looks at Cleo and Shark and Pam. We are all slaves now and massa is still white, powder white. Cleo hands him the pipe. He brings it to his lips and sucks on his real lover, his real massa. He wishes he were on his plastic horse riding far away.

8

White froth and curdled-cream-colored sand runs through their toes. Footprints form and then wash away as Chris and Robin walk on breaking waves. Flowing, in and out.

Branches snap. He looks up, sees two vultures, their black wings flapping, and then they're floating, riding invisible air currents.

"God, I hate those vulture things," she says.

"We call them *cobeau*. The Bahamian air force."

She frowns, reaches for his hand and holds it tight. Cold fingers. He holds on.

"After chemo, I took a shower, shampooed my hair. It fell out. I ended up shampooing my scalp. I couldn't believe it was my hair, my scalp. I couldn't look in the mirror. I tried. I crawled into bed and fell asleep and dreamed I was a vulture," she says.

He looks at her and she looks so fragile. Her slimness covered yet exaggerated by her clothes, one of his old, white, long-sleeved, monogrammed dress shirts, baggy long shorts. And she seems to be getting frailer, lighter every day. Like some kind of reverse Samson, as her hair grows back, she loses her strength. He thinks she has started to shake at times, like old people, but he's not sure because when he thinks he sees this he looks away.

He craves coke, gritting his teeth, thinking about basing for the first time three weeks ago. He thinks how every time he leaves

Robin he goes straight to the 69, and he pictures Shark, last night, smoking, yelling, pacing. "I just got me one bellyful of pussy! The tourist gal catch one look at my dick and ask me if I gots a license for it. She tell me dat I should sell it to the porno movies." Shark stopped, his eyes crazy, tortured, rubbing his tummy, scratching his balls. "The spics. Fucking white niggers. Dems fucking me up the asshole." He comoked more, the smoke flowing from his nose and mouth, laughing after each hit. Then he laughed until he choked, his arms and legs twitching. His laugh turned to sobs. Chris grabbed him, hugged him, white spit hissed from his mouth. Chris was so high all he could do was hold on.

"The first chemo." Robin's face cringes. "They fed it intravenously into my arm, and the instant the drug hit, it was like being hit with a sledgehammer. I vomited." She looks at him, her eyes nervous, questioning.

Chris tries to look at her. Can't. Looks away. As the words roll out of her mouth he detaches himself from them, separates along the dotted line. He changes the subject. "When I was a kid, Shark and I would pretend we were dead to try to get the buzzards to fly down to us," he says, shutting his eyes, remembering the fresh smell and spongy feel and the crawling sound of the Astroturf green grass. He held his body so perfectly still that it shook as he looked up at the sky and clouds swirled—the sky became his world. And then the vultures appeared in the void, way up, black dots. Then sweeping jots, like black jet exhaust. Eyeballs swam in his eyes as the birds got closer and bigger, and it was as if he were falling into the heavens. He felt Shark grab his hand as he felt his body flinch, as they heard the flap and snap of the wings. Wince. And then for a split second, the fleshy, ugly bird heavy on Shark's chest. And Shark screamed, "Boo!" They jumped up together, their hearts pumping, a black blur of wings beating, the vulture retreating. They laughed so hard it hurt.

Chris walks faster, pulling her. He tries to block her view of the graveyard with his body. Her fingers pull away. She stops, walks toward it. From the beach side, waves threaten to overflow it; from all other sides, bush threatens to overgrow it. Struggling, scattered haphazardly, as if washed up in the tide, grey wooden crosses made from driftwood stick out of the ground at different angles. A sprinkling of coral white gravestones, names and dates sandpapered by salt air, jut up like badly made false teeth.

"Why's it so close to the beach?" she asks, walking around, trying to read the stones.

"It's too rocky to dig further inland. Doctor Conch said that hurricane Betsy washed all the graves out and every house in the village blew away but his. They had to hole up in Preacher's Cave for days. When he went back to his house, the open coffin of three-hundred-pound Big Bertha was sitting on the floor. As he said, 'She make man out of most the boys on Cupid Cay.' "

Robin looks up from the gravestone, a sad smile spreading on her face.

He feels relief. "He said he drank a toast to her, saying that she's still the most beautiful gal in the village."

"What are the plates and knives and forks for?"

"The villagers come here and have meals with their dead when they feel lonely. They even set out food for them."

She steps among the graves and her legs get tangled in the orange wirelike vine that has crept from the bush, strangling the scrub, crosses and gravestones.

"What a weird vine," she says as she untangles it from her feet.

"It's called love vine."

"Why love vine?"

"Because it has no beginning or end. Like love." And he remembers Shark telling him that the natives tie love vine around their waist to cure their sex weakness, and he looks out to sea, and he hates himself for not being able to pick her up in his arms and say, "I love you," and say, "I love you so much it hurts." And then to lay her down and show her with his body what he feels. And he hears his mother's voice, drunk, moaning coming from the sewing turret. And he wanted to tell her that he loved her and that she was killing herself with the alcohol and that he would help her and that all she had to do was talk about it and it would be O.K. It would be all right if he could just tell her he loved her and then bury himself in that spot, his spot. He pictures her rocking back and forth on her rocking chair, at first saying the rosary, beads running through skinny freckled fingers, lips trembling, taking short snorts of Bacardi between each prayer, and then toward the end, instead of the rosary, she would be shelling black-eyed peas. The rocking chair would creak, the pea pod would crack and then she would flick the peas to the floor as if she were shooting marbles. The blades of the rocking chair squashed the peas, turning the floor pus green.

"What are you thinking about?" Robin asks, staring at him. "You look so sad."

"Nothing," he says, folding his arms, closing up.

She stares at him, hard, demanding. "I'm not a mind reader," she says, pissed off. "Tell me what's wrong. Please."

"Like I can't even have my own thoughts. Like you want them too," he snaps, and then he feels bad.

She just shakes her head. "You can't give me what I want."

He bites his nails. He's mad at her. He's mad at himself for being mad at her. And he can't think about it, can't show it, can't talk about it with her. So it will go away. So they can go on. So she won't go away. But then it shows itself. And then the guilt. Her alarm watch sounds. She takes the syringe out of her purse. And he feels her pain. The pain that comes without warning. Her face becomes a grimace. He hates that fucking grimace. He hates that fucking pain. And Chris remembers last week, the ice cube in her hand against his earlobe, freezing cold, melting frigid drops onto his shoulder, down his naked chest.

"You sure you want me to pierce it?" Robin asked.

"Yes," he answered.

"The stud ear?" she asked.

"Yes," he said, freezing inside as he thought how every time he tried to make a move on her, he froze, and a rush of the night on the beach with the dolphins paralyzed him, and he's a stud with everyone else, everyone he doesn't care about, such a stud he doesn't even feel anymore, doesn't come anymore.

The silver needle shined. He grit his teeth. She plunged the needle into him.

"It hurts," he screamed.

"It's only a little prick, you big prick," she answered. And he opened his eyes and she just stood there, her eyes shut, trembling. The needle dropped. A red dot lit in the middle of his left earlobe. A drop of blood.

He jumped up in a panic, sat her down on the bed.

"Don't worry," she said. "It's a healing pain. Doctor Johnson says the pain is good. It's a sign of tumor kill."

"Bullshit. How could pain be good? Pain means something's wrong. If Doctor Johnson knew what he was doing, why would he be hiding out in this Third World country club of an island? Why wouldn't he be publishing his results? How come every time I pass his house on Millionaire's Row he's adding a new wing?"

Then she went hard before his eyes, shook her head back and forth. "There's a conspiracy against him, against any alternative treatment. Cancer is an industry in the States," she said coldly. She took a deep breath. "I am getting better. I will get better. The treatment is curing me," she said firmly, flatly, in a sort of chant, and then she looked at him, begging with her eyes. "Please believe."

And he remembers going soft, regretting he said what he said even though it was what he thought, and he told himself he had to make himself believe in the treatment for her, for himself.

He picks up two bottles. Throws one up into the air over the ocean, throws the other bottle at the first one. They smash together. He grits his teeth. A shower of shattered green glass splashes into ocean.

He looks over at her as she pulls the needle out and puts it away. She rubs her scalp with her hand, pushing back hair she doesn't have.

"Talk," she says firmly.

"I'm just so sick of the needles."

Her hands clench. She shrugs her shoulders, shakes her head. "How do you think I feel about them?" She wanders away.

He stares at the sun, feels it burn, shuts his eyes, watches the orange flash inside his eyelids.

He opens his eyes. She's sitting on top of a sculpted, heart-shaped tombstone. In front of another gravestone is a bed of newly dug dirt covered in a hill of gaudy plastic flowers stuck into Styro-foam crosses, hearts and circles.

She sits birdlike, in an impossible position, picking at herself.

He forces himself to walk up to her slowly, each step placed as she places a plastic purple rose behind her right ear. She looks so sad and angry and he wants to hug her but he can't. He feels for her. He breathes in hard and then, "What's wrong with you?" escapes. He moves closer, stops.

A quietness, a stillness envelops them. It pierces his ears.

"You're the one who has the problem," she says, her tone in control. Her icy eyes bite chunks. The waves roll. And he feels the bad little boy.

He forces the words out, "I'm sorry," stepping towards her.

"For what?" she says, flinging the question at him.

He stops. Her eyes meet his and then move away, leaving him. It hurts.

She stares at the ocean, says, "I don't have strength for you and the cancer. Sorry just doesn't . . ."

"What are you talking about? What's your problem?" he asks, watching her chest heave up and down, listening to her harsh breathing, as if someone turned off the oxygen.

"You . . . ," she says, and then she sighs, staring at him, waiting.

He fights to keep it down, to keep it in. Sit, boy! He gazes back at her on the tombstone. Looks away.

"Look at me!" she says, quick and angry.

He forces himself to look at her, squinting as if he's looking into the sun. "I don't need this," he says.

"Neither do I."

"Let's go," he says suddenly, grabbing her hand. She recoils, snaps back against his touch as if it's a slap. The thought that his touch could repel her stings. He takes a step back away from her. He feels himself start to tremble, tries to stop.

"Fuck you," she screams. "Fuck all the coke you stick up your face," she says in a rush, forcing it out.

How does she know? he thinks, shocked. He tried so hard to keep it from her.

"Do you think I'm stupid? Don't you think I know? Where you

go . . . what you do, when you're with Shark . . . Give me a little bit of credit."

He clenches his hands together, forming one large fist. He glances at her on the gravestone as she brings her legs to her chest. Hugs them. He wants to feel the victim. But he knows she's right but he can't tell her. He wants to tell her how badly he wants to try to make love to her again, how afraid he is to try. But he's frozen.

She rubs her eyes. And then she sits there and says nothing. Just sits there staring out at the sea, dry eyed, scanning the horizon. Sunlight pours over her face. He wants to tell her about the coke, about what it makes him do, about what her cancer makes him do. He tries to hold on, smooth it over, like wet plaster, ease. Erase. But he can't. He holds his head in his hands.

"I refuse to feel sorry for you," she says, trying to stay calm. "I refuse to pity someone who has everything but does nothing. Nothing but float around and fuck himself up. You have a fucking brain," she says, no longer able to stay calm. "Use it. Do something. Grow up!"

"Who do you think you are, my mother?"

"Are you turning me into your mother? Forget your mother. Your mommy's not here." She spits the words out, leaning forward, her face a fire, lips pulled tight.

"Bitch," he says under his breath, taking a step back away from her. He feels himself start to tremble, tries to stop. And he feels it. As if his skin is being bitten by sand flies, no-see-ums, biting grains of pepper. So closed in. He has to get away. His heart beats hard. His head spins. His eyes blur. He can't catch his breath. His body covered in sweat, instantaneously. He runs. Dives into the surf, desperate to drown the fire. He swims straight out. Dizzy. Breathless. His eyes open, the salt burning. He tells himself he's not coming back, the thoughts madly racing through his head. He shuts his eyes and it all turns black and he sees Evalina's black skin in her black funeral clothes. And he just wants to get his mother's funeral over with as he feels the embarrassment for her, that she has to be buried in the old native graveyard, because Monsignor said that Roman Catholic law makes it a sin to bury anyone who has taken their own life on consecrated church soil.

He shoves the thought out of his head. Robin flashes before him, alone in the graveyard, sitting on the gravestone. What the fuck am I doing? he thinks. Something cracks. "Do something," he hears her yell. And she's fucking right. He sees great sucking holes, sees the coke filling them up, sees himself hiding behind her cancer. He knows he should be doing something with his life. He turns around and swims straight back in. Dizzy. Breathless. As fast as he can. To get to her. He runs out of the water, his feet kicking and sticking to the soft sand. He wipes his eyes. And she's still there, in the same place. She looks stunned. He runs up to her.

He pushes the wet hair back off his face. She closes her eyes. Water droplets blow off him onto her. He pictures the gold scepter sprinkling holy water on people in church. He sits across from her on soft grass in front of the tombstone. His upper lip trembles. He tries to talk. Stutters. "It . . . I mean, it, the cancer, makes me feel so small, so weak, and there's nothing I can do and I hate it and I can't even think about it," he says, the words flowing out, fighting to control them. "I have to pretend it doesn't exist and I hate myself for being so weak and . . . that's why I take drugs."

"That's bullshit. You took drugs before me, before the cancer. Don't make me your excuse. Don't make my sickness your excuse." She takes a deep breath. "You make me hide it, like I'm doing something wrong, and every time I bring it up, you close up, change the subject," she says, rubbing her neck. "You make me feel sleazy for being sick."

"You . . . make me feel small."

"It's not me," she says, standing up. "I'm not it. It's cancer. And cancer's not the problem. Coke's not the problem. You're the problem. You need to do something, move ahead, get over it."

"I try . . . I want to be . . . I want to be your knight in shining armor and all that fucking macho shit."

"I don't want macho. I don't want a pretend knight. I don't want a boy. I'm dying, I don't want fairy tales." She catches her breath. "I want a man."

No longer in control. Tears flow. He holds himself, rocking back and forth, back and forth, back and forth. He's exhausted. And he hears her saying she's dying over and over. "I let her die alone," he whispers, over and over. "I let her die alone," he screams, angry. His hands form fists. He slugs himself over and over. Hard. He pounds his chest. Then his head. He doesn't feel it, tries to pound the feeling out.

"Stop," she screams, grabbing his arms.

"Please . . . ," he whispers. She brings her ear down to his lips. "Don't die."

Then it comes out. It's running out of her mouth, sweat running down her forehead and tears running out of her eyes. As the retching continues, he imagines that the vomit is the poison and she is ejecting it out of her body. She turns away, wipes the vomit away with her palm. It forms shiny lines between her hand and her mouth, like a child stretching chewing gum from her mouth and then sucking it back in.

He grabs her head. She tries to pull away. He holds it firm. In a vise. Holds her face in front of his face. Looks into her teary eyes through his tears. "I won't . . . ," he says. "You're right. I will . . . change. Do something. Give. You have me. I'll be there for you. For me." He shivers.

He brings his mouth down upon hers, wet, still glistening with vomit, and he can feel her lips under his lips. Kiss after kiss. Mouth-to-mouth resuscitation.

She strokes his hair, whispers in his ear, "If I was only healthy."

"You're the healthiest person I know. I want you. But I'm so afraid I can't."

"I will get well!" she says. And her mouth slides down. Slippery, caressing and tasting, low and lower. He breathes hard. Every muscle tensing, repositioning, sizzling. The heat from outside. The sun. The heat from inside. The sex. She yanks his bathing suit down. Her hot breath is enough, like grains of sand blowing against him softly on the beach. He hardly breathes as his heart beats hard in his hard dick, as her tongue touches. Blood engorging. Her tongue against balls. They suck in, in defense, like in a cold shower, before he makes his brain relax them. He looks at her, the top of her head like an egg with fuzz. He remembers his mother in the morning, every morning, eating breakfast in bed. He sees the soft-boiled egg and the silver egg holder and the special gold scissors in the shape of a bird. He watches Robin's head, like a baby's head but big. Just as fragile. Like if you squeezed it, you could push it in. His pubic hair. A flat shiny blue-black triangle of curls against the downy bulb of her head as she goes down on him, as she goes down lower, to the place beneath, above his ass. Touching it with her tongue, sending shivers of pleasure in all directions, causing everything to throb. He puts his hands behind his head. Clenches his scalp to stop from grabbing, grabbing himself and ending it with a flick of the wrist. Her tongue goes lower. His thighs strain. He thinks of limbo dancers, of the coconut trees bending in the wind. Her tongue is between the cheeks of his ass. She licks. As he wonders how he tastes. And her tongue gets deeper and deeper. Penetrating. He turns over. He's on all fours, like a dog. He faces a tombstone. A white statue of the Virgin Mary sticks out from the love vine, black rusting rosary around her neck, her arms stretched. She smiles at him. And Robin's tongue is joined by fingers sticking in and out, out and in. He tries to hold on. So much pleasure he leaks, moans from his mouth, sweat from his body, tears from his eyes. And has to turn over. She slides down. And she has him in her, swallowed. He loves the way it looks between her lips. He surrenders and his head falls back onto the grass. He reaches his arms behind his back, grabs the tombstone. He squeezes. Then the sun. He squeezes his eyes shut. The light still penetrating orange under his eyelids. Mouth running up and down. The sound of the waves breaking, her sucking. He tries to pull away. To escape to the other lips, to reciprocate, before it's too late. Her hands hold firm, nails dig into his ass. Paralyzed in pleasure waves. She pulls away. He feels panic. Afraid to open his eyes. It shoots to his midsection. His insides quiver. And then he feels her crawl on top of him, and he opens his eyes, and she's naked and so beautiful, and he feels so much for her and the fear melts, as she gives way, tight and then melting. And their bodies make the sound of air escaping from the spout of a dolphin and he thinks that dolphins are creatures who once returned to the sea and he feels as if he's finally returned to where he belongs. Almost too deep. And full. No longer separate. Together. And he sits up slowly and he feels himself going deeper and deeper into her and she's on his lap and her eyes meet his and he hugs her for as long and as tight as he can. And he pries her mouth open with his tongue. The taste of vomit and love. Then he picks her up and carries her, joined, to the hard sand, where the waves are breaking. He feels the wind brushing his back, and the warm water, a passion tide, inside and outside him, with each wave caressing between his legs, his cheeks, the crack of his ass, and then retreating. And the softness meeting the hardness, the hardness disappearing into the softness. And he goes in with the wave and out with the wave. Weightless. In and out.

"I love you!" he screams, drowning out the sound of the waves as he explodes into her, as a scream of boiling ecstasy explodes from her mouth. He imagines he's injecting her full of life.

9

Half asleep, half awake. The sun streams in. Chris rolls over on his back, pulls the pillow from between his legs, puts it over his face. Water laps against the boat. He thinks, today's the day he's gonna start. He always told himself he would write someday, and Robin keeps telling him he can do it and she bought him paper and sharpened new pencils and he promised her he'd start but he's afraid. And he tells himself not to worry as the memories lap through his head. He thinks of the last two months since he and Robin were at the graveyard. He smiles, his recent past playing in his head like a movie: he and Robin following the endless chain of uninhabited islands, emeralds in turquoise surrounded by pinky white powder, then dropping anchor at random. Just blue sky and blue ocean and islands and them. They go shelling and treasure hunting, and he dives down and gets conch and lobster and fish and they go ashore and pick mangoes and avocados and oranges, and he cooks her elaborate meals, and he feeds her and she feeds him. And they spend most of their time naked. Two hot golden forms in the golden hot sunlight. She gathers flowers and decorates him, placing purple periwinkles in his hair, blue bougainvillea on his balls as he plays her old calypsos on his old guitar in the moonlight. And he can't stop touching her and she can't stop touching him. Even when he takes a piss, she enfolds him in her arms and holds his dick. And after the last drop comes out, it stands up hard. They can't stop fucking each other. And it's like no matter how many times they devour each other, no matter how many ways, his dick won't come down, her pussy won't stop dripping. He pretends he's a pirate and she's a wench, he Eve and she Adam, he a merman and she a mermaid. The boat a white fiberglass cocoon.

He keeps his eyes shut, sees clip after clip of their trips to the cancer clinic, endless needles, the lump under her arm growing bigger and bigger until it pops like a zit, like a boil. He plucks the pillow off his face.

He opens his eyes, blinks, stops, stops breathing, looks. It hits him, wakes him. She's naked, kneeling on all fours. The deck is covered in white paper. A bucket full of black liquid sits next to her. Open empty boxes and bottles of Loving Care hair dye litter the floor. He can't help but stare at her luscious ass, upside-down heart, her thighs and in between. Pouting pink. His eyes plunge in. She bends her head down, stretches her long neck. Her hair is about four inches long all over. She looks like a beautiful boy as she dips it into the bucket. Then head bent forward, she slowly lets the ends of her wet, dyed black hair caress the white paper, mopping, painting. Black streaks. So graceful. So fragile. So powerful. She dances the black onto the white. Her head swinging back and forth. Her eyes are focused, absorbed. He's drawn to her, wants to let her know he's awake, but he's afraid he'd break her concentration, afraid she would lose the look and he would lose this moment. He waits for her to finish.

She stops, looks up at him. The look on her face gets deeper, more defined, as if outlined in black. She stands up. Black drips down from her hair, onto her face, her neck. He stands up, hugs her, smells dye, rubs his cheek, his tongue along the black streaks.

"Give me this," she says, grabbing his dick. "I want to dip it in dye, print it, preserve it for eternity."

"No!" he says dramatically, pulling away from her, jumping into bed, rolling over. She washes off her hair in the shower, wraps her head in a towel.

"Oh yes," she says, climbing onto the bed, crawling over him, sitting. He feels her bottom against his bottom. Their skin sticks.

"It's mine," she says. "Turn over. Give it back."

"You're such a brat. Just print a leaf or something," he replies, hearing the sound of their skin unsticking as she moves off him. The sound turns him on. She shoves her hands underneath his side, trying to turn him over. He holds firm.

"It's just like a leaf. When you get hard and curl up. Like a rolled-up banana leaf."

"Then just print a leaf."

"I don't know where your dick ends and you start, or you stop and your dick begins," she says, tickling him between his legs, his balls. He pulls his legs together, laughing, and then turns over.

"You can do it if you promise me something," he says, staring at her stare at his dick.

"What?" she asks, wrinkling her forehead.

"If we don't wash the sheets." He touches her forehead, wiping away the wrinkles.

She grabs his dick.

"I love to smell your smell, our smell." He sniffs. "I want to fuck the spotted bed into one color. Play connect-the-dots with our spores and juices. I want to turn the sheets splotchy."

"Crusty?" she asks, wetting her lips with her tongue.

"Don't forget earthy."

"You're strange."

"I know."

"That's what I like about you."

"I know. Banana leaf," he says, holding it in his hand, looking at it.

"Well, at least you picked a big leaf. I want it inside of me forever. It's curing me." She laughs. "The only problem is it's attached to you," she says, pouring black dye from the bucket into a cup.

"We're a packaged deal, baby."

"Life isn't fair," she says, pulling on a pair of white lace panties. He sees his mother's white hammock crocheted out of thread as thin as spiderweb, and it was so delicate and pretty it looked like the lace on a wedding dress. She would lie hour after hour in the hammock reading books with drawings of hard, handsome men embosomed in soft voluptuous women on the covers. It was only when she read her books that the lines on her face softened and she looked more beautiful than the cover women. When she was tired of reading she would call out to him, "Chris, peel the banana leaf," pulling the sides of the hammock up tight around her. He would try to pull the hammock open. She would hold it shut and then laugh and let go and he would climb in with her, lie next to her, his head resting next to her breast. She would say, "Chris, should we turn into a banana?" And they would laugh, pulling the sides of the hammock shut around them. And then they would fall asleep together in the hammock banana.

"Stand up," she says. "The time has come to immortalize your best feature." She kneels down, gently picks up his dick by the excess skin under the head. Chris pictures a mother dog picking up its pup by the skin of its neck. She dunks it into the dye. Cool. He looks down as she pulls it out. His new black dick. He thinks of Shark. Thinks how he avoided him for the last two months. Thinks how he hasn't done any coke for the last two months. Thinks how every time he feels the urge he fucks Robin. Thinks about yesterday, he was fucking her as the the phone rang. They let it ring. The machine picked up.

"Chris, mon, what wrong wit you. Why you ain't return my calls? I's giving up on you." The sound of Shark's voice filled him with guilt, made him crave coke.

"You have to talk to him sometime," Robin urged.

"Yeah, but not this time."

"You can't run away forever."

She places his dick against the white paper, prints it like a fingerprint. And it turns him on. She dips it in again and he feels it grow slow. Feels the blood enter. His black dick getting bigger and bigger. She prints the process. Dipping and printing. Dipping and printing. Until it can get no bigger. Then she's pumping. Up and down. He breathes. In and out. Shuts his eyes. Sees the dolphin jumping out and in. Midnight. He was twelve years old, staring at the absolute black water. Shark stripped. A flash of moon glazed black skin and then he disappeared into the water. Chris pulled off his clothes, jumped. And one of the dolphins swam around him in circles, jumping above him and then splashing. The cool, agitated water tingled against his naked skin. A trillion tongues licking, and he felt it getting hard and the dolphin swam up next to him and he grabbed its dorsal fin and held on and it was pulling him and the water was flowing past him, against him, surging between his legs. The dolphin swam faster as the rushing water vibrations got stronger. He held on tighter. He got this sensation in the pit of his stomach, a queasy kind of calm, which started to rise as the dolphin started to jump up and down, and he held on and he was flying in a stream of sensations. A shower of shivers of pleasure, more and more and more and more and then it felt so fantastic that he couldn't take it, hold it, breathe, and he felt he was going to black out. Then the scream, his scream, and the feeling exploded, pumped. He feels the intense pleasure from the tip of his hair, from the tips of his toenails, racing to his balls, climbing up his dick, rushing in slow motion. He opens his eyes, sees his black dick explode drops of white that Robin catches with the white paper, printed with pictures of his black dick, as he hears the sound of the glass window of the stateroom sliding open. Chris feels shock as he sees Robin go stiff and then relief as Shark crawls halfway through the window seeing them, registering shock, a mumbled, panicked "Sorry." He backs out through the window. Chris catches his breath.

"We always used to sneak up, scare each other. It was a game," Chris says to Robin, wrapping a towel around his waist.

"You have to talk to him now."

"Yes," Chris says, kissing her nose. He leaves the stateroom, walks to the stern of the boat. "Shark," Chris yells, walking out onto the cockpit.

"What's happenin, mon?" Shark asks nervously, trying to smile. He sits on a fighting chair. Fishing rods stick out from the sides.

Chris sit on the chair next to him and it's as if he has deflated over the last two months. Shark looks smaller, softer. Chris hates himself for running away, for deserting him for the last two months.

"I's sorry I scare you," Shark says sadly, and this makes him feel worse. "I give up waiting for you to return my calls, for you to visit," and there's an edge of anger in his voice that turns to pleading when he asks, "What I do to you, Chrisy?"

Chris looks away from Shark, feels so bad he can't speak. "I'm sorry," Chris says, struggling, gripping the chair.

"Pussy come and go but I's always here," Shark says. "I don't care if you's being pussy whip to death, dat ain't no reason to give me up. Just tell me what I did to you." His leg shakes up and down. "Is it Robin? She tell you not to see me?"

Chris grabs Shark's hand, tries to talk, and Shark says, "The spics fucking me up. I need you," Shark says. "Chris, you the onliest one I got."

"I wanted to come and see you but . . ." Chris lets go of Shark's hand. And Chris tries to tell him it's the coke and not him he's stayed away from. "You did nothing to me," Chris says. "I'm sorry . . . the coke."

Shark's face breaks into a smile. "I bring you one present," he says, pushing his hand into his pocket.

Shark opens his hand. The small glass vial shines in the sun. Little white rocks, small on his thick, coffee palm. Chris focuses on it, wants it. Feels the high as he's pulled toward the crack, sticking his hand out, his body screams, his brain screams.

Chris hears a noise, turns toward it. It's Robin. The smile drains off her face as she sees the crack. They freeze. She walks up to Shark quickly, slaps the bottom of his hand hard. Shark flinches. The vial flies in an arc, up and out, and plops into the water, causing ripples to spread out farther and farther, come together, then disappear. Fade away like memories.

"He quit," Robin says firmly.

"Can he talk?" Shark asks, clenching his hands into fists, focusing tight on Robin's face. His eyes grow hard. She stares back firmly, not blinking.

Chris looks from Shark to Robin, his eyes pleading. "I wanted to see you but I was afraid I'd do coke," he says to Shark.

Shark's face changes expression. "Cool," Shark says, spitting out the word. Robin wraps her arms around him, and Chris sees Shark try to be stiff, but his body relaxes into her, and then his arms wrap around her. "I missed you," she says.

Shark looks over Robin's shoulder at Chris. He shakes his head. "Why you just didn't tell me?"

Chris shrugs. Shark lets go and Robin holds him an instant longer, then lets go. "I's sorry I scare you dis morning. I thinks Chrisy was alone. And I's wanna put one scare on his ass. Like old times."

"It's all right," she says.

"So you gonna tell me what you all was up to in dat room when I break in?"

"Art," Chris says. "Robin was printing my dick, dipping it in black dye and laying it on paper."

Shark shakes his head, amused. "If you two want a black dick you can have mines."

Chris and Robin laugh. Chris stands up. "Come here, Shark."

"You ain't gonna start dat again, homeboy?"

"Who's taller?" he asks Robin, ignoring Shark. They stand back to back. Robin puts her hand on their heads. "You're exactly the same," she says.

"Bullshit," Chris says. "It's his hair."

"Chris been doing dis ever since we small. He ain't gonna be satisfy till he taller."

"You know I was premature and Shark was a fourteen-pound baby."

"And Chris was born ass first."

"And Shark was born with a hard-on."

Robin laughs. "My mother had an orgasm when I was born. That's why my middle name is Joy."

Shark and Chris laugh. Robin's alarm watch rings. "I gotta go to the cancer clinic," she says, looking at her watch, annoyed.

"I gotta go too," Shark says. Chris feels warm and then fluffy on his lips as she kisses him good-bye. "Meet me at the H.I. when you're finished." He shakes Shark's hand. "I'm coming to see you soon."

"You best not be jiving."

Shark and Robin walk off together, talking. And it's like he's watching the two separate halves of his life coming together. He wonders what they are saying.

Chris goes to his stateroom. She has tacked the print of his dick over his bed. He drops the towel, dives into bed, inhales deeply and smells his-her smell on-in the sheets and pillows and he feels so happy. Today, he thinks. I start today. He gets out of bed, pulls on a Speedo and walks to his desk. He sits, stares at the yellow pads, at the sharpened pencils, the uncracked thesaurus, his old Webster's. Now, he thinks. What do I do now? Write? He picks up the pencil. She says I can do it. She wants me to do it. He writes the name "Robin." He writes it again and again and again, trying to think of something to write about. He fills the whole page full of "Robin's." Then he rips the page out, balls it up, throws it in the trash. He sits, staring at the new, crisp, blank yellow sheet. It glares back at him. He pulls his knees up to his chest, hugs them. His head falls forward. He shuts his eyes, feels jealous of her, that she has her art and he has nothing, nothing to write about. And he thinks about Shark, feels jealous of him, that he's doing something, even if it's selling drugs. And he craves coke, so he could break through the wall. He shoves the thought out. Jumps up. Goes to the bathroom. Forces himself to piss. Yellow pee like the yellow pad. He goes back to his desk. Sits. Stares. His head a blank. Write what you know, they say. He writes the word "coke," then writes the word "pussy." He rips the page out, balls it up, throws it in the trash. He stares, then shuts his eyes, sees Robin's eyes and she's encouraging him. But he just can't, can't think, can't move, frozen. He jumps up, grabs a pencil, the yellow pad, climbs the steps to the flying bridge, pulls off his Speedo and lies naked. He looks at his dick, black, sees Robin's face as she painted the paper with her hair, as she printed his dick. He looks at the blue around him with twinkling ripple tips and he feels the cool in his head. Sees Robin in his head. He tries to describe her. Struggles. Writes. "She's something ephemeral, impossible to define."

He stares at the pad till his head pumps. Who am I kidding? he thinks, standing up, adjusting his sunglass band, putting his arm through the Speedo leg hole. He drops the pad over the side, jumps after it, screaming, flying for a split second, and then he's swallowed in wet and the water is splashing out, sucking him, pulling him down. He stops, gravityless, holds his breath, flying for another split second. Then the buoyancy is pushing him up. He exhales. Bubbles pop. His head pops out into the hot light. He inhales hard.

Floating on his back, he tastes and feels salt. He looks up at the cloudless sheet of sky, puts his Speedo on underwater. He climbs into his Boston Whaler, tied to his yacht, unties the rope, starts the boat. He drives into the center of the bay and then weaves the boat through the inlet, a cut in the rock shoal. He feels the chop of open ocean as he passes Crispy Squash Cay, thinking about when all they had on the small island were bush and battalions of bush bugs, which were these two-tone, faded beige crabs with bread-plate-size backs and foot-long legs. Then the bulldozers attacked the island and built a Club Med. He and Shark would wait for a dark night after a rainfall, when the bush bug holes would be full of water. He recalls those crab-hunting nights, putting on ski caps, socks and gardening gloves, long-sleeve shirts and long pants—his armor against the mosquitoes and cut-up bush. He had to breathe through the space between his two front teeth to stop from sucking in the fat mosquitoes as he crawled in the bush listening for the crawling sound of the bush bugs. In between the bush there was mud, which was crispy on the top but when you stepped on it, your feet would break through and, below, it was squishy and would ooze white. It was like the creamy vanilla pudding topped with a hardened layer of burnt sugar that Tantie called cream hooray because every time she cooked it, he would yell, "Hooray!" Tantie said, "Dey does copy her recipe in the hotels and calls it some French stupidness like crème brûlée." They would hear and then see the bush bug's beige shell shine in the moonlight. He and Shark would shine their flashlights into the crab's eyes, which were like tiny pointed fingers with dried black-eyed peas at the ends. The eyes were the only part of the crab that would move. Then they would sweep it up delicately by grabbing its slippery back behind its biters and time would freeze during crab hunts and before they knew it, they would have a crocus sack full of crabs and the sun would be rising and the mosquitoes would disappear. They would peel off their clothes and swim naked in sunrise.

Chris heads the boat straight into Holiday Inn beach. The mass of people, little dots on the beach, grow larger and clearer, as if sprouting arms and legs, as he gets closer to shore.

He turns off the engine, drops anchor. He swims and then walks onto the crowded beach, into the assortment of tourists. A group of scruffy looking English navy men with short white bodies and short hair leer lustily at the group of milk-fed, midwestern spring breakers, all healthy pink and scrubbed looking. Then he spots Tantie, her hands tying braids in a girl's hair. He walks up to her.

"Rude boy, it been long time since you come to see me," she says, trying to sound angry, but her face is lit up by a big smile.

"Sorry," Chris says guiltily, sitting down on the sand next to her. He thinks how he wanted to visit her but then he would think about Shark and he couldn't deal.

"Don't worry, boy," she says. "And tell dis beautiful chile I's the bestest plait-header."

"She really is," Chris says to the girl. "How much she charging?"

"Ten dollars," the girl answers.

"So cheap," Chris says, winking at Evalina. "You look great," he says to the girl.

She blushes. He focuses on Evalina's black fingers as she braids the girl's hair. Streaks of sunlight turn blond streaks to gold. Then he sees the ring Tantie has on her little finger. He stares. His heart beats hard. It's his mother's engagement ring. He doesn't know how she got it.

He takes a deep breath, hears his mother telling him about the ring, about her mother, his granny Josafina, about when she died. "The week before you grandmother died, she went into coma. So I put a lighted candle by she bed. She wake up and blow it out. She say, 'Not now!' She ask everybody to beg God to take she on Easter because she want to go to heaven the same day as Jesus. And den she say she can't die happy till I engage to marry."

Chris remembers his mother's ring catching and flicking back sparks of light as she said, "Dat very same day I went to visit you father. He took my hand between the jail bars and he slip dis ring with five diamond stones on my finger. He point to the first stone and say, 'You.' He point to the second stone and say, 'shall.' To the third stone and say, 'be' and the fourth, 'my,' and the last, 'wife.' One stone for each word," she said, grabbing his right hand, kissing each finger.

"Dat very same day, you daddy get pardon. And it was the day before Easter and I takes him to you grandmother and I show she the ring with the five diamonds and she kiss you daddy hand and even though she know him well cause she his cousin, she ask, 'What you name?' And he say, 'Odillo Roberto Angostura,' and she say, 'Into you hand I, Maina Zurcher Tucker D'Antonio Madina, leave my most precious jewel.' Dat night when the clock struck twelve, she tell me to light she candle and it was Easter and she die."

Evalina finishes up the last braid on the girl's head. The girl pays and Tantie says, "Thank you, baby. You look more pretty dan pretty self."

"Ten dollar for cornrowing white people good hair. The world making joke," Evalina whispers to Chris as a man with "Entertainment Manager" printed on his T-shirt says through a bullhorn, "It party time. Fun and games. We's gonna have Bahamian crab races, rum drinking contest, soca dancing contest, egg toss contest."

"I want to talk to you bout Shark," Tantie says. Chris just stares at the ring, stunned. Memories flood. He remembers when his mother fired Evalina which was the last time he thought she talked to her. And he was fucking maid Fanny, who used to bring up more than his breakfast every morning, spreading brown sugar on his fourteen-year-old hard roll. He sees his mother after she forced his room door open, sees Fanny's frenzied face as she flopped on top of him, sees his mother's furious face as she stamped toward him, freaking out, red-hot. Come exploded out, shot white-hot. His mother put Fanny out of the house and packed his bags and said, "I'm sending you away to school."

He pictures Evalina's plump black cheeks glistening with tears as he said good-bye to her. She gave him a brown bag saying, "It's your favorite, mango bread." He hugged her. And Evalina said to his mother, "How you can send away your only chile? How you can send away my boy-baby?"

His mother's replied, "He not you boy, he mine, and it your fault, you in charge of the maids. You fired."

"Mistress, you can't fire love," Evalina said. She packed her bags and left the house the same day as Chris.

He looks up, away from the ring. Evalina stares from the ring to him. "Boy, time come," Evalina says, grabbing his hand. "Let we go up the beach a little. I's got tings to say."

They reach their spot under the cannonball tree. He sits down next to her. And she looks confused, like she's trying to figure out where to start. Her forehead glistens. The sun shines. She tries to smile but she can't. He looks into her eyes from behind his sunglasses. He aches.

"It about you mama," she says, picking at her fleshy arms. Chris grabs her hands. His muscles tense up. "It's all right," he says. "I don't care about the ring."

"You mama and I make up," Tantie says slowly. "You know we ain't talk since she send you away to school. We's too proud. Pride feel no pain, boy. About six month ago, I bounce she up by the hospital. I stop and she see me and she stop too. We freeze. Something crack on she face. We's fall into each other arm. I feel she body hold the pain. I shut me eyes and I get dis picture of she and me walking on the same path, only I went ahead and left she behind." Evalina takes a deep breath, squeezes his hands. Chris hears shouts and squeals from the tourists playing games up the beach.

"You mama so lonely. She can't ask for no help. I offer to carry she load. At first she refuse, but finally she give in. I sits with her each morning. We's talk bout tings, mostly you and Shark, and drinks tea and eat scones together. One day, she say, 'You knows, before when I wakes up, I roll over in bed, and tink, what the use getting up, no one cares. But now dat you comes over for tea, I get up each morning and tink, Come on, Maria, get out of bed, Evalina will soon be here for tea.' " Her hands are shaking.

Chris tries to picture his mother and Evalina sitting on the bed drinking tea together, and he draws a blank.

"You mama sick, but don't tell no one. Only the good Lord know she torment, alone in dat cold castle house." Evalina struggles with the words. "I . . . I beg she to let me share she pain but she point she skinny finger at me and say 'No, I's fine. Truly I am. I don't want to be a burden.' Why wouldn't she let me help she carry she load?"

Evalina wipes her eyes, adjusts the bandana covering her head. Sweat beads like oil on her forehead. Chris looks down, writes the word HELP in the sand and puts an exclamation mark after it. Then rubs it out.

"Well, one day bout a week before she join Papa God, she fall, and I try to pick she up but she wouldn't let me and dat's when I knows I needs help and I look round and I sees something like light coming to us. Dat light turn to person. I's recognize he face. It Jesus. Instead of asking him to heal she, I say, Lord, you's the key to eternal life, take she and give she a better place. And it was den you mama tell me she have the cancer, and dat it come in she breast and she ignore it and it spread to she lungs. You know she always had sensitive boobie. When you was a baby she tot-tots hurt so bad when she feed you dat tears be falling down she face. Finally I can't take it no more and I take you from her and put you next to Shark and let you suck one boobie and Shark the next." Evalina clears her throat, shakes her head. A tear drips from her left eye. "The very same day she tell me she have cancer, she take off she wedding ring and put it on me finger. She say, 'Dis for my Chris. Wear the ring till he see it and when he ask about it, give it to him.' But I takes it off and couldn't put it on till dis morning . . . I tink it you mama send you to me."

Evalina places the ring on the palm of her hand. It seems to be spitting multicolored specks of sunlight directly at him. He looks from the ring to her palm.

Evalina takes a deep breath. "You mother say to do dis, to tell you dis." Her finger and her voice tremble as she says, "I," and points to the first stone in the ring. Then she points to the next stone and says, "love," and the next stone, "you," and the next, "very," and the last stone, "much." Evalina closes his hand around the ring. "She say dat you the only good ting she do in she life and please forgive she and den she point at the windows and ask twice was I going in the direction she point. I say, 'No.' I take the plastics off the couch. Dat very same night you mother walk the path with the Lord."

Chris sits exhausted. Something grinds deep inside. He looks at Evalina and she looks back at him as if she's trying to read him and it's as if her big brown eyes are a flashlight and he's a bush bug. Then she takes his hand and she kisses it and she says, "I love you very much too and don't forget, God give us all to each other cause we needs each other." And Chris takes Evalina's hand and he kisses it. "Go on, chile," she begs. "Find a gal to love you. Have yourself some babies to love."

Steel drum music drifts from up the beach. Chris looks up at the thick trunk of the cannonball tree, at the short crooked branches growing directly out of the trunk with round, cannonball-like fruits hanging. He wishes one would fall and knock him out. He hears the pan tunes and remembers the words, hears his mother singing to him as they rocked in the hammock,

> Sing to me that old Bahama Lullaby
> Like my Bahama mama used to sing
> Sing it sweet and sing it low
> That's the way it used to go
> Where magic music glows

Her eyes well up. "Never be fraid to need someone," she says, and then a shadow, and he thinks it's a cloud passing over the sun. He smells her smell and he feels her hands resting on his shoulders and he knows the touch and he looks back, stretches his head back and up. Robin.

"What's wrong?" she asks, taking off her sunglasses.

"Robin, this is my Tantie Evalina," he says, plastering an empty smile on his face, ignoring her question.

Evalina tries to smile, shakes Robin's hand. "So you's the gal my

Chris can't stop talking bout. How an ugly boy like Chris get such a pretty ting?"

"He has the kind of ugliness you can't get enough of," Robin says, running her hands through his hair, sitting down.

"Like you know. He be wicked, but he be good," Evalina laughs.

"She knows how good I am," Chris says, winking at Robin, touching her knee with his.

"And I know how wicked he is," Robin says.

"When dey picknies, every time I change Shark and he diaper, dey tiny toeties stick up and pee on me face. Gal, I wanted a girl baby so bad. I get sick of pee all over me face."

"That's why you have such a nice complexion," Chris teases.

"Gal, watch him, he could charm the fin off a shark," Evalina says to Robin. "He grow up to be so whatless. He was the sweetest little ting ever. He wanted to be a dancing priest."

"A dancing priest?" Robin asks, chuckling.

"Yeah, he dancing and dressing up playing priest, talking all kind of make-up Latin and giving he dog Hercules communion. Dat dog must be go straight to heaven."

"I still might be a priest," Chris says. Robin and Evalina laugh.

"You and Chris and Shark come to my house sometime and I'll make up some Cream Hooray for dessert."

"Chris says you're the best cook in the world. Will you teach me?"

"Sure and den yous got to marry and give my bad boy here plenty baby for me to help raise up."

"What do you think, Chris?" Robin asks.

"I think it's time to say good-bye," Chris says, and then Robin's alarm watch goes off. He tries to hold the smile on his face and Tantie sees and frowns.

"God bless you," Evalina says. "I'll live to see both you and Shark settle, praise the Lord." She touches Robin's cheek and says, "My sweet boy here crazy in love with you. Make he happy."

"I'll get the boat," Chris says, leaving Robin, jogging up the beach. He reaches the Holiday Inn, walks into the screaming, laughing crowd. He watches. White eggs fly in the air. Back and forth. The contestants take a shot of rum, spin around and then throw the eggs to their partners. Then another shot, another spin, another step back and they throw the eggs again. He watches the girl whose hair Evalina had plaited. Rum drips down her chin. She tries to catch the egg, stumbles. The egg hits her breast. Yellow yolk slips, staining skin and peach bathing suit. She falls. Legs spread-eagled.

Chris walks away, opening his hand, focusing at the ring resting on his palm. So delicate and beautiful. He looks at the lines on his palm which form a deep M shape, and his mother is telling him that the M on his hand stands for *mother* and when he looks at it, he should always think of her. He places the ring on his little finger. It fits snug up against his knuckle. He feels the water touch his toes and he shuts his eyes and keeps walking. He walks until the water is up to his neck, his chin. The water feels rubbery, as if it wants to push him up and out. He takes a deep breath, opens his eyes, looks at the boat, dives under, swims blindly, refusing to think the thoughts swimming around in his brain. He swims into the abyss, telling himself, "No," and he feels as if he has become part of the emptiness of the ocean as his body yearns for air, begging, as he re-fuses to surface because this new sharp pain overlaps the other smooth, bland pain that he feels somewhere deep inside.

Air! Air! Air! his brain says. He refuses to listen and then pictures his dick turning into an umbilical cord and then he's strangling, struggling to get free. He pictures Robin in his mother's pink coffin being lowered into the ground, like a petit four into a glutton's mouth. He takes mouthfuls of air, his chest moving up and down. He swims to the side of the boat, climbs in, pulls up the anchor and starts the engine. He drives the boat close to the shore. Robin steps in.

"I have great news," she says, beaming.

"What?" He smiles like an artificial flower: no life but never dying.

"I only have to give myself shots three days a week now. It means I'm getting better. I mean Doctor Johnson tells us not to try to fig-ure out how we're doing from our treatment but it must mean I'm doing better."

"That's great," Chris says.

"I told you I was feeling all that tumor kill, all those healing aches and pains."

"Great," Chris says, thinking, Fucking quack.

"You know how I knew to come down here?"

"How?" Chris asks, feeling her excitement. She's getting better, he tells himself. Just forget. Try not to think.

"I was killing myself. I had just given up on the chemo and I was putting all my energy into my art. I was creating these intense things and with each one I finished, I felt a little less alive." She takes a deep breath, shuts her eyes. "I'm on the subway and there's this bag lady and her eyes are shut and her clothes are dirty and her legs are black-and-blue and bloated. There's a hairy mop covering her feet and next to her there's this man with an old man's face and a young man's body and a turquoise hat and he's eating sunflower seeds. He bites them in half and eats and puts the other half in the woman's mouth and then he takes some red-and-blue capsules and opens them and sprinkles yellow powder all over her face. He keeps going until her face is covered in yellow. It looks like pollen. Then he lights a cigarette and blows smoke into a bottle and then holds it up to her nose. I could see such care on the man's face, such care for the woman. I felt jealous of them, jealous that they had each other and I would never find anybody and I left New York the next day. I told myself I couldn't die until I found someone to love me that much and I found you and I love you so much, I want you inside of me."

Chris cuts the engine and his little boat drifts against his big boat, and he jumps out and ties the rope. He reaches his hand out to help her out, and as his hand touches hers he sees her tender dreamy look, like an astonishing light that yanks him, and he sweeps her up in his arms and he blindly gropes for the words to tell her about his mother, about how he let her die alone, about how worried he is about Shark, about Shark telling him the spics are fucking him, about how he thinks the cancer doctor is a quack, but she looks so good, so happy.

She grabs his hand, pulling him up the stairs. She lies in the white hammock hanging from the railing on the flying bridge. "Come here," she says, holding open the hammock. He lies next to her in the hammock, grabbing the sides, pulling it shut, making a hammock banana. The sun filters through; it's like being covered in a lace doily. He shuts his eyes, fighting tears, buries his head into her side. And then on top of her and his lips touch her lips and his hips touch her hips, undulating together, their own type of island dance. His insides tell him to move off and lie next to her and hold her in his arms and talk to her. Lips and hips grow sharper, lighter, tighter. He swallows, pushes up off her.

"What?" she asks.

He looks at her sex-blushed face and as the words bubble up from within, they dry soundlessly on his tongue. He's not sure whether he can't tell her because he's selfish or selfless.

His mouth tastes dry as he lies, "I just want to say how happy I am that you're getting better."

And it's so much easier to just sink back into the silent sexual cave. He gets out of the hammock, pulls off her sangria-colored bathing suit bottom. He kneels on the floor in front of her and she turns around, sitting in the hammock like it's a swing. He grabs the side of the hammock, his eyes closing as his head falls forward, and he inhales her lovingly, his heart heavy, open, his mouth spreads her gently, slowly, opening, like opening a present, anticipating the surprise, wanting the surprise, but not wanting the anticipation to end. Everything revealed by scent. Like wine. The aroma of raw moist ecstasy. Awakens tangled memories. Rises as a vapor through the nostrils to the brain. One of sour, two of sweet, three of strong, four of weak. The smell of the islands: fish markets mixed with blooming blossoms—windswept, sun-roasted, and it belongs to him, her smell is his world.

He's sticking out of the top of his bathing suit. A round red pulsing bulb. And he yanks his Speedo down, hearing a rip, and the ripping sounds so good, and it's like he's been released, as he tries to go deeper between her legs, pushing his head in, pulling the hammock toward him, his tongue stretching out, licking, straining. Her legs scissoring his head. He moans into her. Like trying to yell underwater. He comes up for air. Wipes his hands on his face and be-tween her legs and dives back in, spreading their lubrication on himself, grabbing himself, beating, faster and faster, tighter and tighter, and she moans and he can't stand it anymore and he stands up and her eyes open up. She spreads her legs as open as possible, spread-eagled. He positions himself, placing just the head inside, and he swings the hammock forward slowly, entering, getting lost, slow and slower, bit by bit. And he remembers being in the ham-mock with his mother and they had fallen asleep and his father woke them up by swinging the hammock lightly at first and then faster and faster and faster and as the air swished through the tiny holes in the hammock he felt his mother's grip on him tighten. They all started to laugh together. He felt so good he thought he was flying. And he's flying back and forth, in and out. The ham-mock swinging. Fast and faster. And it's too much pleasure and his legs start to tremble as her legs wrap around his waist and he cups Robin's ass for support. And she screams and it runs through her body, his body, and it's a scream of pain and he freezes, afraid to move. Pulling out. And she holds him. Her hand grabs his dick. "No," she says. He just stands there, not knowing what to do. As he gets smaller, her hand grips tighter.

She breathes heavily. "Before I came down here," she says, her voice strained, "I had this metabolic treatment in Mexico. I had to get up at five in the morning and they would drop off a thermos of coffee and a plastic cup full of castor oil and some brown sugar. I had to drink that down." She chokes. He feels his stomach groan. "And then, and then, a few hours later I'd have to give myself a cas-tor oil enema mixed with soap, and then I'd have to give myself at least six coffee enemas during the rest of the day. Somehow it was supposed to clean you out and the caffeine in the coffee was sup-posed to kick the liver and cause extra bile, which would digest out the cancer cells. And I just got weaker and the treatment almost killed me." She shivers. "They told me it was my fault."

He shivers. Looks at it small, stuck to her hand, and he thinks of the old lady snot trees which have small sausage-shaped beans and when you crack them, they leak sticky snot stuff.

"When you touched me that way, something happened and I remembered the treatment. And I'm sorry and please, please don't stop," she begs.

He kneels back down on the floor in front of the hammock and kisses the lips between her legs over and over again and it refuses to go back up. And he remembers the months and months of kneeling before the statue of Our Lady of Lourdes at Mary Star of the Sea Church, the statue found in Preacher's Cave that was supposed to have swum ashore from a sinking Spanish ship. He remembers squinting at the rows of votive candles glowing ruby red, lighting up row upon row of rum bottles, crutches, dark glasses, wax lungs, stomachs, hearts, gifts of thanks, paying homage to her virginity, to her intercessory powers. He sees his mother's pale white face, like the statue's pale white face, as she prayed novena after novena that his father would come back after he left her for maid Fanny. And he went with his mother to pray every day because it hurt him too much to let her go alone, and he spent so much time on his knees that he developed hard pads on them like monkeys have. He pictures his mother and Robin in a cage, like he kept the bush bugs. They are fighting over the scraps of old sour vegetable he's feeding them to purge them before he kills them. As his tongue goes into her, her pelvis pushes down into the hammock and he keeps trying until the lips between her legs dry up and his mouth dries up and his tongue gets sore, sticking to her like communion to the roof of his mouth. He gives up, crawls up, hugs her. She gives him the look that says it's all right. He sees the poisonwood branch, the stick covered in velvety, sticky green leaves with tiny black flecks like freckles, and he's a child again and Shark is rubbing the branch all over his body. Shark is laughing and taunting, "Mon, don't be a sissy-boy. Do it!" Chris took the branch in his shaking hand, the poisonwood leaves shaking. He rubbed it on his body. And the next day, he woke up to the soreness, his body bloated, red and itching all over. His eyelids stuck together with green pus. Shark was there ready to go fishing. The infection was so bad that he got a high fever. He swallowed pills only to have them jump back out of his throat in a gook of throw-up and his mother brought these big pills that looked like horse pills. She told him they were suppositories and they had to go up his ass. He remembers his father's hands holding his legs down as he screamed and his father yelled, "Don't be such a sissy-boy!" His mother separated the cheeks of his ass and stuck it up. He fought against it with his ass muscles, trying to push it out as if it were a clump of shit, and he sees them lowering his mother's coffin into the brown earth. He looks at Robin, and she is asleep, her head on his chest, her mouth open. He gently pulls out from under her and then he pulls the ring with the five diamonds off his finger and pushes it on her wedding finger. I love you very much, he thinks. He gets out of the hammock. Leaves.

10

Chris drives. Fast. Faster. He doesn't know where. He just wants to get away. He pictures his mother breast-feeding him, tears running down her cheeks. The pain. He feels it. The cancer. A lump. Eating and growing. Her ignoring it. Rocking. Praying. Drinking. Till it ate her breast. Till it ate her lung. He let her die alone. Blamed her. Robin. The pain. She ignores it. Tells herself the pain is making her better. He can't say anything. Seeing the agony on her face when he told her he thought the cancer doctor was a quack. He shakes his head, screeches to a stop at a traffic light. He takes deep breaths, watches a man and a boy fly a kite in a field across the street. The man holds the kite and the little boy holds the invisible string and he hears the boy yell something and start to run and the man lets go and the kite slides up into the air, then stops, and the boy lets out more string and it collapses and then climbs. The kite gets higher and higher, smaller and smaller. A red dot with rag rainbow tail jives in cloud-capped, faded-blue-jean-colored sky. And Chris remembers flying kites with his father. He pictures him alone. And he has this tremendous urge to see him, to tell him that his mother didn't commit suicide. He turns, heads toward his old house, feels the coolness of the air conditioning and the comforting murmur of the engine. He hears "Sano Colito, Sano Colito," which are his father's magic words, which he would say to him when he was hurt as a child. Chris sees the bottle of Limacol. He smells the fresh smell as his father carefully poured the clear liquid onto a strip of cotton wool. He sees his dirt-crusted knee with the slit of red dripping. He shut his eyes waiting, his knees shaking. Then the soaked cotton stinging. His father chanted the magic words, "Sano Colito, Sano Colito." He concentrated on the sound of the words and the pain would go away.

He arrives, parks his car outside, stares at the Pepto-Bismol pink faux castle on the hill above. He climbs over the fence, walks up the path. He stops at the front door, takes a deep breath. He pushes the door open, stares at the black-and-white photograph of his mother dressed as Mary, Queen of the May, in the rusted, fragile, filigree frame. Stares at his mother's waist. So small he feels he could have reached around it with just his hands, and the fluffy triangle of white skirt as if it floats on the black tar below.

He walks up the steps slowly, remembering how his father would sneak up behind him and yell, "Poke a pit!" and then he would chase him and he would slide down the slick oiled-mahogany stair-case banister. He would let his father catch him and hold him down and tickle him under his armpits until he laughed so much he cried.

Chris enters his father's room. It's empty. Plates with decaying food litter the floor. He stares at the plastic roses covered in dusty plastic on the bed stand next to his mother's side of the bed. Chris hears a noise coming from his mother's sewing turret. He walks toward it, picturing his mother rocking back and forth on her rocking chair, saying the rosary, pictures her skinny fingers, her ring with the five diamonds.

Chris pushes open the door. He hears the back-and-forth rock of the chair, looks into the dark room. His father rocks in his mother's chair, back and forth. In front of him is maid Fanny, dressed in her white maid's uniform. He's about to say "Hi," as he hears his father moan. He looks closer, sees his father's naked breasts, two hairy jiggling peaks of fat, and his pinkish paunch, and then jutting out as if being swallowed up by his belly, his father's fat, slick, red dick and big, hairless balls, like a dog's afterbirth, being kneaded with each rock of the chair by maid Fanny's stubby black fingers.

The frame freezes. He can't look away. He remembers the endless stream of hours, days, weeks that he knelt in front of Our Lady of Lourdes praying with his mother that his father would leave maid Fanny and come home, praying that his mother would stop crying and drinking. His mother even started to dress like the Virgin, wearing only blue and white, and she had a beautiful dress that was blue and white with a pretty pink rose on the waist. It was his favorite dress. He walked into the sewing turret and she had the dress in her lap and she had the scissors in her hands. She said, "If I only wears blue and white, the Virgin favorite color, she may bring you father home." Then the sound of the steel blade as the scissors snipped the pink rose off, one petal at a time. She rocked back and forth saying, "He loves me. He loves me not." The petals fell to the floor, one at a time, like dead leaves.

Then Chris hears his father moan, louder and louder and louder. Maid Fanny lets out a sizzling laugh. He turns, runs.

Chris drives, opens the windows, breathes deeply. As if the hot air could cool the burning inside of him. His heart pounds hard in his head as he stares straight ahead, pressing his foot down harder and harder on the gas pedal. The car races faster and faster, so fast that it starts to shake and then lift into the air. He's a child again driving with his mother and maid Fanny is driving the car ahead of them and his mother got a crazy look on her face and started to follow her. Maid Fanny saw them behind. She sped away but his mother drove faster until she was next to Fanny's car. She swerved, banged into her car. Metal screamed. Then his mother and Fanny in the street.

"Stay away from my husband, you black man-hog!"

"If bee does find honey in he comb, he don't have to roam!" Fanny yelled back. "I does fuck him good."

"Because you is animal," his mother replied, "and you gonna find out buzzard can't eat sponge cake. And then it be just you and the vengeance of God. Who don't hear, gonna feel. Marriage got teeth!"

"Don't pelt none of that stank godliness at me. He tell me fucking you like fucking hairdo!"

Chris arrives at Studio 69, raps on the door, softly at first and then pounding, feeling the twacking noise in his brain. "Fuck," he yells, picturing Robin still sleeping in the hammock, his mother's ring on her finger. The hammock turns into a coffin. His knuckles go numb. Mosquitoes charge like the sound of a drill. Bite. He slaps at them, swatting the air. He turns the doorknob, expects it to be locked. The door swishes.

"Shark, Shark." His voice bounces back at him as he walks to the back of the club. Then it's silent. He craves coke. Streams of light filter through cracks of blacked-out windows, lighting up chairs stacked on table tops, and the stage, guitars and drums and horns resting. The steps creak. He opens the door to Shark's office. A rush of light and the smell of burning. He sees the gun pointing at him, shining silver, and then Shark. He flinches. Shark laughs, high and crazy.

"What the fuck?" Chris mumbles, frozen, staring at him. Shark's hair is greasy, matted in clumps. His eyes, it's as if they're ready to blast off.

"Pussy whip," Shark says without feeling, sitting down on the couch, the gun on his lap. It points, a second, silver dick. Chris just stands there quiet, shocked, frozen, thinking, I should leave. "Robin give you permission to see me?" Shark tilts his head back and lights the glass pipe, inhaling, coughing as he chokes on the smoke. "Why you hate me? I did anyting to you?"

"No, you did nothing," Chris says, sitting down on the floor in front of Shark, forcing himself to look at him. "I'm sorry. I already told you I'm sorry. Haven't we been through this?" He can't look at Shark, can't look at the pipe.

"I was here before she arrive and I'll be here after she gone."

"Don't worry, she's dying, remember?" Chris says, and before it even escapes from his mouth he wishes he hadn't said it. He hugs himself, frustrated. He sees the hurt in Shark's eyes. The air burns, smells bitter. His brain cells rain painful desire. He salivates, tastes it, sweet like sugar cane. No. He forces himself to think of something else and he pictures Tantie's pigs, two pink balls of fat, and remembers how whenever it was hot they would sit in the surf. The pigs loved to eat coconuts and would beg like dogs, grunting instead of barking as he and Shark raced up the trunks of the coconut trees. Then one day the pigs went wild, running around in circles, bouncing off trees and one another. The villagers ran out of their shacks to watch. Evalina prayed because she thought they were possessed. And Shark asked her what she had fed them. She held up a Ziploc bag of white powder and said, "Only some dis flour dat wash up on the beach."

"Comoke, mon," Shark stammers, watching him watch the pipe, holding it out to him.

Chris shakes his head. "Robin's getting worse. She's in pain. She thinks the pain is curing her."

"Smoke some coke. Make bad better," Shark says, interrupting him.

Chris looks at the stem of the pipe and then at the barrel of the gun. He takes a deep breath. Resist. Then he looks at Shark. "Mon, blow," Shark urges, sucking on the pipe. White smoke flowing from red lips.

Chris takes a deep breath, sucking up the smoke, the smell, thinking about when he and Shark were altar boys at funerals. Right before they put the coffin into the ground, he and Shark would go up to Monsignor, genuflect together and then circle the coffin, and all the people, all the eyes stared at them as he held the incense carrier up, flicking over and over as Monsignor said, "Accept our prayers like sweet-smelling incense in thy sight, and the lifting up of our hearts as a fitting sacrifice." He would inhale. And he was sure that's what God smelled like.

Escape. The pipe. "It's so fucking useless," he says, grabbing it, bringing it to his lips. He sees Robin's needles as he sticks it into his mouth and inhales. He counts in his head, one–one thousand, two–one thousand, three–one thousand, and then the rush.

Shark starts pacing around the room saying, "Dem cartel niggers fucked me. Dat why the club closed. People's fraid to come. Spics don't own me. I ain't nobody slave."

Chris takes another hit, grips the side of the chair, waiting for another train to run through his brain. And Shark keeps talking, flat and loud, "I gonna fuck those spics. Fuck those spics. Fuck."

Chris grabs the pipe. Inhale, exhale, inhale, exhale. He blanks Shark's words out and concentrates on the high, because he can't deal with his own problems, can't even listen to Shark's. And he's so high. And he smokes more and more and more and more until his head floats off his shoulders, and he floats away from himself, shutting his eyes.

Then, a voice crackles loudly. Chris's eyes snap open.

"Shark, Shark, it frenzy time. Pregnant bird bout to drop white egg. Yankee twerly, up early, trying to bungy him. Snow's gonna fall somewhere between Congo Town and Peace and Plenty Inn." Chris recognizes Harry's voice as Shark grabs the portable VHF, jumping up, all action.

"Les go, mon,"

"Where? What?" Chris asks, confused, dazed.

"We got one blind date with Abominable Snowman," Shark says, excited, grabbing Chris's hand, pulling him out the door. He stumbles, fireworks exploding in his head, and even while he follows Shark he wonders what he's doing, why he's doing it, but it's like his brain can't stop his feet.

"We's gonna steal the spics' load," Shark says as Chris watches the speedometer, seventy-eighty-ninety. The Ford Bronco bucks wildly on the wavy beach road. They hit a bump; Chris's head smashes against the roof. He braces, feet firm against the extra-thick burgundy carpet and hands pressed against the velour, zebra-upholstered roof. Chris concentrates on the overgrown orange fuzzy dice bouncing from the rearview mirror. Shark stares ahead, his eyes like a compulsive gambler at the casino. Shark picks up the VHF. "Where dem mosquito? Come in, Tweed."

"Dis be Tweed. Dat ugly wimp in the blimp, quiet like clam. You best chill. Dis gonna lead to a spill. See you at the funeral." Shark changes frequency on the VHF from channel nineteen to sixty-eight.

"What the fuck?" Chris asks, shaking.

"You know dat DEA dude with the spots on he face dat works the blimp? I gives him pussy for info. He my agent now. He's contact Tweed when tings coming down and Tweed does VHF me."

Chris shuts his eyes, trying to make it stop, trying to think, but he's still too high and he feels his head floating as he pictures the blimp floating over the bush below. He remembers, the first time he saw the blimp, he thought it was a UFO and then he found out that it was part of the War on Drugs, part of Operation We See You, a kind of flying big eye loaded with all sorts of top-secret radar to track the drug planes and boats. The Americans thought of everything but getting the blimp driver laid, Chris thinks. Shark's Operation We Fuck You jabbed the cyclops of Operation We See You. Tons of U.S. tax dollars wasted on the mediocre milking of some agent's dick.

Chris forces his eyes open, checking the speedometer. One hundred. Shark's eyes dart between the road and the sky. They turn the corner, sliding, brushing the bushes. The sound of celery crunching and then a shower of green.

"Slow down!"

"Don't be fraid, sissy-boy," Shark yells.

"Look at the road. Shark! I'll look for the plane," Chris says, coming down, stamping his foot down on an imaginary brake.

"Watch for falling snowball."

The car shudders as Chris stares at the shaking sun roof, thinking it's going to shatter. The plane followed by the helicopter passes overhead. The plane banks left, then right, rising up and up and up as the helicopter anticipates and mirrors the moves of its prey. The car passes a picnic crowd on the beach. The plane dives, the helicopter dives.

"Drop it!" Shark yells as the plane does an about-face, as if trying desperately to fart the helicopter out its backside. Shark joins the dance and spins the Bronco around, pirouette. Then Chris sees her flash before his eyes. Frozen as a photograph. In the middle of the road. He stares. Shark doesn't hit the brake. He's looking up. Chris hears the scream. "No" flows from his throat. He sees her mouth open. Then her body bounces. A smacking, hollow sound. Her body white, limp, sprawled. Legs spread-eagled, real spread out. Her "It's Better in the Bahamas" T-shirt stained red.

"Stop!" Chris screams.

Shark ignores him, stares straight ahead.

"She'll die. Turn the car around," Chris cries, grabbing the wheel. The car swerves, screeches. Shark fights to keep control.

"Aye, homeboy, I ain't playin!"

"Stop!"

"Fuck You!"

"That woman will die!"

"Chill!"

"Stop!" he yells, trembling as the engine churns faster as he looks at Shark, at his eyes, like a window that faces a brick wall, a taut smile on his lips. Chris looks away, shuts his eyes, takes deep breaths. Control, he thinks. The car screeches to a stop. He hears the door slam. He opens his eyes as the plane followed by the helicopter buzzes the picnic crowd, a blur, desperately low, as the crowd freezes. In limbo, statuelike. A wax museum scene of the annual Jesus of the Mount Church picnic. The plane like a shark scraping itself on the reef, trying to unstick a remora. Vibrations churn the blue sea into white spray. A swirl of waterspout. Then the plane heads straight for the picnic. People run, taking cover in trees. It looks like a shark chasing a sting ray, the ray going shallower and shallower, the shark grounding itself into the sand trying to catch it. The ray, up in the surf, flips itself onto the beach. The tip of the plane wing hits the sand. Sparks fly. People scream. A bouncing ball. Fish out of water, floundering. Ear-shattering sandpaper scream of metal. The final cry. The plane comes to a broken, complete stop.

The plane door opens. Two men stumble out and disappear into the picnic crowd. People rush toward the plane. The helicopter, jet black with gold stripes, *Coke Buster* written on the nose, pounces down, blowing beach. A desert sandstorm. People fall to their knees, covering their eyes, fighting the surging sand and air. Three Don Johnson wanna-be DEA officers, silk suits, automatic rifles in their hands, run out. The blade stops moving. Stone silence.

Chris sits in the car, tries to bring himself down, calm himself, taking deep breaths. He shakes. Got to get to the woman, he tells himself, wiping the sweat off his face. He jumps over to the driver's seat, tries to start the car. No keys. He leaps out as the crowd stops, stares in disbelief at the officers, as if aliens have landed.

"Please remain calm." An electronic voice echoes from the heli-copter. Chris looks in the cockpit and sees the pilot as somebody yells, "Dem Yankee can make talking twerly but them can't stop we." People laugh. "Kindly point out the men who were operating the aircraft. Please form two lines for interrogation," the helicopter seems to say.

Chris runs to the group, searching for Shark. The crowd starts to mumble. "Anybody seen Shark?" he asks, as people talk louder and louder. "What dem GI Joe playing at? Dis ain't America. Dem honkies tink it still be *Roots*." The crowd walks forward slowly as one of the officers, a slapping-up-whores, kicking-down-doors type, fires a round into the heavens. Chris flinches as he feels the ear-splitting shots in his brain. He has come down. He wants to get the hell out of there.

The crowd hesitates, stops. The officer smiles with new confi-dence. Superior firepower. Then from the center of the mass flies a handful of egg salad. It hits the officer smack on his take-control grin. He has egg on his face. This sets the people off. People grab anything they can get their hands on—sand, turtle fillets, macaroni pie, Beck's bottles, coconuts, and more egg salad come flying from the crowd. The officer's confidence gets coated with food. People rush to the plane. Conch fritters, guava duff are crushed into the sand. The frenzied people rush toward them. The officers retreat, lose the food fight. The helicopter takes off. Now, fast forward, everyone races to the plane. They pick the bones clean, suck it dry of coke. Everyone with bags of coke in their hands. They're run-ning. Small children, too weak to carry the bags, drag them.

Shark steps out from behind a coconut tree, his body pumping up and down in swagger. "Stop!" he yells harshly. His voice startles. There are muffled voices and the party stops. No one moves. Eyes scrutinize him.

Chris runs up to him. "The keys. To get to the woman."

"What woman?" Shark asks.

"The one you ran over."

"You crazy?" Shark yells, clenching his fists. "Please," Shark begs in a low voice, "the peoples."

Someone in the crowd yells, "How dis Shark load? He name print on it? Dis people load." Shark looks toward the voice.

"The keys," Chris screams. "You're a fucking murderer!"

The people stare. Reflex action, the arm comes at him, a black streak, fast. It smacks him hard, too quick for pain, just numb disbelief. Chris's legs give way and he feels himself fall onto his back in slow motion. Shock. Thin warm blood pumps from his throbbing nose. It runs down his face, over his chin, gets sopped up by his black shirt. He opens his mouth to breathe and smells-tastes blood, sees the stars behind the punch. He fights, tries to get up from his back, feels too faint, hears Shark say, "Dis my load. Thanks for helping unload. Now, younna best put the bags in the back the car."

Chris pushes himself up to a sitting position, feels dizzy, breathes heavily, watches as Shark pulls out a wad of bills. The people stare at the money. "Dis Shark load for true," someone yells. Shark gives each person a hundred-dollar bill as they load the bags into the Bronco. The people look down, take the money silently. Shark grabs a handful of hundreds and gives it to the church deacon. "Buy yourself some electric bells."

"Thank God for the manna from heaven," the preacher replies.

Chris tries to push himself to his feet. He feels to vomit. Stops. Then a siren and flashing blue lights. The police car comes to a screeching stop. An officer jumps out, dressed like a tourist attraction in a starched white shirt with gold shoulder stripes and black pants with a red stripe running up the legs.

"What dis?" he asks, taking off his white helmet. Its gold tip shines in the sunlight.

"Just a picnic," Shark says, strutting up to the policeman with a wad of money.

"Look like cocaine to me," the policeman says formally.

"Looks like flour to me," Shark says as he pastes a hundred-dollar bill onto the policeman's sweating forehead. He peels the bill off. Shark pastes another. The policeman removes it. Then another. And another. "Looks less like coke," the policeman says, laughing. The crowd laughs. Shark sticks on another bill. "Now it look like flour," the policeman says, smiling, getting into his car and driving away.

Shark walks up to Chris beaming, the dollar signs in his eyes. Shark grabs his hands. Chris cringes when Shark touches him. "Sorry," he says excited, "I didn't mean to hit you."

"The woman," Chris trembles. "Me . . . You hit her . . . We have to help . . ."

"I finally fucked the spics. Dis dere load," Shark says, smiling, ignoring him. "Dey gonna have to fucking deal with me if dey want it back."

"Shark, you might have fucking killed someone."

"How many peoples die to fill you face full of comoke? Pussy whip, you play, you pay."

The girl spread-eagled, his mother dying alone, the needles sticking into Robin, the coke sloping up his brain. "Fucking nigger," Chris says, pictured his father's dick being pumped by maid Fanny.

"Who you is?" Shark asks. "You ain't no better dan me. Fucking hypocrite!" Shark throws a five-kilo bag at him. It smacks him hard across the face. An icy snowball. He gets into his car, screeches away.

Chris lies on his back, shuts his eyes to stop the spinning. Chris hears an ambulance siren. His eyes snap open, his fingers clawing the sand. I have to get up, he thinks. His head stabs. He pushes up into a sitting position. He feels his face, feels sweat. Then a portion of the sand a few feet from him comes alive. Chris wipes his eyes. There's a rush of struggling newborn turtles toward the sea as birds shriek, swoop down gluttonously, capturing them in their beaks.

Chris stumbles to his feet, picks up the bag of coke and one of the turtles, walks to the water and releases the turtle into the surf.

11

The five kilos lying, lounging luxuriously on the side table. Tempting, tantalizing, talking to him. Take me, I'm yours. He shuts his eyes hard, willing it out. But it stays in, shines inside eyelids, five kilos of raw ecstasy. He grabs a bottle of Añejo, chugs it, not tasting it, wanting to drown in it. Sleep, he begs, pulling the white sheet over his head. It feels crispy. Little grains of sand, abrasive. Saltine crackers. The fucking sand, the fucking powder. He gets up and yanks the sheets off his bed. Fluffs them. They float in the air like clothes on a clothesline. He remakes the bed quickly and crawls in. Sleep, he tells his body as he puts the pillow under his head, feeling something slippery, slimy, like dead fish. Ignore it, he thinks. The sheet isn't covering the mattress. The polyester below. He gets up, remakes the bed. Enough, he thinks, shutting his eyes again. Holds them. A line of light pierces through a crack in the curtains like a laser aiming straight at his eyeballs. He gets up, pulls the curtains together, gets back into bed, takes deep breaths. Feels the elastic of his underwear pulling, cutting into his skin. Ballet dancer's balls in tights. Drag queen. He reaches down and yanks off his underwear. Now he feels it between his legs. He gets out of bed, walks to the head, turns on the light, stands above it. Dick in hand; it won't come out. He strains. His father's dick being pumped by maid Fanny, his future, and he thinks about the note Robin left stuck to the fridge with a baby conch shell magnet, "I waited for you. Always, Robin." And the "always" burns in his brain as he pictures the growth next to her breast. He imagines it popping. Pee spurts out.

He gets back into bed, shuts his eyes tight. The five kilos prick like black sea urchin spines stuck deep into his brain. "You play, *you pay*" echoes in his head. Tortured for all those sins, mortal and venal and anal and vaginal. He has to get rid of it, destroy it. Now, before it's too late, before it kills him. He jumps out of bed, grabs the bag. He stands there. Indecision. Up his nose. Down the toilet. Yes, he's gonna flush it. For him. For Robin. She walks through the bedroom door.

Chris freezes. Robin flinches, looks at him and then the bag. He drops the bag. It opens, spills a little powder cloud on the baby blue carpet. They both look at it. He stutters "No, I . . ." Her face goes hard, eyes cold. Her hand comes at him. The slap. Inside his brain. The left side of his face stings. It hurts all over.

"Fuck you," she screams, fleeing the room. He follows. Grabs her hand. She recoils. He tries to explain. Can't.

"Don't even try . . . ," she says harshly, breathing heavily. "You make me sick." Then the sound of the door slamming shut. Then he grabs the bag, goes into the bathroom. Opens it. Down the toilet. He tries. Malfunction. Suicide. Paralyzed. Too heavy. Muscle fatigue. Muscle failure. He looks into the head. Flash of the woman bouncing off the car, of his mother, of Robin's waterlogged wig. He collapses next to the toilet and grabs a handful. Coke clenched in his hand. He unclenches, puts his mouth on it. Feels it against his lips. Eats it. A child eating sand on the beach. His nose in it. Snorting. Evalina's pigs sucking up slop. In the fetal position, folded into himself, he feels the ache of tears blur numb as he starts to fall into the high. His heart beating. I'll beat you there. I'll beat you. I'll meet you. Kill it. He fists some up his ass, packs the cone full of ice cream until it's stuffed, until he stops feeling the coffee enemas squirting up her ass. Takes another handful. He throws it up into the air. It snows down on him, covering him like a powdered doughnut. Ho, ho, ho, don't blow no snow. He packs more up his nose. Handful after handful. He's so high and wants to get higher, wants to get further away. He covers his dick and balls with coke, like building a sand castle on the beach. The sexy white, like a tan line, touching him between his legs like lace panties. More. Up his nose. His hand above his mouth. Coke runs through his fingers like that sweet powdered candy that comes in colored straws. Halloween gluttony. Till death do us part. Melts in your brain, not in your hand. He's breathing it instead of air. The other hand, sweat mixed with sweet coke, on his dick, like a coating of cold bacon fat. He beats it. Hand clenched as tight as possible. Everything so fast. Choke it. Coke it. Come, come-come. I want to go, go-go. The sweat flowing out of his armpits, his ass, everywhere. Another handful, overflowing.

Go with the flow. Further away. Go further away. Dick in hand. Unfeeling. Like a hot dog. I'm going to kill you. He beats it. Caught in the rapids. Too fast. Can't fight the current. Can't fall in. Can't come down. More. More. No down. Just out. Milk it till it comes dry. But no feeling. Like scrubbing clothes on the scrubbing board. He sandpapers it. I'm gonna come dying. I'm gonna die coming. They're coming. Coming to get me. Coming for the five kilos. Got to get away. Get it away. Suck it up. Stuff more cotton up. Hide. More up his nose, in his mouth, up the ass. Cut the pain. Frosting a cupcake with salve. He's on himself, in himself, butt-fucking himself, a six-foot, three-inch dick. Keep going so they will stop, so it will stop. It won't. Help! Help! On his back. He can't get up. He couldn't get it up. The cancer doctor laughing, laughing. Treat it. Coke to the rescue. Cold sweat turns to hot sweat. He screams. Burning. Begs. Coke, more coke. To put it out. Water on the fire. Got to go underwater. He shoves his head into the toilet. Stop. Stop! She's on top. The woman, spread-eagled, aiming spurts of blood in his mouth every time he breathes. He chokes, can't breathe. He pulls out. Sputtering. Bangs his head against the toilet bowl.

Inhale-inhale, inhale-inhale. Bang! Pain. Bang! Pain. Shark's fist, Robin's hand smashing his face. His heart pounds harder and harder as he pounds his head against the toilet. With each bang he runs faster and faster. From himself. The streak turns into a dot and then spins. Trapped in the middle of a Ferris wheel, drunk spinning, faces peel away, turn into skulls. Bone white. Coke white. Faster and faster. So dizzy. Skulls pierce every orifice. His armpits, his nose, his ears, his mouth. He fights to get them off. Invisible sand flies, piranhas attack. He scrapes. Tries to dig them out. He cracks. From himself as it starts to flow. Bleeding blood red. Then pink. Coke-mixed blood. His heart beating so hard, going to implode. More coke. More pounding. He, fighting the trap, looks at the bag of coke on the floor, falls forward, mouth and nose first into it.

12

Chris hears a noise, wakes up, feels his head pound. He tries to forget last night as he keeps his eyes shut, telling himself to fall back asleep, telling himself it was all a nightmare. He hears Robin yell, "Fuck you," over and over in his brain. He sticks his fingers into his ears, curls up tighter into a ball. Then he hears her voice. "Christopher." His eyes jolt open and he snaps fully awake. The light blinds.

Robin's face flickers. He tells himself he's dreaming. Then he feels the coke bag, plastic and powder sticking to his face, the frigid bathroom floor against his belly. He shivers, shuts his eyes as the radio from the stateroom plays: "Dis ZNS Freeport, the voice of northern Bahamas. It twelve o'clock at one oh seven point nine, Bahama time–quality time, and you know who love you so."

Chris tries to forget last night. He's wet. Sweat flows like grease, like when you prick a sausage. He smells like stinktoe tree. He fights his eyelids as they try to stick together. The radio plays, "Bahama news at the top of the hour. A tourist woman was hit and run yesterday at Peace and Plenty Inn. She in serious condition at Angostura Hospital."

He sticks his fingers into his ears, opens his eyes, tries to talk, but no volume. Robin gets down on the floor.

"Chris?" He hears panic in her voice and feels shame. Exposed, skinless. He can't—can't face her—can't face it.

Leave me alone, he thinks. Please. He turns away from her, faces the toilet. Her fingertips touch his forehead. He flinches, moves away from her touch.

"Are you O.K.?" Her voice sounds strange, as if she's talking long distance over a phone.

"I don't feel good," he says, his head pounding.

"Me either."

He squeezes his eyelids tighter.

"Please." Her voice harsh now.

"Don't," he says, feeling slit open.

"What's the use?"

"Yeah, what's the fucking use?" he mumbles as he tries to juggle the blame. He tries to hate her but he only hates himself. He looks at her and she looks back at him with penetrating disappointment.

I don't need you, he thinks, as he detaches, listening to the familiar sounds of water lapping. The boat bobs. In his mind, he just sails away, far away.

"Have a nice fucking life, Christopher," she screams.

He slams his eyes shut, hears her walk away. Sneakers squeak across the deck above as he hears her screaming "Christopher" over and over and something clicks and before he can think, he jolts up and out of the bathroom, running, his heart pounding, his head pounding and he's breathing heavy and his lungs hurt. He smells dried blood in his nostrils as he tastes the coke aftertaste in his mouth and throat. He runs out of the boat along the dock and she's in her car. She doesn't see him. He hears the car engine shriek to a start as he screams, "No," and she doesn't hear. He jumps in front of the car and he realizes he's naked and he's covered in white powder and he thinks of the bums in Robin's subway, how the man sprinkled the lady with yellow powder and how Robin was jealous of them. And he stretches his arms out, mouthing, "Please."

He sees her see him. She hits the horn. One long continuous blast shoots through his body, pierces his brain as he lies spread-eagled over the hood of her car, trembling, catching his breath. He puts his hands over his ears. Robin's head rests on the steering wheel.

He crawls off the hood, gets into the car and reaches over and turns off the engine. Then it's so quiet. Except for her harsh breathing. Shame turns his stomach inside out. He doesn't know what to say. He can't stand the sound of the silence.

"I'm sorry," he says blankly, not daring to look at her, not daring to breathe. But then he has to.

A tear pools in her left eye, slips. Her head falls forward again. Then she sits up and starts to nod her head up and down, more and more violently, and then her head slams against the wheel over and over. He can't stand it, shuts his eyes. Dull thuds continue. He flings himself forward between her and the wheel. Her head bangs into his, slamming his face against the wheel. Sharp pain shoots. She stops. He puts his head on her lap, his face between her legs. He takes deep breaths, smells her, sticks his tongue out. Licks. Nips fabric. Blood drips from his nose. Blood rushes to his midsection. She moans, shoving him off her. He's on the floor. He keeps licking, her toes. His hard-on ground against the rubber mat.

"Fuck me then," she spits out. "That's all you're good for." She kicks. The pain feels good. Chris tries to think of something to say to make it better but he can't stop the thoughts racing through his head. And he's sitting at the top of the steps peeping through the banister slats, waiting. The door slammed open. His father was trying to get away and his mother was on the floor grabbing on to his father, his legs. He dragged her across the floor as she begged, screaming, hysterical, "Please don't leave!" Then the slitting sound. His mother was ripping off her clothes. "Fuck me!" she cried. "I'll do it good! Better dan dat black bitch!" His father looked up and saw him. Their eyes met. Then he picked up his mother, carried her back into her room. The door slammed shut.

She stops. "Anything," he says calmly, and he doesn't know where the calm comes from. "Just don't leave." He slides up, slumps on the seat next to her. His hard-on sticks up stupidly, and he's angry at it and it looks angry at him, hard and red and pulsing.

"It's over," she says, choked up, looking away from his eyes at his hard dick, as if she's talking to it. "Get out."

The car is hot and steamy. He squints against the sun's glare. "Please," he begs, rubbing his eyes. "Don't."

"I can't handle it. Can't be your mother. Your nurse." She breathes heavily. "Please. Get out. Leave me alone."

Something slips inside him. He grabs her hand. It feels dead. Then her finger. He sticks his tongue out, licks her finger, licks the ring with the five diamonds on it, thinking, I love you very much. Then sucks it. She pulls away, shaking her head. The ring cuts his tongue. He tastes blood.

His voice breaks as he tries to speak, and he stops and takes another breath. "I wasn't going to do it. I was going to get rid of it. And then . . ." And he stops because he can tell she doesn't believe him and he's not even sure he believes it.

Her lips part. Her eyelids tremble. "I need. I can't fight you and the cancer," she says firmly, quietly, her face tight. She stares coldly at him.

He looks away. "Help me," he whispers. He can't meet her eyes. He stares at the red bruise on her forehead.

"Help yourself," she says, agony in her voice. "Just leave. Now."

A great wave of feeling for her washes over him. He just sits there, unable to move. He feels the seconds pass slowly.

"You're killing me," she says weakly.

He opens the door. Gets out. Shuts the door softly. Watches dizzily, feels himself slowly go soft, drain, as she drives away.

13

Chris wakes up, takes a deep breath of fresh sea air. He sniffs the spotted sheet, smells Robin's smell, craves her. He jumps out of bed, opens the curtains on the porthole, walks over to the full-length mirror. A sunny stream flows, lighting up particles of otherwise invisible dust. Floating. His tan skin glows. I did it, he thinks. One month.

He touches his reflection. Clear eyes stare back at him, no more red, no more dark circles. He flexes his muscles, rubs his stomach and then pinches, less than an inch, picturing the small roll of fat sucked out, along with the coke craving, by liposuction. He remembers a month ago, after she left him. It was like after his mother died. He felt totally and completely alone. He craved coke, the bag, what was left of it, sitting on the bathroom floor. He stared at it, picked it up, wanted to dive back into it. Then he heard her voice, "You're killing me."

He opened the bag, strained, then poured. The coke fell into the toilet in one glob then floated, clumped together like cottage cheese. He took a deep breath. Flush. The coke disappeared in a swirl of white water. And he knew he had to get away. He started the boat, headed out to sea away from Freeport, and he was doing it for her. He told himself he wasn't running away.

He climbs up to the flying bridge, looks around. His boat is still the only one in the harbor. Only the natives know how to navigate the intricate channel into the hurricane hole. He smiles to himself, still not numb to the beauty of the morning light, thinking the only mornings he used to see was when he stayed up all night. He's awed by the amazing range and subtlety of blues. So much sky and water. A blob in the water in front of the boat is a darker blue, like the shadow of a cloud on the water, only there are no clouds. The blob moves. It swims toward the boat. Chris thinks goggle-eyes, diving into them. A splash and then his naked body wrapped in cool. The blob parts, divides as Chris swims. Goggle-eyes dart around him in a mad rush, millions rushing-crushing into one another, leaping out of the water as if it's boiling, and all he can see is a flash of oversized eyes and then a sizzling splash sound, quick as a blink, as the fish are absorbed back into the murky, moving cloud. And Chris becomes a moving spot of clear within the cloud because through some sort of fish radar, the goggle-eyes stay about a foot away from him. And he thinks it's like swimming through eyeballs.

Chris swims away from the school, his body on automatic, feet kicking, arms pulling as he tries to forget he has a body. Like a Buddhist monk, he chants "Robin" over and over as he swims. And he misses her so much, thinking how two weeks ago he couldn't take it anymore, driving his skiff for hours to the closest phone. He sat outside the bright yellow-and-pink shack in Cupid's Cay village for more hours still. He tried to get up the nerve to call her. And he finally did. She picked up, said "Hello." Her voice so close. He hung on, couldn't say anything. Then she said, "Christopher?" He hung up. He wasn't strong enough yet. But now he is, he thinks. Today's the day.

He swims and swims and then the feeling flows into his body, takes over, and his body starts to fly by itself. He turns, flies back. He has almost reached the boat when he sees a conch through the water resting brown-green on the sandy bottom and he swims down and picks it up. He sits on the transom, his legs dangling into the water. He cracks the conch, thinking about the years of practice it took him to learn to crack conch properly. He hears Doctor Conch saying, "Dere be time in every boy life when he best learn what to do with he conch." He gave him and Shark a conch hammer and a thin-bladed knife.

"Men," Doctor Conch said, handing them each a small conch, golden brown on the outside, pink on the inside, "you must hold she firmly in you hand, like so. Den take you hammer and hold it so.

"See dis space," he said, pointing between the second and third row of points on the spire of the shell. "Now pound she good, right between. Den crack she a little: knock a slit in she. Now, take you knife and juck she hole, in and out. Now juck she good, boys, cause she don't want to come. Now dat done, turn she over," he said, turning his shell over, "and she comes."

Doctor Conch's conch came sliding, sliming out of its shell. He and Shark turned their conchs over, and nothing.

Chris turns his shell over and the conch comes sliding, sliming out. He cuts off the pieces of grey conch slop from the white meat and throws it into the water and his legs and feet and toes are surrounded by bathing suit fish, nibbling away at the sinking slop. He dips the conch meat into the ocean, squeezes lime, Angostura bitters and Matouks pepper sauce on it. Then he eats his breakfast, picturing Shark chewing the gelatinous wormlike conch roe like it's Juicy Fruit, hearing him say, "Conch pistol's what make me so rich with dick." Chris remembers laughing. "That's what made you so rich with bullshit," he said.

"Aye, Chris, I ain lying," Shark said. "I's dead serious. I still don't eat much white-people food. Dat does make you soft. You never catch me eating orange sherbet or white shit like dat."

And then he sees Shark's black fist coming at him, and he hears himself calling him a nigger. He flinches. It hurts. He prays that he's all right.

He grabs a pen and writing pad, climbs back up to the flying bridge, sits on a lounge chair. The sun beats down, heating him. Gusts of breeze blow, cooling him. He shuts his eyes, feels sweat start to form, soak into the yellow writing pad resting on his stomach, covering his genitals. He drifts back to a month ago when he first came here. It seems like an eternity. It seems like yesterday. And he had no plan. He thinks about when he first tried to write.

Nothing came to him, nothing came into his head. But he forced himself to sit there for about a week listening to a voice inside that kept telling him he couldn't do it. It hurt. But he kept hearing Robin telling him he could, that he could be a writer or an artist. And after about a week it started happening. It just started flowing out. And now he couldn't stop it. It controls him. He has to do it. He writes until he's exhausted. And it's like he's getting all this stuff out, releasing all this stuff that was weighing him down, stopping him from doing anything. He's on the last page of the yellow pad. He writes, "Brian sees the one-piece pajama suit with the S on the chest. The feet were hard on the bottom, like monkey pads. And his mother told him the S did not stand for Superman but for Special-man and she said, 'You're my special little man and you are the most important thing in my life and I love you more than life.' And she would come into his room in the middle of the night and snuggle up next to him and cry, and she would wrap her arms around him, and he would hug her back and say, 'Mommy, don't cry.' " He stops writing. He has filled up a full pad. He hugs it, stands up, starts the engines, pulls up the anchor.

He navigates the boat through the channel, watching the bottom. It's all sand, divided into wide ridges like ribs. Then it's all covered in little clumps of turtle grass, like the thin hair that first grew on Robin's head. Then he's over the shallow reef. He watches the depthometer, holding his breath. He has four feet of water. *Paradise Overdose* draws three and a half feet. The ocean floor turns all rainbowy as he glides over purple and yellow sea fans waving through the clear water and clumps of brain coral—a mad scientist's laboratory of fat brains and staghorn coral—on top of a field full of deer, and lettuce coral—an underwater farm of stiff golden lettuce. Multitudes of minnows and pilchards drift in clouds. Further down, grunts, snappers, porgies, angelfish, a moving, multicolored mass. Then he leaves the reef behind. The bottom drops off as he passes over the continental shelf. He sets the automatic pilot, heads straight for Freeport, heads straight for Robin.

14

Chris wakes up to thrashing on the bed, a split second, all too fast. Nothing solid. He gropes wildly as a hand slaps loud and hard over his mouth, up against the bottom of his nose. Stinging, sweaty, smelling of perspiration mixed with musk cologne. He chokes, sucking through his mouth, forgetting he can breathe through his nose. He fights. The hand over his mouth gives way enough for him to turn. He sees a brown man with wild uncircumsized eyes wearing a green surgeon's mask, holding a machete.

Chris squirms, cold steel stinging his temple. Where am I? he thinks, looking through the porthole, seeing Freeport.

"Don't move," the man orders. Then the sound of the cock of the gun. He feels the cock in his brain. His body goes rigid, flash-frozen in pulsating fear. Chris's eyes move back and forth, searching. He sniffs air through his nose.

"I'm gonna take my hand off. Scream, and my amigo will slit you open. Comprendes, hijo de puta?" the voice hisses. A low growl of a laugh escapes from the other man behind the surgeon's mask.

"Be stupid and die, gringo," the man holding his mouth says roughly. Chris feels the metal move from his sweating forehead, the hand pulls away. Release. He inhales, wants to fight. He tries to stay calm, to hold in the shivers. "Turn over," the man orders, shoving him with the butt of the gun.

He lies face down on the bed, sees the brown hand, the silver knife. He smells himself and Robin on the spotted sheet. Wrapped in a blanket of fear. Time drags. "What . . . ?"

"Shut up!" The man ties the rope around his wrists, pulling tight, scraping, and then once around his throat. A noose. And then back to his back. The final knot. Control, he thinks, as his biceps, triceps strain. The man yanks the cord, like fingers down his throat. Choke. His neck jerks back, his arms wrench up.

"Up," the man commands.

And Chris is on his knees facing the stern.

"Turn."

Chris turns around, slowly, desperate to see the man, as if this would help. First he sees the gun and then the tan hand holding it and then the face smoothed, features smothered by a tan stocking.

"Where the product? Where you hide it?"

"What?" Chris asks, trying to understand, trying to read the man's face through the stocking. Blank.

"Our load," the man screams.

"Load? I've been away for the last month. On the boat. I just got back yesterday. I don't know what you're talking about."

"We've been waiting for you, hijo de puta." The hand hurls at him. Shark's black fist: You play, you pay. He shuts his eyes before the hand smacks his face, shoves his head sideways. He hears the slap deep inside. His head flies to the left, his neck stretching against rope and pain. And then on the other side of his face. He bites his tongue. Cringing. His head flaps right, stinging all over. He smells, tastes blood.

"I like kill people," the man grunts.

"Don't," Chris pleads, searching for some sense. He braces for another hit. He tells himself he can't lose control.

"Where's Shark? Your partner."

"Shark's not my partner," Chris says. "I'm rich. I don't need to fuck with that shit."

"Fuck us, we fuck you!" the man growls. He grasps against the rope ripping against his throat. Then the man snatches him by the hair. He looks at the other man's eyes and then the knife. "Where's the fucking coke?" the man asks.

"I don't fucking know," escapes in a scream. He fights the rope, choking. The gun, a flash of silver. His head. He doesn't feel it. He wobbles, gropes to stay on his knees. Warm blood trickles.

"Where's Shark?" The man grabs his crotch, squeezes, twists his balls. "I'll make you eat them."

Chris coughs, swallows the pain, fights the faint, pleads, "I'm sorry! I don't know!" Then grabbed by the hair again. He shuts his eyes, afraid to look. He's shoved down on the bed, and he feels the gun up against the back of his head. "Tell us," the man says. Chris grits his teeth as he feels the cold steel on his neck snake down his backbone. Sweat drips. Then against his naked ass. He tenses. "Speak, maricón!" the man yells, sticking the barrel of the gun into his asshole, pushing against his insides. His ass muscles fight letting it in, his ass filled with hard cold. Chris yells, "I don't know!" His mind races out of control. Trying to think of something to say to make it all disappear, and all he can think of is the suppositories up his ass and Robin's coffee-enema cancer cure.

"The last time I was with Shark was a month ago. He punched me. Ask anyone. I haven't seen him since. I hate him. I want you to fucking kill him. You want money, I got money," he pleads.

And he feels the gun pull out. He breathes. "In the closet, the Tide box." The man slides the closet door open, grabs the box, looks inside, smiles, says nothing. He walks up to Chris and yanks him around by the rope. Then he snatches a scarf up off the floor, rolls it into a ball, shoves it into his mouth. Chris tries to spit it out, retches. The man sticks silver duct tape to his mouth, forces him out of the room, pulling the cord tight around his throat as he rams the gun hard against his head. Chris strains. The scarf muffles the sound of his scream.

At the back of the boat, his legs now tied together. He wrestles the rope. It rips against his neck. Both men are there now. They pick him up, hold him out over the back of the boat. He looks down at the water, breathes rapidly through his nose. "Save yourself. Tell us. Tell us or we'll kill your girlfriend."

The tape is ripped off. The scarf is yanked out. He has nothing to say. They stare at him and he feels if he yells they will drop him. He gulps for air, thinking of Robin, praying, Please, God, no! The man laughs, a horror-movie laugh, and Chris fears the feel of the water. They stuff the scarf back into his mouth and one man has his legs and the other sticks fingers under his armpits and he prays as they swing him out over the water. His heart stops. Then back again. He smashes against the deck. And the man barks, "Tell Shark he's dead."

He hears them walk away and then the sound of tires screeching. He tries to turn over, tries to squirm out, to untie the rope. It's so quiet. He realizes that he can spit the scarf out of his mouth. He spits, the scarf and a clump of spit. The backed-up scream bursts.

15

Chris bangs on the door of Robin's house, hearing the man in the mask say, "I'll kill your girlfriend," over and over. His stomach churns. He's afraid for her even though he's sure the man was bullshitting, that he didn't even know he had a girlfriend. Chris shakes his head thinking, I don't have a girlfriend. I haven't seen Robin in over a month. "Fuck!" he screams. He stops banging on the door. His hand hurts. He touches the rope burn on his throat. It stings. Fuck Shark, he thinks, fuck him for getting me in this shit. Fear shoots as he pictures him dead, killed by the Colombians. The last word he said to him, "nigger." He gets back into his car. Drives. I got to help him, he thinks.

He parks, walks to the front door of Studio 69. Mosquitoes hiss in his ears. He stops, pushes the door open. Everything is dark, black and so quiet. He yells, "Shark!"

"Shark-Shark-Shark!" echoes back at him off the walls.

He stares at-in the darkness. His eyes adjust. Chris works his way past broken chairs, overturned tables. Glass crunches under his feet. He smells rancid rum. A spot of light glows through the eyehole on the door of Shark's office at the back of the club. Chris stumbles toward the eye of light, his arms in front of him. His heart beats in his throat.

His hand shakes on the doorknob of Shark's office. The light

through the door hole, a spot, settles on his forehead. He thinks of
the gun against his head. He takes a deep breath, turns the knob,
pushes. The door swishes open. He stumbles forward, blinded by
the light. He hears steps behind, sees a blurry black figure moving
in the bright, out of the corner of his eye, in his blind spot. Someone grabs him. He falls forward.

"Chris." The arms release him.

The man rolls off him, stands up. Chris grabs his hand. He looks
at his shaken face, his square-cut hair. "Tweed."

"Mon, like I almost crap," Tweed says, breathing hard. "Like
pussy fall on me lap. I tinks you spics, up to old tricks."

Chris catches his breath.

"Cartel Colombians. Drug thugs," Tweed says, excited. "Dem
lords badder than bad. Dey own we country, make us into monkey.
Dat load dat Shark box you over last month. Dat belong to dem.
Thief from thief does make good laugh." Tweed waves his arms dramatically. "Dem send one spic to say deys want the load back,
quick, on the fast track. Shark only playing fool, acting cool. Shark
say he ain't no soft man, no nigger boy, no black toy."

Chris paces, feels the gun inside his ass. "What?" Chris asks exasperated.

"Mon, Shark ain't studying he head. He brain dead. They tell
him, 'Plomo or plata,' lead or silver, money or the bullet. Shark bit
bullet." Tweed clacks his teeth together theatrically. "It like *Miami
Vice.* Spics like white on rice. Dey march in with so much gun, we
ain't know where to run. Shoot-out at cocaine corral. And Shark's
men in the Colombian pocket. Dey puts down dem guns and say,
'Fuck it!' "

"Shark?" Chris asks nervously.

"He disappear into thin air. Black into dark, so fast, he leave trail
of spark. Dis island Colombia now. Younna better learn Spanish if
you want to manage." Tweed shakes his head.

"Fucking death wish," Chris mumbles to himself, walking back
out to his car. "Where do you think he is?" he asks Tweed.

"Try the ghetto," Tweed says, following him.

Chris opens the car door. Heat escapes like out of a sauna. His face cringes as he starts the car, flicks on the air conditioner, rolls down the windows to let the hot, fatty air escape. He touches the steering wheel. It burns. He sits with the car door open trying to think, waiting for it to cool. He waves at Tweed. Then drives and drives and drives, as if suspended on the heat waves, the asphalt like a winding piece of slick black licorice. He searches.

He makes a left turn. A stink flows through the air conditioner as he enters Freeport's ghetto, Mango Estates. Houses, all identical, white, concrete and rotting, sit on dusty gardens of struggling weeds and piles of garbage. Chris thinks that his father built these houses for the people after he bought their homes and land to build the strip of hotels on Lucayan Beach. And Chris is a child again, holding the stack of crisp contracts tied with red ribbons and sealed with even redder wax. He thinks back to the colorful shacks on the beach, smells the old village: bread baking in outdoor ovens, fragrant fruit trees salted by ocean air, fresh-dug earth in the flower-pot farms. He hears the sound of his father's gold Angostura crest ring as he would rap determinedly on the doors. Most doors swung open from the power of his father's knock to reveal shy, astonished black faces, and his father would say, "I's here to see the head of the household on important business." They would be told to sit on the couch, usually made of crates and pillows, and they would be given lukewarm sour-orange juice. Chris would swish the juice around his mouth, placing his thumb on the heat-softened seals, then lifting it off, and then trying to follow the curlicues of his fin-gerprints in the wax. His father would say, "Just sign and you family will get work and also a concrete house in the new, modern Mango Estates in exchange for you sorry piece of land on dis ugly beach." His father would wink at him as the natives placed a shaky X on the dotted line.

He opens the windows, breathes deeply, as if the hot air could cool the burning inside of him. His heart pounds hard in his head as he stares straight ahead, pressing his foot down harder and harder on the gas pedal. He screeches to a stop, parks, walks to the cancer clinic, shivers, pushes open the door, is slapped by hospital smell, frigid air-conditioned air, fluorescent light.

Robin. She sits, long tan legs crossed, drawing pad on her lap.

Panic shoots. He feels like he's on the ledge of a tall building, looking down. She looks up at him, expressionless. He hears a clock tick loudly and he thinks it's his heart. He forces himself to look back at her, picturing himself, scruffy hair, face covered in stubble. Her eyes question. He takes a deep breath as he walks up to her. Her little lips part. She trembles, rubs her neck.

He tries to talk and his teeth clack together like those wind-up teeth. And she looks deeply at him as if she's trying to look into him and he meets her look, holds it, and her face changes and she radiates feeling and concern and he wishes he could kiss her pussy, has this incredible urge to just bury his face in her pussy.

He grabs her hand. She stands. He leads her out. They get into his car. Light swims on the five stones on the ring on her finger. I love you very much, he thinks. They face one another. Her eyes question. Chris takes a deep breath. He rubs his eyes. His voice breaks as he tries to speak, and he stops and takes another breath. He starts the car. Drives. He looks at the road. "Baby, everyone thought my mom killed herself. But she didn't. Evalina told me my mother died of cancer and she told me when I was a baby my mother would cry when she breast-fed me because her nipples hurt and how she kept trying and crying and that's how she was," Chris says, and he looks over at her, the words coming out faster and faster, the encouraging look on her face sucking them out, and he feels if he can just get them out it will be all over, and the problem was holding them in, and out they come, and he couldn't stop them even if he wanted to. "And I couldn't stop thinking of her dying alone in that big house with no one. And I should have been there." He pauses for a breath. "I feel her feeling the lump in her breast grow bigger and bigger and her ignoring it until it got so big it ate her lungs. And Evalina gave me the ring." He grabs her finger. "And she said my mother told her to give it to me and to tell me she loves me very much. And too much cancer . . . I left her, just like my dad . . ." He lets her finger go. "I went to see my father to tell him that my mother didn't commit suicide and he was fucking with the fucking maid. They played me like a yo-yo: one minute they were so loving and the next they were so mean and I loved them and I hated them and it's like throughout my life everything I get is snatched and it's like I can't enjoy it because I keep waiting for it to be snatched. You . . ."

"I need you," she says, her voice barely audible, looking away, twisting the ring around in circles.

Chris trembles. "I . . . I can't help but think of you as dying and I try to force myself to think that you will live, that you will get better, but why should you be any different from everything else and I'm so afraid for you, of you, and I want to believe in the cancer treatment because I know you believe and I want to believe for you, for me. It hurts." He breathes deeply. She brings her face close to his. He feels her breath. She shuts her eyes for a moment and says, calmly, softly, "You. Just you. I don't need you to think any special way for me. I know I have a deadly disease. But I can fight it. But I need you with me." She clears her throat, touches it with her hand. "This month has shown me how much I need you."

He concentrates on her wonderful smell, watches the sunset over the trees, an orange haze settling into black night, barely lit by a slit of moon. His headlights, like two bright eyes, stare into the dark. "I based out with Shark. The pain got further away the more I smoked. Then somehow we were chasing this drug plane and the car hit this woman. Shark left her there, kept chasing the plane. I'm scared. He wouldn't stop and I tried to stop him but I could have tried harder but it was like I had no control. Thank God an ambulance came. It was like the woman was you—I quit. You have to believe. For the last month. For you. For me. I started to write." He pulls into the dock. She looks at him, as if she's looking through a windshield in a storm. He stares back until she blurs. Tears flow. He licks them, drinks them, feels so much better, like he's floating, a bubble. A great wave of feeling for her washes over him, and he has to let it out. He leans forward, grabs her. "Help me," he whispers.

"Help me," she whispers into his ear, hugging him back, tight.

He draws back. Looks at her. She looks back. He kisses her wet cheek. "Live, live with me. Move in," he says. He touches the tips of her hair with the tips of his fingers as they walk back to the boat.

"I want to read what you wrote," she says, sitting on the couch. He hands her his writing pad. She looks at it, at him. She sits, starts to read. He sits across from her, watches, tries to read her face. She turns the pages. He can't stop looking at her, can't believe she's giving him another chance. She looks healthy, beautiful, tanned, her hair now shoulder length, sleek and thick.

She closes the pad, looks back at him. His heart beats hard. He holds his breath. She gets the same intense, dreamy look on her face as she does when she works on her art. He feels as if he has just burst through the ocean's surface. He gasps for air.

She gets up, says nothing and leaves the room, walks into the bathroom. The door shuts.

He hears water running, sits, waiting, wondering. And he can't believe she's here once again, on the boat with him. He tells himself he's not dreaming.

She comes out of the bathroom naked. He looks at her, at her perfect pussy. His dick stands up hard. She grabs his hand. He follows.

The bathtub is filled with bubble bath, surrounded by flickering candles. Steam rises, bubbles hiss, water drips, Marley plays on the stereo, "Don't worry about a thing, cause every little thing is gonna be all right." His body sizzles as she undresses him. His shirt, one button at a time. Then his shorts. His zipper. No underwear. Dick springs free. She leads him to the tub. He gets in, sinks into the feeling. Feels revealed, as if he's floating in a glass jar of formaldehyde. And it feels good. He feels so light. His muscles relax, bones crack. Tension dissolves. The round head of his hard dick bobs in the white like a red-brown bubble. Robin kneels beside the tub. "You are very talented," she says. "I want you to know that you are very talented." Her lips on his lips, her tongue on his tongue, above the popping bubbles. He remembers how his mother liked to blow bubbles, and he remembers how when he was a child she used to buy that bubble syrup that came in the plastic bottles and they would sit across from each other and blow through that little plastic thing with the hoops on each end. And he pictures the pucker of her pale lips when she blew bubbles and how she blew so softly that bubbles always came out and he would always blow too hard and the soap film on the plastic hoop would just pop and turn into a wet drop. And sometimes a spray of bubbles would come out of his hoop at the same time a spray came out from hers. Floating, fragile, clear, multicolored balls. And he would watch the delight on her face as his bubbles would stick to hers. The water washes, cleanses, fresh, cool. He's floating underwater in a passage cut by the current through the reef. He flows with the flow, doesn't fight it, weightless. He shuts his eyes, smells flowers. Roses. Robin's fingers gently rub his scalp, shampooing his hair. Then she grabs his hands and pulls and he stands, steps out of the tub. The sound of trickling water. They walk into the cabin. She dries his hair, wrapping the towel around his head like a turban. She dries his face, kisses each eyelid, his neck. She dries his chest, kisses each nipple. His stomach, licking his belly button. Then his ass, between his cheeks. She kneels on the floor. He watches the top of her head as she dries his feet, between his toes.

She walks him to the bed. She smiles when she sees the come-spotted white sheet. It glows. He lies down. Robin crawls on the bed, kisses each of his balls, the left, then the right. She puts her arms around him, brings her mouth to his ear. Her lips quiver. "I missed you," she says, and she lies upon him, her head resting on his chest, her warm breath caressing his nipples. And he stares down at her. He can't believe she's in his arm. He can't believe how good she looks, feels, smells. They lie together in a shaft of moonlight shining through a salt-streaked porthole. He synchronizes his breathing with hers. Then he can't fight it anymore. He has to. He crawls between her legs, kisses her pussy over and over, his favorite smell, his favorite taste. Pink tongue on pink lips, so silky as he licks and licks, as his tongue goes inside Robin deeper and deeper, feeling. Her pelvis goes up. Way up. She is up his nose, in his mouth. He holds on with his hands and his tongue. Pulling-pushing, up and down. Tug of war. She pulls his head up. He pushes his head down. And he locks his head between her legs and flips, slips his body around until it's in her face and she swallows him in one hungry gulp.

And she does it to him as he does it to her. She jerks wildly. He jerks wildly. His head rocks, soaked in waves of pleasure. Shrill. An alarm. On the edge. He brings the plastic bubble rod close to his lips. About to blow. "Go, yes go," his pleasure cells yell. He exhales. Billions of joy bubbles float throughout his body. "Yes! Ohhhh, yes!" He explodes. Their bubbles stick together. Their screams melt together, form one scream, one bubble as they come together. Popping. Came together. He grabs her quickly, pries her mouth open with his tongue, sucks the come out, takes it all into his mouth, soft and slippery, passion afterbirth. He spits the come out onto the sheet. Frothy and white.

The come and spit sink into the mattress, forming another spot.

"See Spot run," she says.

"Run, Spot, run," he says.

"If I die before you, will you come and feed me like the natives do?" she asks.

"Not only will I feed you, I will think of you and come for you," he replies.

"Let's shake on that," Robin says as she grabs it and holds it in her hand, clasping it like a rope, as though, if she let go, she would fall.

16

Chris wakes up, feels for Robin. Not there. He sits up, smells bacon frying and hears cups clinking, silverware tinkling. He inhales her smell on the spotted sheets. Chris hears footsteps, turns. Robin carries the silver tray that he used to snort coke from, singing, "Happy one month to us."

A single candle sticking into the omelet flickers. Next to it orange juice, a slice of papaya with a slice of lime on top, buttered toast and a blood red hibiscus. She places the tray on the bed, sits next to it.

He sticks the hibiscus behind her ear and stares at the flame, orange top, blue bottom. Then at her. He kisses her lips, makes a wish and blows out the candle.

"To a month of living together," she says.

"To always together." Their glasses clink.

"It's your favorite—asparagus, bacon and sour cream," she says as she pulls out an asparagus and holds the milky white tip up to him. He bites it off. She eats stalk.

"Perfect," he says, savoring the taste, watching her eat, thinking how lately she's been eating a lot but keeps losing weight.

"Today we're going to make the sheet surprise."

"Finally. You're gonna tell me," Chris says, as he thinks of going with her to buy the white sheets and the different color dyes. He pictures the mixed look of absorption and happiness on her face as she mixed the colors on the dock, one at a time, in the galvanized wash tins, stirring, her hands a spoon, and they turned muted shades of brilliant yellow, aqua, pink, red, purple, orange as the sun-bleached hair on her arms lit up gold in the sunlight. She would check the tins all day and when she was sure the sheets had absorbed the exact amount of color, she called him. He grabbed one end and she the other and they stretched them out and hung them on a line he rigged up between the posts on the dock. And the sheets looked like thin slices of rainbow and when the wind blew, they breathed. Every time he asked her what she was going to do with the sheets she would grin and answer, "It's a surprise."

"I'm gonna show you later," she adds, cutting a piece of omelet as he thinks of her cutting the dyed sheets into strips and then rolling the strips into balls.

"I'll miss your different-colored hands. They made me think of Easter, of coloring eggs," he says, thinking about spreading out the *Freeport News* on the kitchen table with his mother and Evalina and Shark. And then the tart smell as Evalina poured the boiling vinegar water into the glass bowls. As the vapor rose, he and Shark dropped in the color pills, which would kind of hop when they hit the hot liquid and then sink slowly to the bottom, followed by a trail of tiny bubbles, and the pills would disintegrate, leaking into a fragile ribbon of bright color until they took a spoon and swirled the color into a uniform shade.

"I loved to draw on Easter eggs with a candle," she says. "I loved the way the invisible writing would show up after the eggs were dyed."

"I always made a rotten one. I'd dip it from color to color until it turned putrid brown. My mother always told me to stop but I knew she liked it," Chris says. He remembers when he was a child, sitting on the balcony waiting, listening for the sound of his mother's car because she said that when she got home they would color eggs and when he heard the car pull into the driveway he got so excited that he ran, leaped over the white hammock catching the back of his foot and then he fell forward so fast that he couldn't even stick his hands out to cushion the fall. When he touched his face, it was wet and dripping. And his mother was there before the scream had finished coming out and she was screaming also and she picked him up and put a silk scarf on the blood and applied pressure and it stabbed as she took him to the hospital. He started to cry and she looked at him with sad eyes and said, "Don't be scared." And he said, "I'm not scared. I'm crying because we won't get to color eggs." And she said, "Christopher, we'll color eggs every day dis week." And he was so happy and was not even afraid as Doctor Baboo took out a big syringe and held it up to him saying, "This isn't going to hurt." He felt his mother's grip on him tighten as he shut his eyes and the doctor injected the needle into his cut. All he could see behind his eyes was a complete week of coloring eggs.

Chris takes the last bite of his omelet.

"I have another surprise for you," Robin says, dabbing her mouth with a napkin. "Shut your eyes."

"O.K.," he says, closing one eye and then the other, then opening one and then the other. She laughs.

"Shut both your eyes at the same time. Keep them shut." She grabs her parsley-colored paisley scarf from the table, wrapping it around his eyes, tying it in the back, blindfolding him.

"Kinky," he says, and he hears her leave. Watches the black behind the blindfold, listens to the licking sound of the water against the boat and then her footsteps. He hears her sit on the bed next to him.

She unties the blindfold. Bright, fuzz, and then he sees it. "Cream hooray," he says, smiling. She brushes her cheek against his and his unshaven face makes a sizzling sound against her skin and she says, "Evalina gave me her recipe. Go ahead—taste it."

"You don't just go ahead and taste cream hooray," he says. "I'll show you." Chris taps his finger carefully on the crispy crust that rests on top of the creamy pudding. "You have to separate the hooray part from the cream." Then he pokes under the crust with the end of the spoon and pries off the top. "Kind of like opening the top off a paint can," he says, picking up the host-sized wafer of burnt sugar. Robin does the same thing.

"Now, hold it above your head. Repeat after me. Say, take this all of you and eat it."

"Take this all of you and eat it."

Then they chew the sugar circles. It sounds like breaking glass.

"There used to be a guy on the island called Crash, the Glass-Eating Man. He worked the native shows. He was huge and blue-black. He would grease up his muscles with oil and wear a G-string and a bone through his nose and paint up his face like a cannibal, with white sunblock. He had the longest, thickest tongue I've ever seen. He would lick the air back and forth, in and out. He would choose a woman, grab her drink and chug it in one gulp and then he would eat her glass. He would just chew it up and swallow it. Then he would hold a microphone up to his neck so you could hear the glass crunch and then the swallowing sound of the slivers going down his throat."

Robin touches her neck.

"Crash was the stud of the island. The women whose glasses he ate couldn't resist him."

"I don't believe you," she says, spooning up some of the cream part of the cream hooray, closing her eyes as she tastes it. A small drop of white dribbles out of the corner of her mouth. Her tongue licks. It disappears.

"I swear. I used to follow him after the show. He screwed the women on the beach. He didn't even bother to wash off the oil and sunblock. I won't tell you what he did with the bone in his nose." Chris takes a spoonful of pudding, sucks it into his mouth and swishes it around as if tasting wine.

"Mmmm," Chris says. "Tastes like orgasm."

"I'd like to taste an orgasm," Robin says. She winks at him. He shuts his eyes, tastes the cream hooray in her mouth and his mouth as he licks, as he feels the cool drip-drop flop on his genitals and spread. He opens his eyes to see the cream hooray, white on black pubic hair and on brown dick and balls, and it starts to flow as he starts to grow and she says, "Another surprise," as she starts to lick the drips like a lollipop, like a kitten licking cream, her tongue flicking, coated in white, and it feels so great that he falls back onto the bed. He's tasting the feeling with his whole body. Each lick, a sliver of elation, makes him quiver as he feels his thigh muscles shiver and then tense. He feels her tongue against his balls, sucking the smaller one in and then the other. The pleasure. The surrender. The trust, knowing she could bite down on them like jawbreakers. Yet she treats them like a mother bird with eggs. And he thinks how his mother kept her promise after he fell and they colored eggs together for a whole week and there were so many eggs they couldn't eat them. Robin licks away all the cream hooray. And then he feels her mouth swallow it, her lips suckling it up and down, milking him, a firecracker. Lips light the fuse, sizzling lower and lower as he relaxes and waits, relaxes the muscles fighting to be tensed, to pop the pleasure out, and then it starts to come all by itself and she stops, pulls up and off. And it stops, right before overflowing. His breath comes up short.

He opens his eyes and looks up. She says, "Surprise!" Ties her scarf around his eyes. And she pulls his head down. Down. And it's dark and smells of her and cream hooray and his mouth opens to taste the smell and his tongue is out and he's licking and licking and he doesn't know what part of her he's licking and he tries to feel it with his tongue but it's all silky and tastes sweet and rich. He realizes she has spread cream hooray on her body, as he follows the tasty trail, as he imagines he has the glass eater's long, fat, purple tongue. And he thinks as he licks that it's like he has finally crawled into that secure space and will never have to leave. He exhales hot air. Then his tongue feels what he thinks is a breast as he tastes the cream hooray and her nipple gets hard, pushes out to meet his tongue, and he's sliding down, and then her navel, his tongue flicking in and out, and he strains to slow down as his tongue follows the trail down but he can't because it's so slippery and soft-subtle and good that he just can't eat enough and then he feels and tastes pubic hair in his mouth and he feels so happy he moans. Then she moans, only it's louder and shriller and he's hearing it as if it's coming from her other lips. He licks her around the edges, imagines he's a hummingbird and she a blood red hibiscus. The beak of the hummingbird enters the hibiscus like a dipstick pierces, gently, softly, flickering tongue ballet of balance. Wings move so fast they can't be seen. Then like a dog. Beefsteak tongue laps her up. Parts the sea. Cracks. Tastes. Her warmth melts, creamy and ripe, changing, every time similar but subtly different. He takes a good mouthful, his tongue scoops her like the spoon in cream hooray and he lets it reach the inner crevices of his mouth. His heart floods as she floods. He drinks it. Drunk with it. Drowning in it. Till he has licked up all the cream hooray. He slides up. Fast! And his mouth is eating her mouth as her mouth is eating his and he feels her legs wrap tightly around his back. He's push-pulled under, under toe, undertow. He taps into her, applies pressure, the war drums beat. A losing battle. Slow and subtle at first, then hard. Pumping. He sees Shark with the pile of Easter eggs they couldn't eat after the week of coloring and he feels the cricket bat in his hands. And Shark picked up an egg and his muscles pulled taut as he pitched the egg at him and it flew through the air. A blur of color. He swung the bat and, pow! the egg exploded. Her toenails scratch his lower back as she rips the blindfold from his eyes. He explodes white, coming into the white light.

Inhale. Kiss. Exhale. Kiss. Repeat. Spots float before his eyes. Another spot leaks onto-into the sheet.

"Cream hooray never tasted so good," he says.

"Coming never felt so good," she says.

He synchronizes his breathing with hers and shuts his eyes and feels full, complete, drained. Tries to place the feeling deep into himself so he can pull it out anytime he needs it.

He slips out of her, rolls off her, pulls her on top of him. Hugs her tight. Feels the cold wet under his ass and likes the feeling. He thinks of all the spots on the sheet. The sheets reek of her and of him, their spores and juices. He won't let her wash them. All yellow-brown, the color of the brown-yellow sargassum weed, which floats like a cloud on the ocean. He pictures them living in their own cloud, clouded with exquisite pleasure and pain. They cling to one another like the seaweed, fighting the pressure. Tangled, arms, legs, and torsos entwined, genital to genital. The boat their bed, their own little island floating in a broth of killing things. He thinks

that all seaweed will eventually be cast ashore, dry, turn black, crisp
in the sun. Turn to dust, dust to dust. She rolls off him. He spoons
himself up against her, tries to fit himself into her, like fitting his
fingers into a silk glove, the air between them making a farting
sound. He imagines he's stuck to her. How can I be without her? he
thinks, and he feels cold and pulls the sheet up over them and then
tries to push himself up even closer to her, mold himself around
her, like Jell-O in a Jell-O mold. His stomach feels like it's full of
Jell-O as he hears Shark saying, "Dat must be Jell-O cause jam
don't shake so," every time he saw a woman with big breasts. And
Chris thinks about Shark. He can't believe he can't find him, and
he pictures Tantie on the beach two weeks ago. She hugged him,
pleading, "Please find him."

Chris lies in bed, Robin's alarm watch sounds. Chris shuts his
eyes. She sticks the needle into her arm.

"What ever happened to Crash?" she asks Chris.

"He married one of the girls whose glass he ate. She owns a glass
shop and he can eat up as much glass as he wants."

"Bullshit," Robin says.

Chris turns to Robin, "So what about the sheet surprise?"

"We have to take the boat out," Robin says.

Robin unties the ropes. Chris climbs to the flying bridge, turns
the two keys, pushes in the left button, then the right. The engines
crank, spit out smoke, churn.

"Where to?" Chris asks.

"Mangrove Cay," Robin answers. She climbs the flying bridge.

The ocean is flat calm. The boat cuts the sheet of glass, chopping it, piercing its skin, spewing foam. Chris steers with his feet on
the wheel, staring at the colors.

Chris squeezes Robin's soft hand as they watch a flying fish, a
winged spear, glide through the air.

"Is it a bird? A plane? Superman?" Chris asks, smiling.

"You're Superman," she says, looking amused. She kisses him on
the forehead.

Mangrove Cay appears, a dot on the horizon, which slowly
changes into a streak of an island. He pictures the boat wrecked,

rotten ribs sticking out, skeleton white against the sand white of the beach, pictures himself and Robin and Shark trying to survive the savage sea, cramped together on a tiny dinghy, clawing, mile after mile, day after day, against the tidal waves, the great white sharks. The equatorial sun beats down. Bright dim hope. Each anticancer injection. Thirsty for water, they catch a fish with their hands and suck the moisture from it. Slowly the boat sinks. The sinker plops into the water, pulling the bait down with it.

Chris cuts the engine, drops the anchor. It's so quiet.

He climbs down the steps. "So what are we going to do with the strips of cloth?"

"Art."

"Yeah?" Chris says, glancing at her.

"I want to wrap the cloth strips around the mangrove banyans."

"Come again?" he asks, bewildered.

"I want to wrap the banyans, make them different colors."

Robin goes to the cabin and returns to the cockpit with one of the garbage bags full of the colored strips of sheet. Chris savors the expression on her face.

"The things you do for love," Chris says, as he starts to inflate a rubber raft.

They swim out to Mangrove Cay, towing a bag of colored material on each of their rubber rafts.

Robin sits on her raft and opens the garbage bag. She untucks the end of a rolled ball of colored strip and wraps the material around a mangrove banyan, a long wooden arch of root that stretches above and out and into the ocean.

"You want me to make like a cast on the roots?" Chris asks.

"Yes," Robin says. Chris wraps other banyans.

He feels so happy and he imagines the colored material balls are Easter eggs as he unravels them and wraps them around and around and around the mangrove banyans.

And they wrap and wrap and wrap and talk and talk and talk and Chris thinks it's like they're painting nature, like they're gods creating. He feels above it all.

They swim back and forth to the boat to get more bags of material. And then there are no more bags and they have wrapped the entire island, which is about fifty yards around, and they paddle back to the boat together. They climb up to the flying bridge. Chris grabs his pad and writes. Robin sketches. When the sun starts to set, she grabs his hand. They stare at Mangrove Cay, at the wrapped mangrove. It looks so beautiful in the changing light of the sunset, like the island is wrapped in neon.

"I never liked mangrove before," Chris says. "I thought it was just ugly swamp. It's like I'm seeing it for the first time," Chris says. "It's beautiful."

"That's what the surprise is," Robin says. "That's what art is. Letting you see something, something you've seen a million times before but never seen." Chris looks at her and an ocean of feeling sweeps him away. It's like he has never seen her before, like this is how she must have looked all the time when she was healthy.

The sun is getting lower and lower, closer and closer to the sea, and he goes to the fridge and gets a fat mango. He cuts it, gives Robin a cheek, and he takes the seed. The flesh of the mango is the same color as the setting sun. He imagines he's biting into the sun as he bites into the pudding-orange tart sweetness. Sticky mango juice runs down their faces.

"Let's jump into the sun," Chris says, running and climbing up the flying bridge. Robin follows.

"You have to jump into the water the second the sun is swallowed up, the second it flashes green," Chris says. Robin grabs his hand. They are hand in hand. They watch the sinking sun, the rising moon, the miles and miles of twinkling ultramarine below and wrapped Mangrove Cay.

"It looks like a flower," Chris says.

"A firework," Robin says.

"An orgasm," Chris says.

"A Hallmark card," she laughs.

"Like fuck me, I'm sensitive."

"With pleasure," she says.

Then it's time. They jump off together, splashing hand in hand into the sunset.

17

Chris drifts awake, keeps his eyes shut, a bald black under his eyelids, a filmy paste taste in his mouth. He sees endless hours of sleep. Like the sleep is a trap, like the sticky black glue his mother would spread on cardboard that the mice would scamper to eat, only to get stuck, little mouths licking till the poison in the glue caused their skin to ooze like tartar sauce. Robin sleeps and sleeps and fights and fights. He searches and searches, feels trapped in an endless search for Shark over the last two months since he was attacked by the Colombians.

He opens his eyes. Spots like fragments in mica flit in disappearing frenzy. Then clear. He wipes his eyes to look at Robin, hears her saying last night, "I'm so tired all the time. I'm afraid I'll give in to the sleep." Her voice like an embrace. And she has his dick in her hand, in her sleep, in her special way, holding yet not really holding it, like an object too precious to grasp. He focuses on her electric touch, and it makes him feel a little drunk as his whole body tingles and it grows, molds into her hand, and then he pulls out.

Rain starts to sprinkle and then pound in spurts against the boat. Then the fresh, fresh smell. And it's late afternoon and the sun is out and it keeps drizzling and Chris hears Shark say, "When rain falling same time sun out, it mean the devil and God fighting for fish-eye." He rubs his eyes, sitting up, staring down at Robin. She's asleep on her stomach. He stares at her ass, two egg-bubble cheeks, and he thinks of his bubble float, made out of two Styrofoam eggs. He's a child and his mother is teaching him how to swim. She smiles and says, "You can do it, Specialman." His eyes follow Robin's long legs, stopping at her perfect feet. And he can't help himself. He sticks his shaking pink tongue out and brings it down into the crack of her ass, licking, tasting. He feels her wake up. She spreads her legs, opening up her body. He follows the crack of her ass, licking in the place below her ass. Then he eats her pink softness, softly. And he tastes the ripeness of the blood between her legs. He pulls the tampon out, the cord between his teeth like dental floss as he thinks back to his first communion. He was eye level with Monsignor's crotch, looking up as Monsignor dipped the white host into the golden chalice as he held it, dripping red, up to his mouth and he said with a crooked smile, "The body and blood of Christ."

Chris shook, "Amen" coming from his mouth.

Robin moans. Her hands push the back of his head farther in, her nails digging into his scalp, and he fights to stick his face-tongue in deeper. He grinds his midsection into the bed as he grinds his tongue into her and he pictures his shaking pink tongue sticking out. The host, in slow motion, Monsignor's dirty nails, as it touched the tip of his tongue like a waxy feather. And he's light as a feather, flying. "Chris! Chris! Christopher!" Screams push from her mouth as she comes as he comes pumping into the sheet. The orgasm boomerangs around, coming back at him from her, from her other lips.

"I always wanted to wake up coming."

He laughs. She laughs. His head bounces up and down as the laugh ripples from her stomach to her groin. He hears a gurgling sound, lets her special smell splash over him as he sucks in air, his nose in her splash of pubic hair.

"When I was little, my mother taught me to swim and I had a bubble made out of two Styrofoam balls and as I learned to swim better she took off one of the balls. Finally there was only half a ball left and she took that off and I swam with no float at all. I was so happy. My mother jumped up and down and clapped. She said we should have a splash party. She got down on her knees and giggled and starting slapping the water, splashing and laughing, and I splashed the water also and we splashed as hard as we could and we laughed as hard as we could. I feel like I just had a splash party with you."

He wraps his arms around her, imagining he's stuck to her, entwined, colored material wrapped around the mangrove, arms like branches, and she says, "I don't want to die."

"Don't worry," he says anemically. "Everything is gonna be all right."

She pauses, pushes his hair off his face. "It will be all right." She tries to sound reassuring.

And Chris thinks it's like they're all leaving him, his mother, Robin, Shark. He can't believe he still can't find him.

"Look," Robin says, pointing at the sheet.

"What?"

"We're finished," she smiles.

"I certainly am." He pants, dramatically.

"No—the sheets." She puts her hand over his mouth.

"What?" he asks through her fingers.

"The spots." He kisses her palm. She enfolds him in her arms.

He looks. The sheets are now one color, all the dots connect.

"We won."

"Yes," she says, yawning.

Chris buries himself in the spot and he feels the growth under her armpit against his lip. He holds his breath, hears her fall back asleep, remembers going to see Evalina last week, lying to her. He just couldn't stand her pain anymore. He told her that he heard Shark was safe and living in Miami. And she said, "Praise the Lord," hugging him, and he felt so ashamed. And his stomach feels like it's swallowing itself, and he knows the only thing that helps is to continue searching for Shark, and he knows it's useless, but he can't stop, can't stop the feeling. He extracts himself from her embrace, climbs out of bed. Dresses.

He drives frustrated. He knows Robin's getting weaker. He knows there's nothing he can do but be there for her. He knows Shark is probably dead. He drives fast with the windows open, scanning the sides of the road.

Chris passes the row of base houses on Bass Lane. He slows down. He feels the pull of the coke as he passes, imagines how delicious it would feel to get high. He swallows, pushes the thought out of his head as he looks at the mass of whore faces, all blank, until they spot his Jag, which causes them to switch on artificial I-want-you eyes and smiles, some waving, flashing tits as they grind their hips in mechanical provocation.

Then he sees the face, hits the brakes before he can think. He stops, looks. Peroxide hair with black roots shines in the afternoon sun. Pam staggers up to the car, leans against the door, peering into tinted windows. Her nipple pokes through her ripped shirt. He presses the window switch. It slides down.

She sees him, recognizes him. "You got coke?" Pam asks.

"Get in," Chris says, flicking the unlock switch and opening the door. "You seen Shark?"

"No," Pam says, slamming the door, slumping in the seat, trying to smile. Chris drives, thinks, not knowing what to do, wishing he hadn't stopped.

"You got snow, smack?" she asks.

"So how are you, Pam?"

"Fine, Chris. It's better in the Bahamas. Fine, Chris. I can't wait to blow."

"I don't have any."

She grabs the door handle. "Don't . . . don't hold out on me." She starts to cry, black tears flowing from the black smudge of eye makeup down her cheeks.

"God, I hate this island," she says, trembling. She clears her throat, wipes her eyes with her sleeve. Chris reaches over and strokes her matted hair, and it feels like the inside of a Teflon frying pan. She smiles at him, insincere, grabbing his hand from her head, pulling it to her mouth, sucking his finger.

"No," he cringes. She jumps back against the car door.

"Stop," she says. "I'll fuck someone else for it."

He can't wait to get rid of her. He feels the coke craving, hits the brakes. She gets out, gives him an acid look, slams the door shut. He drives away, feels relief as if he's driving away from a part of himself he hates. Then he thinks of Robin, the girl spread-eagled. He stops, makes a U in the center of the road. Pam sits on the side of the road, folded into herself, a crumpled piece of paper. He stops, gets out of the car, touches her on the shoulder. She moves sideways, slightly beyond his touch. "It hurts," she says, looking up.

"I know."

"It'll be over soon as I get some."

"It won't be over till you stop," he says, sitting next to her on the side of the road.

"What have you become? I know you. I fucked you," she says harshly.

"What have you become? A coke whore?" He spits the question back at her, hoping to shock her into reality.

"Fuck you!" she says hatefully, standing up, walking away.

He follows her. She stops, hugs herself. "I wish I could go home."

"Go."

"I have no money."

"I have money," he says, pulling bills from his pocket. He stands, helps her up. She stares at the money. "Get in," he says, sticking the bills back into his pocket, opening the door. And he thinks, if I could just get her away from here, as he drives fast around the landscaped roundabout, a blaze of flowers.

They drive in silence. Chris tries to think of something to say. "Where you from?"

"New York," she answers tightly. She bites her lip.

Chris pulls into the airport, into the commotion of taxis arriving and leaving. White-skinned tourists coming in and red-skinned tourists going out.

Chris parks in front of the airport entrance, in front of the No Parking sign.

"Let's go," he says, getting out, going around to her door, opening it, grabbing her hand. She follows, her face blank. A policeman walks up to them. "Mon, younna can't read sign."

Chris pulls out a twenty-dollar bill, stuffs it into the policeman's hand. "We's in a rush. Watch it for me."

The policeman looks at the twenty, smiles. And he hopes Pam will also just take his money and go. They walk up to the Bahamas Air counter. "A one-way ticket to New York," he says.

The ticket lady puts down a plate of food she's eating as if he's disturbing her. He pulls out a wad of bills, counts out the hundred-dollar bills.

"Which flight you want, mon?" the lady asks.

"The next one."

"Flight 272A, Freeport–JFK."

"I'll take it," Chris says.

"It depart in five minutes," the lady says.

"Good," Chris says. Pam starts to say something. Chris looks at her. She stops.

"Any luggage?" the lady asks.

"No," Chris answers.

The ticket lady takes the money, gives him the change. He grabs it. "Gate five-A," she says, and Chris grabs Pam's hand and pulls her toward the gate. She looks at him as if she's dizzy, as if things are happening too fast. They arrive at the gate. Chris pushes the change into her hand along with the ticket. She stops. Please go, he thinks.

"Lady, the plane gonna leave. You best go quick," the man at the gate says.

Chris watches her back as she walks to the plane, holds his breath, counts, one–one thousand, two–one thousand, three–one thousand, nervously. She stops. No, Chris thinks. Then she walks up the steps. One step at a time. She enters. The door shuts. Chris breathes. He stares until the plane taxis away.

Shark just left the island, that's why I can't find him, he tells himself, walking back to the car. He's hopeful for Pam, feels as if he was finally able to do something, to help someone. Then he thinks of Robin. He drives back to the boat, watching the sunset. He can't wait to hold her, his hands tracing the curve of her back, feeling the warmth of her, synchronizing his breathing with hers. He can't wait to listen to the sound inside her stomach. He'll tell her about Pam. And she'll make it better. Just get home to her. Everything will be calm, he tells himself.

He arrives, walks down the dock, unlocks the door of the boat. Enters. He flicks on the light. "Robin."

No answer. Silence as he walks through the galley toward the stateroom. Maybe she's sleeping, he thinks, and he feels his eyes start to shut and he holds them open and they burn to close as he rubs them. He opens the door to the stateroom, enters quietly, hears a groan. Then another.

Wide awake, slapped hard in the face, he rushes toward the sound.

"Where are you?" he screams, trying to turn on the light, knocking over the bird-of-paradise plant, tripping, crawling on all fours to the noise. Another groan. He stands, opens the the bathroom door. His insides jump.

Robin sits on the floor next to the head, pale, her body tied in a tight knot.

"I have to go to the hospital." She winces against pain that seems to be shooting through her body.

He picks her up, grabbing the sheet off the bed, wrapping her. He thinks of mummies, reverse Pietà as he carries her to the car, floating in a stream of panic. And he sees her hold in the moan, in suspended animation, swallowing the pain to try to soothe him as he tries to soothe her.

He lays her down on the back seat. Hysteria swells, the waves not breaking, swelling larger and larger till they grind on the reef. He fights the swell. Each moan another swell, threatening to pull him under. He turns the car keys. Nothing.

Oh God. Dead? Dead battery. Paralyzing pain panic. He hyperventilates. The smell of fear rises off him. The smell of the inside of old sneakers. Deep breaths. Easy now. Easy does it. The car starts as he thinks his heart will stop.

"You must have slept on a pea, princess," he tries to say calmly. Silence.

He looks at her in the rearview mirror. The sheet sticks to her, blotting her up, blotting her out, transparent, like gauze. He imagines wringing it out like a sponge as he wipes the sweat from his forehead, collecting the juice like sap from a maple tree and injecting it back into her, as he tries to concentrate on the road, the night black as Ash Wednesday ash is placed on his forehead, from dust to dust, to protect him, like the blessed palms on Palm Sunday. He prays even though he doesn't believe. He prays because there's nothing else to do.

"Hail Mary, full of grace, the Lord is with thee, blessed art thou among women, and blessed is the fruit," he mumbles, searching for some calm, as everything goes in slow motion. Sticky with sweat, he feels stuck to the road. He reaches Queen's Highway. It's barricaded. He swerves, goes around it, bush scratching the side of the car. He wonders what the barricade is for or if there was a barricade. Seeing things, his heart thumps. Beats in his eyes, in his ears, his chest. And then he remembers the carnival. It's carnival night. He was going to take Robin to see it. He thinks about turning around but it will take too long to go another way.

His heart pounding, driving, louder and louder. A muted moan escapes from the back seat, from between grinding teeth, sending shivers, chills through his body as he grips the wheel tightly, trying to keep it steady. The more he tries to keep them steady, the more they shake.

More beating. Drums. He hears drums. His headlights light it up like spotlights. He slams his foot on the brake, his hand on the horn. The crowd surrounds his car: Indians, devils, clowns, skeletons, sailors, bats, jab-jabs, witch doctors. Drums pound. Whistles blow. Horns honk. Pans tink. They dance around the car, two steps forward, one step backward, beating on rum bottles, paint containers, car parts, dust bins, biscuit tins. Burning torches in people's hands. The car shakes with the beat. Bodies move to the rhythm as if screwing the air, and then each other, in the front, and then back-backing, one leg in the air like dogs peeing, jerking, never missing a beat, jucking in and out, around and around. He's caught in a whirlwind, a waterspout going around and around, sucking him in like water going down the toilet. They are sucked into the devil's triangle. He rolls down the window. The smell of sweating bodies, strong pot, stale rum.

"Help," he yells.

A man dressed as Jab Molassi, molasses devil, skin smeared with black molasses, slavery chains on his arms, sticks a bottle of rum in his hands saying, "Relax yourself, have a rum, white."

"Help," he yells again. Muffled by the chorus of the calypso.

> Mas in you mas
> Fire in you ass
> Carnival is bacchanal
> Life too short, so make it sweet
> Screw till you fall off you feet,
> Sing back to back
> Belly to belly
> Don't give a damn, cause you done dead already
> Carnival too sweet you know
> Don't stop the carnival

The carnival. The crowd, rum-coke-frenzied faces. Red eyes blinded. Hearing only the beat. They stare into the car, smiling, laughing, making faces. He's in a fish tank. A cage at the zoo. Animals circle. A crawfish. Claws bounce against the car to the beat. A skeleton with a sign around his neck, BASE OUT, crawls onto the hood of the car. A woman dressed as a pirate pretends to stab his tire with her dagger. Moses bangs the Ten Commandments against the hood of the car. He's caught in a trap. Three blind mice, no tails. A man appears in the back window, all rippled, hard muscles, black naked body, white war paint, tiny G-string forms a grotesque mask of a devil's face, his dick hanging in the long purple tongue, Afro pubic hair tumbling out of the top. Chris stares at him stare at Robin and smile. His breath fogs up the glass. The sheet has fallen off her. The man climbs up on the back of the car, grinds his midsection against the glass, his tongue-dick growing, slapping against the rear window to the beat of the drum, leaving a mark like a squashed horsefly. The more Chris yells, the more they laugh.

He opens the door, steps out, fights so he's not swept away by the crowd. He grabs a person that is dressed as a bird-of-paradise, an overgrown fire orange piñata, by his fiery leaves. "Mas, mas, you know me by me nose hole?" the man yells.

"The girl is sick. I have to get her through the crowd to the hospital. Help. Please."

The man understands, dances to the head drummer. Chris watches the drummer's black muscles surrounded by black veins like electric cord. Sweating, pounding away on the drum, changing the rhythm. Faster and faster, till his hands are a blur. The crowd moves with the beat. It controls them, like possession. Faster and faster. The bird-of-paradise runs in front of the car, an escort. Finally he's in the hospital parking lot.

The bird-of-paradise and an egg-shaped man dressed as Humpty-Dumpty after the great fall help him carry her into the hospital. They meet nurse He-she dressed as Carmen Miranda with a fruit-cocktail head and a nurse's cap on top.

"She sick. Critical," Chris yells.

"Only Doctor Baboo be here," He-she says. "The rest be at the carnival. He in delivery. Les go!"

They rush Robin into delivery. Doctor Baboo moves from between a woman's legs to Robin.

Chris leaves, collapses in a chair in the lobby. Thinks, Please don't, don't die, as he watches the expectant father pace around and around and around the waiting room.

18

R o b i n sleeps as Chris rubs aloe jelly into the cracked skin of her hand. A cockroach crawls from under her bed. Chris stamps on it, crunch-splat, as he looks at the intravenous feeding into her. He sees sea roaches creeping from the rocky shadows and then lowering their asses into the water. Their asses enlarge as they drink through them. And he thinks he should buy a Roach Motel, where they check in but don't check out, like the hospital. Millions of muted noises echo. He counts the endless stream of hours, days, weeks that he has sat next to her bed waiting and he realizes it has only been about a month.

The woman in the next room cries over and over, "Thanks for coming, son." Like a chorus of a song, Chris mouths the words with her.

He closes his eyes, tries to fall asleep. He sees eyes inside his head. Dead eyes like a bag of marbles. He pictures them, agates and crystals and steel ball bearings.

"Whoever lose have to do it," Shark said. Chris eyeballed the two marbles left in the ring, concentrating on Shark's marble, a clear sphere from out of the stem of a pop bottle. Chris's fingers flicked, and then the clack of glass against glass as his marble stuck. Shark's marble flew.

And then later that afternoon, Sister Immaculata walked, her habit an animated white tent. Shark sprung from behind the tree, his bare feet trampling the dirt, black hand yanking Sister Immaculata's white veil. She shrieked, then fell to the floor. She tried to cover her naked head with her hands. Chris stared transfixed at the round sphere covered in black five o'clock shadow.

He opens his eyes, stares at Robin's head. It floats like a buoy anchored to the ocean bottom. She opens her eyes. His heart beats fast as he watches her heart skip on the monitor. He takes a deep breath, holds her head in his hands, cradles it, trying to take some of the pressure off her neck. She tries to smile. It hurts him. He tries to tell her she doesn't have to try to smile. But he can't, so he touches her lips. And he brings his face close to hers, feels caught in a sweeping current.

"How do you feel, baby?" He strokes her hair.

"Better than you look," she answers softly.

"Thanks." He forces a thin smile.

"Why don't you go?"

"I want—I need to stay with you."

"You're making it really hard to have an affair with the doctor."

"You're making it really easy for me to have an affair with He-she."

She yawns, shuts her eyes. He kisses her eyelids, grabs her hand, strokes it, saying, "Sano Colito, Sano Colito, Sano Colito." The woman in the next room starts to chant again, "Thanks for coming, son!" over and over and over. Chris puts his fingers in his ears, but he still hears her.

He gets up to stop the sound. He walks, glances into her dark room. Her creased black face, crumpled carbon paper. "Thanks for coming, son. Thanks for coming, son." Louder and louder as he walks toward her. Her cobweb-colored Afro crushed into her pillow. She starts to whisper. Chris can't hear her. He turns around to leave. She starts again, urgently, "Thanks for coming, son." He walks to her bed cautiously. She's wearing a black nightgown with small black embroidered roses on it. He sits on the bed next to her, clasps her bony hand. He brings his ear to her mouth, hears the dreamy sound in his ear say, "I'm sorry." And Chris feels something way down inside groan silently. He kisses her wrinkled lips. She smells of a handkerchief perfumed with Limacol. She shuts her eyes. His voice shakes as he says, "I'm sorry too, Mom." He lets go of her hand, leaves.

Chris goes back to Robin's room, sits on the floor, grabs her hand, feels her hand in his hand move. He opens his eyes. Her eyes open up.

"How are you, baby?" he asks, standing up, sitting next to her on the bed.

"Good," she answers as she squints at him as if she's trying to figure out who he is. She squeezes his hand, looks away, chokes as she says, "Don't think I'm dying because I want to." She takes off the ring with the five diamonds, puts it in his hand. "I love you very much," she says.

"I'll wear it till you get better."

She closes her eyes. He slips the ring onto his pinky, collapses on the floor next to her bed. And a tidal wave of emptiness rushes, the hollow nothing filling from stomach to neck, and there's nothing he can do because he's nothing. And he hears her say, "I'm dying," over and over, and it's the first time she has ever said it.

Chris gets up, looks into the mirror on the hospital wall, looks into his eyes. He sees his eyes and more eyes circling around and around, doctors and nurses eyes playing ring-a-rosy. He sees the bowl labeled EYEBALLS as he pictures the haunted house in first grade. Dark, black, big eighth-grade ghouls dressed in white, hissing and booing, and the table. Dracula holds his hands down into the bowl labeled EYEBALLS. He feels them wet and juicy, feels his own eyes cry wet as Dracula laughs, as he picks up one of the grape eyes and forces it into his mouth as he fights and screams. He looks away, goes back to his spot on the floor, next to her bed. He hugs himself into a ball, puts his head between his knees, his arms around his legs. His head pounds. He thinks he should take a migraine pill, but he wants the pain, so it can cover and dissolve the other pain, and he thinks, How come you get to die, Robin? And Robin saying that she's dying makes him believe it. He opens his eyes to stop the thought. And he looks at his wrists and he pictures cutting them, like slicing cheese. He picks up a pen and writing pad from the table next to her bed. He tries to think of something to write. He can't, hasn't been able to write a sentence since he put her in the hospital. He rubs the pen across his wrist and imagines it's a knife. He clicks the metal end of the pen and the point pops out as he pictures all the needles she stuck into her body, and it was all a waste, and he starts to laugh and he can't stop as he draws, following the veins of his arms, tracing them in black ink from inside his elbow all the way to his wrists, and with each vein he pushes the pen down harder. Then the palm of his hand. He connects his wrist to his palm lines, marking them in black. He stops when he sees the M on his palm and he hears his mother telling him that the M on his hand stands for *mother*, and when he looks at it, he should always think of her. And he remembers his mother bringing him a crystal bowl full of plump grapes and she had removed the seeds and peeled each one. She fed them to him. One at a time. Soft and wet, juicy. Like coke. Oh God. He tries to push it out of his head, but it flies right back in and sticks, buzzing around like a bug to a bug light. The craving won't die until his brain gets zapped.

He leaves, walking fast until he reaches the hospital door. Then the hot air. He runs into it, racing the thoughts in his head. You're all alone. Because you're not good enough. You can't. He runs faster and faster, away from the hospital, away from Robin, letting it all go, not daring to think of the consequences. He follows his body as it follows the coke craving. On autopilot, his body runs by itself. Sweat drips down his face. He tastes it, feels it, his chest tight. Dead end. He stops at the Stop sign, pounds into it. His fists. The sound of muffled metal as he sees his father and the punching bag. "Fight like a man. Harder. Harder. Till it hurts!" his father yells. The pain burns his red knuckles. He gives up. Fuck you, Dad, he thinks, running, seeing his father's red dick being pumped by Fanny's hand. He arrives at Mango Estates, at the row of base houses. He stops, breathes it in deep gulps, slum smell, like buckets of scalding piss. He walks with purpose. Body in street-smart posture, the no-body-fucks-with-me look planted firmly on the face. A pack of emaciated dogs bark at him. One jabs its nose into his crotch. He punches it hard on its flat head. It sounds hollow, like when you thump a watermelon. The mongrel whines pathetically. The other dogs follow hungrily, keeping their distance now, their tails wagging, disturbing clouds of flies. He slaps at them, at the air, blanking them out. The coke pulls. He imagines diving into the clean white. A used rubber sticks to the bottom of his shoe. He walks to the house with the sign painted on the wall in flat paint:

IF YOU WANT THE BEST
COME IN FOR A TEST
ASK PAPA BASE
FOR A TASTE

The color of dry blood. Chris pushes the door of the base house open. A crack, it creaks, he walks in, into a wall of hot, smelly dark, tries to focus. Someone, something, grabs him, shoving him. His body thumps against the wall.

"Spread them," the voice orders.

Chris goes rigid, feels the hands on his body, touching, along his arms, his chest, his back, his thighs, his ankles, and then jutting up quickly between his legs. Then the hands are gone. He turns around. He feels so dirty, like when he was fourteen and he was so stoned and he came to Mango Estates with Shark and they fucked a whore and he didn't want to touch, only come, as she looked at his semisoft dick with contempt as she said, "Hurry up hard, I ain't gots all day." And he tries to forget this scene even as it unfolds, folding it up into smaller and smaller pieces, until it's small enough to swallow deep into the unconscious, even before it happens.

Chris's eyes adjust to the dark. Beams of light flow through the cracks of the boarded-up windows. Pipes and bongs light up, glow white, then red, lighting up, lit, beady red eyes, dead—like those he just left behind in the hospital. The dragging on pipes tangles with the shrill laughter of the cocaine high, tangles with the chemical smell of the ether, gas, ammonia, tangles with the smell of garbage, shit, vomit and piss. He walks toward the pipes, toward the knots of basers, tied down, sprawled on the floor, in knots, tied to their pipes. Glass crunches. He steps on something spongy, smells decaying rat. He hears something, feels something between his legs. Again. He looks down. A woman grabs his groin firmly, "Crack for some crack, whitey?" she asks, spreading her legs, holding her feet up toward the ceiling, her tight white skirt ripping as her whole hand slips into her hole.

"I do white boys good," she hisses, flicking her tongue out like a snake. She licks air.

Chris looks away, down at her protruding ribs, at the scabs on her knobby knees, one dribbling a trickle of blood. Just get it and get out, he thinks. A part of him wants to turn and run. Another stronger part makes him stay till he scores the high.

"Let me put hot chocolate on you vanilla bean. I's queen of fuck. White, baby, for some black," the woman begs. The voice cuts. He recognizes it, looks closer. It's Cleo. He recoils. Dick way up in his body. He remembers fucking her as Shark fucked Pam. He pictures Cleo's breasts glistening and slipping from side to side, flowing up round and down into teardrops. She holds on. A tug of war. The crowd laughs, high pitched and high.

"O.K., baby, seventy-five cents for suck, fifty cents for fuck, Coooome. Come baby."

Chris can't get away. He pulls, skids, catches his step. Cleo catches his leg. He's dragging her across the floor. Just get it and get out, he thinks.

Then a man like a pile of yellow bones gets up off a soiled mattress in the corner. He walks slow, pulling on a pipe. His piss-colored face spotted with flat red zits. His head pulled off balance by a pile of thick dreadlocks. Chris looks away from his bulging eyes, like lychees, looks at Cleo, who has now crawled up his legs, her face pressing into his groin. He feels her hot breath between his legs. She looks back at him and says, "Don't I know you?"

Papa Base grabs her by the hair, shoves hard. Her head snaps against the concrete floor. Her hand opens, quarters fly out, scatter across the floor, tinkling like money in the church collection plate.

"I's Papa Base, the dude with the irie taste," the yellow man says, his voice mucous.

Chris looks at Papa Base, at his T-shirt. Reads it:

STICK YOUR NECK OUT FOR YOUR KIDS.
STOP DRUGS.
TIRED OF THE JONES.
USE THE PHONES.
373-2309—A DRUG HOT LINE.

Papa Base opens his hand, beautiful rocks on his palm like little hearts. Chris feels them in his heart, white, like hearts of palm. He can't move.

"One heart, one love, one Jah. Twenty-five dollar for one stone, bald head."

Chris tastes the high. Doesn't answer. Can't.

"O.K., ten dollar. What the raas you waiting for? Freebase ain't for free," Papa Base says. "Yaah, you head crack up. You spooked. Fire for Babylon."

Chris reaches into his pocket. Empty. Fuck. The man who patted him down must have stole it. Or Cleo? He has to have the crack. He pulls his pockets out, looks at them. Desperate. He takes off the ring with the five diamonds.

Papa Base smiles. Chris hears, "Mama." A black boy in a pair of dirty underpants, big brown eyes. The boy drops down on the floor, cradles Cleo's head.

"Mama," he screams. Chris thinks, God, it's Roscoe, and he re-members making drip castles with him and Gwen and Robin. He reaches out to him, to hold him, to save him.

"So you like boy, bump head. Mon, he too young. He ain't ripe yet. You'd split he," Papa Base says. Roscoe bites Chris's hand hard. Chris screams, pulls his hand away as he hears a familiar scream in back of him.

He recognizes the voice, freezes. Shark. It registers. He rushes into the back of the room, tripping over people.

"Fuck mon," people mumble. "Dat dude head crack too bad. Spooky dupey pink shit."

Chris hears Shark's voice again, yelling from behind the door. He shoves it. It's stuck.

"Shark," he screams.

"Fuck you," Shark yells.

"It's me. Chris. Let me in," he cries, banging on the door, his fists pounding, not feeling.

He walks back, runs, his shoulder hits hard against the door. Pain pulsates. It gives way, flies open. He flies forward, fights to stop his body from falling forward, he trips, feels his body hit the floor. He looks up. The gun points at his head. Shark lies on his back. Chris exhales.

"Shark," Chris cries, feeling the happiness flow. He crawls toward him on the floor. "I thought you were dead."

Shark sits frozen. Chris waits for him to put down the gun, waits for the recognition to click on his face. Shark's face creases up in confusion. His eyes blank, sunken deep into his head.

"Fuck dose fucking spics. Dey won't fuck me. Dis my fucking island," Shark rants, waving the gun back and forth in the air. Chris's eyes move with the gun. Every time it points in his direction, he flinches, resisting the impulse to cover his face with his hands, as if that could stop the bullet.

"It's me. Chris," he says, trying to keep the alarm out of his voice as he sees the spoon, the burner, the needle on the floor next to Shark. "Chris," he says, soothing, over and over and over.

"Dems all over," Shark says, grabbing a belt from the floor, wrapping it around his arm, putting the end in his mouth, pulling, picking up the needle, stretching out his arm. Chris wants to grab it. The tip of the needle shines as it touches the vein standing up on Shark's black skin. Chris looks away, sees a flash of Robin injecting herself. Then looks back at Shark as he pulls the needle out. And something snaps, Shark exhales, relaxes, and it's as if the drug brings him back.

"Chris, don't ever do none of dis," he says, putting the needle on the floor. "Never do no smack."

"No," Chris says, staring at Shark's ripped T-shirt, at his white pants, a big yellow stain at the crotch. Shark's seems to have shrunk.

"It's over, Chris. I'm over. Mon, the onliest way to shed nigger skin is to die."

"It's not," Chris says.

Shark smiles at him bitterly. He shakes his head. "You's white and you got money." Shark opens his mouth and sticks the barrel of the gun into it.

"No!" Chris screams, his body tense, ready to pounce, focusing on the gun. His mind rushes, trying to think of things to say, to make it better, to make him stop, but his mind is a blank. He takes deep breaths.

Shark pulls the gun out and laughs and laughs and laughs. And the laughing scares Chris because it doesn't sound like Shark. Chris forces a smile on his face. "You're scaring me," he says, trembling.

"The fun just begun, Chrisy." His eyes get wilder.

"Let's go, Shark," Chris tries to say calmly. He moves closer to him, inching his way slowly.

"Where? Spics everywhere. Dey's under me skin," Shark says, putting down the gun and scratching hard, all over his arms and legs, his chest and between his legs. Chris focuses on the gun, to make a grab for it. It's so close. He edges up, concentrating on it, working his way forward, bringing his hand forward. There're only inches between his finger and the gun. Shark snatches it, laughs again.

"Not slick enough, slick," he says, pointing the gun at Chris.

"I can help," Chris begs, trying to ignore the gun, to look into Shark's eyes.

Shark looks away, pauses, the gun drops down. Then he looks into him. "You and me's different, no matter how we's try to pretend," he says desperately. "I won't be your nigger friend. I don't want to be anyone's nigger. The spics took it all. What can I do? Go back to moving tourist bags by day and fucking dem white pussy by night? Beg with big black eyes and big black dick for a big green Yankee tip?"

"We'll go see snow. It's you and me, Shark. When you come down, you'll see. And you'll stop talking all this shit and we'll go and see snow, and . . ." He loses control, ignores the gun, crawls across the floor, flings his arms around Shark, hugging him hard. Something cracks inside and he feels his whole body convulse.

Shark hugs him hard and he's crying, and the gun is still in Shark's hand touching his shoulder, and he keeps hugging him and Shark's lips touch his cheek and then his lips are on his, tongue in his mouth. It feels good. Chris pushes away. All out of control.

"I ain't going nowheres but out," Shark says, crazy, slurring, pointing the gun at Chris. "I's gonna beat the spics to it." Shark holds the gun to his head.

"Quit fucking around," Chris yells as he stares at the gun and pictures Shark's dick dripping white.

Chris hears the click of the gun. Shark shuts his eyes, pulls the trigger. Chris anticipates the blast. Nothing. Dead silence.

"Don't! What would I do without you? Evalina?" Chris feels the panic grow.

"Mon, cork dat shit. She like you better dan me anyway. White is right. Black is slack." Shark cries, the tears on his black skin shine.

Shark holds the gun to his temple. His hand shakes. The bullet blasts. The thrust causes Shark to miss, the bullet hitting the ceiling. Fine white powder floats down.

Chris smells gunpowder. He can't hear. He sees the determined look on Shark's face as he holds the gun back up to his head. He charges forward, yelling, "No!" and then his hand is on the gun, and then another explosion rips and the noise and flash cuts and he doesn't know what has happened. He feels the warm, wet splatter drip. And he sees spots, his head screaming with the blast, echoing. He pulls himself off. Shark lies on the floor, his eyeballs swimming in their sockets. Red drips out from the side of his head, trickling down his neck, staining his "It's Better in the Bahamas" T-shirt.

19

Chris slides down onto the floor next to Robin's bed. He shuts his eyes, sees Shark's eyeballs jerking around. He tries to stop the memory of yesterday, to pluck it out before it all floods back. A red tide. Once again he sees blood. Blinded, as fear pumped. He forced himself to look at Shark's head, covered in a veil of blood. Then, afraid to touch. But he had to, to stop the flow, to save Shark. He yanked off his white shirt. His hands shook, afraid there was no head, afraid there was no skull, that his shirt and hand would just sink into the brain cavity, afraid his brain would then overflow and he would have to stuff it back inside his skull. Chris's white shirt turned blood red. He wiped and squeezed and wiped. And then a gash on the side of Shark's head, from his eye to his ear, the size of his middle finger. Chris tied the shirt tight around his head, then pushed down hard, applying pressure.

Chris feels a touch. He flinches, opens his eyes.

"What's wrong?" Robin asks, running her hands through his hair.

She looks awake, so much better. He doesn't want to tell her, but he has no choice.

"Shark shot himself," he says, trying to sound calm.

"What?" She sits up, her face strained.

"Coke," he says in a choked voice.

"Is he all right?" she asks, alarmed.

"I don't know. He was stoned out of his mind. He thought Colombians were after him. I don't know. He wanted to die. He's down the hall. I tried to stop him."

"You were with him?" she gasps, clutching the sheet.

"I didn't," he says quickly, shaking his head. She looks at him. He looks back. She can tell he's not lying.

"I was going to; I was crazy." She looks so sad. He stops.

"Talk," she urges, a brave look on her face.

"I don't want . . ." He struggles, not wanting to say anything that would hurt her.

"Treat me like I'm well," she says.

Chris looks away from her, at the No Pest strip hanging from the ceiling, freckled with dead flies. "I couldn't take this hospital," he says slowly, calmly. "You sick. Sleeping all the time. I felt alone. I couldn't stand it. I just started to run. I ran to a base house. It was like I was being sucked and I had no power and I was about to buy some crack and then I heard Shark. He was crazy. I kept trying to stop him. Then the bullet so loud. And blood . . ." His voice cracks.

"Don't," she says, holding his hand.

Chris's head falls forward against the side of the bed and he takes a deep breath and inhales the sterile hospital odor rising off the sheets. Then the shudder deep inside. He doesn't feel alone anymore. He lies next to her on the hospital bed and hugs her, feels her healing warmth.

"I won't. Not after what happened to Shark." He wipes his face on the sheets. He buries his head.

"Let's go and see him. The doctor told me I should walk more," Robin says, sitting up, her lips pulled tight.

"Sure?" Chris asks, helping her up. She stands, shuts her eyes. "What's wrong?"

"I feel a little dizzy."

"Maybe we shouldn't."

She flashes him a determined look.

They walk down the hall slowly, trailing the intravenous like plastic entrails. She pulls as he pushes the portable device the intravenous hangs on. The wheels of the device squeak.

"Somebody tell this bag that two's company and three's a crowd," Robin says, breathing deeply.

"We'll get rid of it soon," Chris replies, thinking that the bag is always there, a chaperone. He imagines it growing bigger and bigger and being slipped over her head, over her body. A body bag.

They pass the old lady's room. She sleeps.

"She never cries for her son anymore."

"Maybe he came to visit her," Chris says, hearing Shark's voice, a low moan coming from his room by the nurses' station. They walk slowly together. Shark's voice gets louder as they get closer. He screams. Chris cringes. Robin stops.

"I better go back," she says.

"I'll walk with you."

"No."

She walks back to her room. Enters. He runs down the hall and peeks.

"I see you," she says. "Go, help Shark."

Chris runs back down the hall, stops in front of Shark's room, takes a deep breath, stands, feels exhausted, adrift in uselessness. And he's back at the base house and Shark has just shot himself, and then so many empty faces, red pickled eyes, watching. "Ambulance!" he heard himself scream.

"Mon, we got no phone and no ambulance coming round here anyways. Let he die in peace," Papa Lick said. "Pig get fat but hog get slaughter." And then high laughs from the crowd. As if they were laughing at him. Adrenaline pumped. He picked Shark up in his arms, ran toward the shafts of light. Someone held the door open. He was slapped by so much bright. Chris ran as fast as he could, his sweat mixing with Shark's blood, dripping all over, down his arms, his legs. His sneakers slapped the asphalt, leaving slippery blood prints.

Chris stands by the door, listens to Shark scream, "Fuck you. Kill me. Fuck." Then there's a momentary lull.

He forces himself to walk into the room, to look at Shark. He sees the black body against the white hospital sheets, Shark's head bandaged in white, swollen. His features distort, strain as if his face is a lump of black clay being pushed and pulled out of shape. Drops of sweat drip.

"Help me," he begs, rolling and bucking on the bed, fighting against the white cloth restraints that tie his arms and legs to the metal bed railings. The bed rattles. Shark tries to punch and kick.

"I'm gonna get help," Chris says. He runs to the nurses' station, grabs He-she by the arm, pulling him. "Shark. He needs something. To kill the pain." He-she follows Chris.

"Please," Shark shrieks.

"Please," Chris begs.

"Mon, I can't give him no ting. Pain killer will cause he brain to swell. Could kill he. The doc say dat the brain does be like egg yolk. When the bullet graze he head it cause he brain to ricochet, bounce off the next side he skull. The pain's from the next side he brain swelling up. From the pressure as the brain push to get out."

"There must be something," Chris says.

"I's sorry," He-she says, touching him on the cheek, leaving the room.

Chris walks to the foot of the bed. "The pain will end soon. It's Chris. You're in the hospital," Chris says with as settling a tone as possible. Shark looks at him with glazed eyes. Chris hears Shark telling him, "Drugs easy money, capital E, capital Z, money. I owes it all to you."

Shark lies still. Chris stands next to him. "You're gonna be fine. You're in the hospital. The pain will end."

Shark's body relaxes. Chris loosens the restraints on his feet and arms. "Just relax, relax," Chris says, pulling a handkerchief from his pocket. He drips some Limacol on it, touches Shark's forehead.

"That's good," he says. Shark lies still. Chris exhales, thinking, Thank God, touching Shark's lips with the cloth. His eyes open up wide. His head strains forward. He bites. Chris pulls away, holding in the scream. Shark spits. Chris wipes the gob from his face, sees blood on his hand. Shark yells, "Kill me!"

Chris can't stand it. He can't stand to see Shark like this. He shuts his eyes, sees yesterday, sees a flash of his body, his clothes, covered in red. He wanted the blood off, as if by getting rid of the blood he could erase what had just happened to Shark. He walked straight into the shower, turned on the water, stood shivering in the cold. Red water fell from him, running between his toes. He ran out of the shower. He was on the flying bridge, looking out over open ocean, at the rising sun, a red ball turning the air heavy and liquid red, bleeding red into the sheet of smoky water. He looked away, down at his white pants, now colored red. He pulled them off, pulled off his underwear, dropped them into the water, watched them float. A stain on the red-blue sea. He stared directly into the sun until he felt thin splinters of fire stinging behind and in front of his eyes, till all he saw was a red blur. He felt his body all sticky, as if it was still covered in blood and the blood had turned to tar, and he pictured himself and Shark as barefoot boys, feet melting into the road like toasting marshmallows. He rubbed his body to get the feeling off and pictured Robin and himself staring at wrapped Mangrove Cay. He pictured Robin and Shark dead. He jumped.

Shark screams, "Fuck." Chris opens his eyes. Evalina stands staring at him, at them, quietly. She looks small, her back bent. Chris walks toward her. She looks away. Her eyes are far away. Deep circles underneath. She mops the back of her neck with a handkerchief, breathes heavily. Chris puts his arms around her, hugging her. She shakes. "I's been here all night."

Her head rests on his heart. "He'll be fine," Chris says, trying to sound positive.

Shark screams. No words. Animal sounds. Chris grits his teeth, fights the urge to put his fingers in his ear. Evalina hugs him hard, shuts her eyes. He clenches his hands into fists.

"Why?" she asks, dazed.

Chris feels trapped in a slavery movie. The massa sells the slave's son. He's ripped from his mother's hands. She grabs the massa, begs for her child. His mind races, trying to think of things to say, to do. Chris holds Evalina up. All his life he has depended on her and he thinks back to when he was small, burying his face into her white apron, hiding because he was afraid, in the shack in the bush. She said, "Chris-baby, don't be afraid. You in God house." And he turned around and opened his eyes, looked at the crosses drawn in chalk on the floor, at the people in front of the altar, their eyes and heads wrapped in white cloth. Each held a burning candle, the only light in the Shouter church. They swung together, left to right, moving to the tempo, singing,

> Jesus lover of my soul
> Let me to thy bosom fly.

Tantie started to clap so loud he felt the wind from her clap fanning his head. Beads of sweat flicked onto him. They ripped off the white cloth, and everyone started to roar, "Catch the spirit!" They fell onto their knees, dancing, moving backward and forward, rolling their bodies, dancing the candles in their hands. Hot wax dripped and dried white on black skin. And everyone was swinging with the music as if it was magic they couldn't resist, and it got faster, louder, hotter. People clapped as their feet slapped against the floor, marking the rhythm. And Chris couldn't help but sing also, as loud as he could. As if being touched by some invisible force. Muscles on people's faces froze. Eyes stared at nothing. Shoulders twitched. Knees shook. Bodies jerked out of control. Chris felt as if something was touching him, and he wanted the touch, and he let it flow and an electric shiver pierced him. He went stiff. The shaking took over. He felt so happy.

Then it was as if he was waking up from a dream. He felt Evalina's arms around him as she said, "Praise the Lord, my baby catch the spirit. Pray with me, boy."

Chris hugs Evalina harder, as if this can stop the shaking. Shark moans. "Evalina, pray with me," he whispers.

She pulls away, shakes her head. No. This hits hard.

"If dere a God, would he do dis to my baby?" Tantie asks, desperate, as if she doesn't have the strength to speak.

Chris feels the words come out of his mouth, "But Evalina, there has to be a God. You told me," not believing he said what he said.

Evalina sighs, looks away from him at Shark. He follows her eyes to Shark. His body thrashes against the bed. The railings bend. The white sheet falls below his waist. His dick, his balls. He stops moving. A dribble of piss pooling on his balls. Evalina walks up to him, swabs the pee up with her handkerchief, gently lifts up his dick, wipes it, covers him up.

Then the power flows as if Evalina has been plugged back in. She walks up to Chris, hugs him so tight he can hardly breathe. Other straw market vendors enter the room. Chris takes a deep breath, smells palm thatch. They walk up to Evalina, one by one, and hug her and with each hug Evalina seems to get a little straighter and bigger. Then, last in line, being pushed in a wheelchair, an old man, white Afro like spun sugar, his skin like chamois leather. Chris stares at his one grey eye and his other brown eye, smiling. Chris can't believe his eyes. He's looking at his childhood.

"It's great to see you, Captain Doctor Conch," Chris says, shaking his hand.

"You must be tink I's dead? Aye boy? I does still be strong enough to crack a conch or two."

Chris smiles. "I heard you were living in Bimini."

"I move back to Grand Bahama bout a month ago. When I hears bout Shark, I must come." Doctor Conch takes a bottle out from under the shawl that is covering him.

"It be fill up with conch tonic. Give it to Shark when he a little better and he be fix up."

Chris takes the bottle and pictures Doctor Conch cracking conchs and then hanging them by the horns and catching the drippings in a pan. And then he would mix the drippings with eggs, aloe juice and rum and beat it all up, and grate a little coconut to float on top. He and Shark would beg for a sip of conch tonic. Doctor Conch would let them have only one sip, saying, "Too much of dis be make you boys false ripe and mannish. I feel younna gonna crack enough conch and gal as it is."

Chris pushes Dr. Conch's wheelchair. The congregation makes a space for them at the foot of the bed next to Evalina.

"Lead us not into temptation, but deliver us from evil. Father forgive me because I have sinned. Let us pray," Evalina says.

They form a circle around Shark, and bow their heads.

"I knows you hear cause I's believe. Praise the Lord. We beseech you," Evalina prays. "Save my boy so he can repent and turn he head back to the Lord. Protect he from the malice and snares of the devil."

Chris listens to the sounds of the prayers flowing around him, like fingers soothing his whole body, like wings beating, lifting him up. He feels his lips start to move and the words are coming from him and he's praying with them. And then they all join hands, Evalina on one side of him and Doctor Conch on the other. Chris feels something, something good and safe and joined. And he knows that something's there with them even though he can't see it. He feels it flow in and out of him, to and from the chain of joined hands.

Tantie prays, "Jesus say, when two or three does be gather in he Father name, he be dere with dem." Chris looks at Tantie and she is wearing his mother's old blue-and-white dress, only she has added a piece of bright purple to make it fit. He pictures his mother cutting the rose off the waist. He shuts his eyes. She loves me, he thinks.

Chris feels an arm on his shoulder. He turns around. It's Robin. A hush passes between them as she joins hands with him. Evalina holds the hand with the intravenous and says, "We also pray for dis sweetheart here dat my other boy does love. Take all the cancer out of she body. Halleluja."

"Halleluja," the group replies.

20

Chris sits beside Evalina on the cot she has brought into the hospital room. Shark sleeps. Chris pictures Shark floating under an endless sea of sleep. Every once in a while he seems to try to surface when a slur of sound flows from his mouth. Chris wonders if he will ever wake up, wonders, if-when he does, whether there will be anything left of him. Yet he's relieved the screaming has stopped.

Evalina's lips are moving. He knows she's praying. She rubs her eyes. She looks at him looking at her, grabs his hand and whispers, "Leave it in the hands of the Lord."

He squeezes her hand. "I'll be with Robin," he says.

He leaves, heads down the hall, walks into Robin's room. He stops, stops breathing, looks, feels the look on her face. It hits him, wakes him. She sits upright, Cover Girl mascara brush in hand. She touches the brush to her eyelashes, brings the pad to her face, winks. She does this again and again and again. He feels the intimacy, feels himself blush as he watches her brush, wink, brush, wink. Draw with her eyelashes. Her eyes are focused, absorbed. He is drawn to her. And he wants to let her know he's there, but he's afraid he'd break her concentration, afraid she would lose the look, and he would lose this moment. He waits. He could watch her forever. My God, she's beautiful, he thinks.

She stops, looks up at him. The look on her face gets deeper, more defined, as if outlined in black. She's gonna be all right. She stands up. Tiny black dots under and over her eyes. She hands him the pad.

He stares at the delicate black blink marks of her eyelashes on the white paper. And he thinks, My God, it's beautiful. He keeps staring until he falls into it, traveling to the place where she lives when she's healthy, a place of passion and magic. A place of art. He sees flocks of birds flying, schools of fish swimming, sea fans on a reef bending with the current, a field of wheat blowing with the wind, the waves, miles and miles of endless ocean. He stares, refusing to blink, his eyes starting to burn, the blink marks starting to blur and move, and he sees flames flicking, them fucking, fucking, fucking, the big bang, and he blinks and he sees a whisper.

"It's called *Butterfly Kisses*. Sixty-nine winks with the left eye and sixty-nine winks with the right," she whispers.

He puts the pad down, hugs her, licks above and below her eyes, licks up the mascara freckles.

"I'm so happy," she says, handing him the pad.

"I know. Cause you're working. It's the first time since you've been in the hospital."

"I'm getting out. The doctor told me. On Saturday." A great smile on her face. She opens her arms. Chris feels himself moving toward her and then they are hugging deeply on the bed. His lips touch her cheek and slide to her mouth, and then her taste in his mouth, her cool smell.

"As soon as the doctor told me, I got this great urge to create." She grabs his head, her hands on his cheeks. "I thought my art had a life of its own, but now I know how connected it is to me. When I stop the art, I'll be dead."

Chris feels her breath against his face, and it feels like energy flowing.

"I was using all my strength to fight the cancer. Physically I couldn't do it. Couldn't make art. I know I'm gonna be well cause the art came back."

Chris swallows to keep down the emotion. He kisses the skin between her fingers.

She hugs herself, shuts her eyes. "Oh Chris, I can't believe in a few days we'll be back on the boat. Alone. Together," she says happily.

"And when you get even stronger, we'll sail away. Go wherever you want. Hop from island to island," Chris says. He buries his head into the spot, feels excited, like when he was a child and his mother would come and take him out of school. He would be afraid that something was wrong until she said, "I think it's a hop island day." Then the fear would melt into excitement. They would drive together, just the two of them, as far east as they could go, until the Queen's Highway dead-ended into the ocean. And then she would let him pump the car horn until they saw Almond coming in his boat to pick them up from a sliver of island called Deep Water Cay that was surrounded by only shallow water, so shallow Almond couldn't use his engine. He would have to pole across the flats to get them with his special bamboo pole, which, he said, "be the bestest piece of bamboo ever to float cross the Atlantic from China where it grow." Then they would be on the boat and he would hold the middle of the pole and look up at Almond's almond-shaped eyes and almond-colored arms and hands above him as they pushed the pole into the mud. When they arrived at the cay his mother would give Almond a picnic basket. He would excuse himself to go and eat with his dead wife. Ever since she died, Almond lived on the island alone. He would sit in front of her grave and eat and talk and laugh.

He and his mother would walk hand in hand down the beach until it broke away into pancakes of sand. All exactly the same size, about two feet around. A line of white sand connect-the-dots stretched out over the turquoise sea. And they would hop from spot to spot. And then the line of dots would end at a small island that they called Double-Breasted Cay because it was shaped like two breasts. They would sit between the breasts, in the island's cleavage, under the one coconut tree. His mother would spread out the picnic and they would eat and talk and laugh.

"What are you thinking?" Robin asks, stroking his hair.

He pushes his head up. "I'm dreaming about island hopping," he answers, "about our boat trip. Just you and me, together, forever."

"I'm dreaming about your taste," Robin says, looking deeply into him.

"Shut your eyes," Chris says, breathing deeply.

She shuts them. He sits up, pulls a perfect mango Julie out of his pocket. He rips off a strip of the skin with his teeth.

"Open your mouth," he says. He holds the mango to her mouth. Her lips tremble.

"Bite."

She bites down. Juice drips. Orange on pink lips. She licks. He holds one hand over her eyes. He feels her eyelashes against his palm. "Feel the boat rocking gently. Feel the sun burning hot. See the islands in front of you, one after another." He rips the rest of the skin off. Juice flows. He bites yellow mango flesh.

He takes his hand away. She opens her eyes, takes another bite of mango.

She kisses him, pushing a sliver of mango into his mouth with her tongue. He swallows, shivers.

"I'm not dreaming," she says. "Soon we'll be on the boat."

"Tomorrow," he says, lying next to her on the bed, burying his head back into the spot. He feels like a man who's boarded a train as it was halfway out of the station: breathless, happy, relieved. He thinks of the one time his father went with him and his mother to Double-Breasted Cay. It was right after hurricane Betsy and the water between the sand dots was chalky, not the usual turquoise, and each dot was outlined by froth like whipped egg whites. He picked up handfuls of the froth and threw them up into the air. They would separate and turn into billions of floating, popping, hissing, twinkling bubbles.

The hospital room door opens. Chris turns over and sits up. Tantie Evalina pushes his father into the room.

His father looks nervous as he says, "Chris?"

Chris stares at him, shocked. He looks so old, fragile. His father's wheelchair turns into his mother's rocking chair. He pictures it, fat, hard and red. He feels the anger like a sharp knife cutting from inside out.

"You daddy call and tells me he wants to come to visit Shark. We just finish seeing him and I tells him you in here," Evalina says. His father smiles in such a way that it is hard to think of him as an old man and not a child. He stares, waiting.

"I got to go," Chris says, getting up off the bed. His father looks sad.

"No," Evalina says urgently.

They all look at her. "What?" Chris asks, sitting back down.

"For me," Evalina says.

"So what do you want?" Chris asks his father. His tone casual. His father's face drops.

Robin looks at him, begging with her eyes. The look reminds him of his mother. And he pictures the black woman pointing at him, his mother's face draining, turning white, as she pulled him away, as the woman said to her little son, so he could hear: "Dat you half brother, you and he gottie the same father and he give you he name and dis does make you good as inside, a true Angostura." And Chris remembers taking a shower with his father when he was a child, his eyes reaching the level of his father's groin, as his father's soapy hand cupped his own crotch. Chris looked, unable not to look, and it was all so big and hairy and he felt so small and bald. His father squeezed himself. Chris saw the one ball, like the balls of bread he would make by squashing up the white insides of the Wonder Bread that his mother made him eat because she said, "It have to be better dan island bread cause it come from America." It hung inside the sack like an egg in a small brown paper bag, and there was only one. His father said, "Boy, look dis, I's only got one ball, but I still can't keep from the gals, and dem can't keep from me. This one ball be hot enough to drive dem all crazy with heat. God help your two grow up to be like my one." Chris remembers reaching down and feeling himself, and they felt like two raisins.

Evalina looks from him to Robin and then to his father. A sorrowful look crosses Evalina's face as she walks up to him, grabs his hand, pulls. He doesn't know why but he just follows her out of the room to the hall. He's afraid to look back. He starts to pace in the hall.

"Love what good, Christopher," she says firmly. "Forgive the bad. He don't have much time left. You'll be sorry."

"There is no fucking good," Chris spits out at her, shaking his head, folding his arms.

She looks hurt, reaches into her pocket, takes out a folded piece of paper. She places it on his folded arms.

Chris grabs the paper, unfolds it. It's a check to Evalina for fifty thousand dollars. It's signed by his father.

"What?" Chris asks confused.

"He gave it to me," she says softly. "I only had to ask him once. I need it to save Shark's life, to pay off the Colombians, so dey won't kill he." She pauses. "Dere's good. Plenty."

Chris just stares at the check and then at Evalina and he doesn't know what to say and he tries to stay mad at his father but he can't, because of what he did for Shark.

"He told me not to tell you," she says, and she grabs him and hugs him and whispers, "Heal. We's got so much sickness and it all out our control, but the sickness between you and you daddy can be healed."

He walks back into the room. Robin looks at him, then shuts her eyes. His father looks at him.

He struggles, grabbing the side of the wheelchair. "How you keeping, boy? You need anything. Money?" And there's a tremble in his voice and Chris feels pity and he know his father's only way of showing love is with money. He looks at his father and the creases on his face soften and it's as if he's about to decompose.

Chris catches his breath, feels drained. He can't fight anymore. Chris looks at the brown age spots on his father's hands, like stains, like washed-off dye. Chris walks forward and he bends down and hugs his father stiffly. He feels his father trembling hug back, smells his father's Brylcreem smell, remembers looking down from the top of the hill on Double-Breasted Cay, seeing something floating, flashing slips of brown light at him from a patch of froth. He hopped on the dots until he got close and then he jumped off the farthest dot and swam out. He thought it was a bottle and when he reached the froth, he saw what looked like a giant brown eyeball floating. Then he realized that it was a glass ball float. He was so happy, because he had been looking for a glass ball his whole life. He grabbed onto the ball and it was so big he could just stretch his arms around it. He swam, floating on it, pushing it, until he reached Double-Breasted Cay, and then he rolled it up the beach until he got close to where his parents were. He picked it up and held it in front of his stomach. The glass ball felt cool and slick against his navel, and the ball was the same color as his skin, and he imagined the ball was part of him, his stomach, and he was pregnant. When his mother saw the ball she clapped and said, "I told you. I told you dat one day you'd find one. All you had to do was have faith." He gave her the ball. "You make me so happy," she said. And he hugged her from behind, his arms around her, her arms around the ball. Then he felt something behind him and it was his father and his arms stretched around him and his mother.

And he looks over at Robin and she grabs his hand. Kisses it. His father follows the look. He wipes his forehead, rubs his eyes, smiles weakly.

Evalina hands Chris two paper bags. "We gots to go now."

"I miss you," his father says. "Please come see me."

"I will," Chris says. "I miss you too, Dad." And he waves good-bye.

Chris opens one of the bags, looks inside. The smell of hot bread fills the room.

"I'm very proud of you," Robin says.

"Hot cross buns," he says, handing Robin a bun with a cross of creamy frosting on the top. "One Good Friday when I was little, Tantie baked a batch of hot cross buns and I licked off all the crosses when she left the room."

"That's what made you so holy," Robin says. Then he licks the cross off his bun.

Chris opens the other bag. "Hooray," he says. Robin smiles.

And they tap their fingers on the crispy crust of burnt sugar that sits on top of the creamy pudding. And they reach under the top with the end of the plastic spoons and pry it off. They hold the round circle of burnt sugar above their heads and say, "Take this all of you and eat it." And then count. "One. Two. Three."

"Hooray," they say together. And they are munching the burnt sugar. Chris watches Robin as she puts her fingers in her mouth, pink tongue tip tasting a bead of white.

21

R o b i n rolls over, stretches, squints against the sunlight, her black hair glinting. "Is it tomorrow yet?" she asks in a sleepy voice, yawning, rubbing her eyes.

"No baby, it's still today," Chris answers. He slides next to her on the bed. She sinks back onto her pillow. He plays with a wisp of her hair.

"I brought you another surprise," he says, handing her a paper bag.

She looks puzzled as she takes out two eggs and two empty pickle jars. "What?"

"You can tell your future on Ash Wednesday by putting egg whites in water."

Chris walks to the sink, turns on the tap. "I can't wait to go swimming," Robin says.

Chris fills the jars. "Tomorrow," he says, walking over to her.

"Did you see Shark while I was asleep?"

"Yes," he answers.

"Any change?"

"No, but yes. Somehow he looked better. Maybe it's just wishful thinking." He feels guilty that he's so happy that she's getting out when Shark is still so sick.

"Hold the egg in the palm of your hand."

"You think I can hatch it?"

"Don't make fun. As Tantie says, 'Folk custom got plenty brain.' Think about tomorrow." He wraps her hand around the egg.

Chris holds the other egg, sitting next to her on the bed. "How do you feel?" he asks.

"Like a chicken."

"Hold on to my hand and shut your eyes. Try not to cluck." She shuts her eyes and then he shuts his eyes and says, "Jesus, in this egg white I beg to see the future you have chosen for me."

Chris opens his eyes, cracks Robin's egg with one hand, pours it onto his cupped hand, letting the white slip through his fingers. An egg white stream flows into the water-filled jar. The yolk rests on his palm, a big yellow eye.

"Open your eyes," he says. He sucks the yolk into his mouth, holds it open for Robin to see.

She leans forward, her mouth open, her tongue out. She touches the yolk with her tongue. The yolk pops. Yellow drips out of the corner of his mouth. He swallows. She laughs.

He cracks the other egg, places the two jars on the windowsill in the sunlight.

"Now we have to wait for the sign to form," Chris says.

Chris hugs her, buries his head into her side, holding his breath.

He breathes, stays in his spot, listening to her breathe, and he's a child again watching the air fill up the red sail of his little sailboat. Her remembers how he and Shark would sail from island to island, fishing until they caught a grouper, and then they would go ashore and make boilfish and grits with the grouper's head. Shark would check to see if the soup was ready by touching the fish's eyes. When it was just right he would pluck the fish's eyes out, and Shark would eat one and give him the other one. The eye would sort of pop when he bit into it.

Chris pulls out from Robin's side. She looks over at the bottles. "What do the eggs say?" she asks.

Chris walks over to the window, grabs the two bottles.

"This is yours," he says, handing one of them to her. She looks into her bottle. "What do you see?" he asks.

She stares. "I see a boat sailing across the sea."

"Let me see?"

She hands him her jar. "A boat means a trip. Means you're going on a trip," he says, looking inside her bottle. He sees a coffin, a coffin in a rainstorm.

"What?" she asks, catching the look on his face.

"What?" he answers, forcing a smile, thinking it's just a lot of bullshit.

"What's in yours? What does yours say?"

He looks inside his jar. "I see a cathedral with lots of turrets. It means we're going to get married. On my boat. I'll marry us because the captain of a ship can marry people."

"Aye aye, captain. Come here and hug me." He lies on the bed next to her. Hugs her.

"I have a wave in a bottle," she whispers into his ear.

"What?"

"In New York I have this wave in a square plastic bottle. It's been packed in a trunk since the seventies. So I guess I have a wave in a bottle in a trunk. The wave is Tidy-bowl blue. You plug it in. It goes back and forth like a seesaw. That's how I felt in the hospital. Like that wave."

"Tomorrow we release it." He kisses her neck.

"Tomorrow," she repeats, touching the spot he kissed.

"I have a Virgin in a plastic bottle. My mother bought it for me in Lourdes. That's the place where the Virgin appeared and the place where they make quaaludes. The plastic bottle has a plastic Virgin standing up in a plastic grotto with a plastic cathedral behind her and above her head on a plastic halo it says, 'Je suis l'Immaculée Conception.' It was full of liquid and had fake white snow stuff in it. It snowed when you shook it. I dropped it and it cracked and all the liquid dripped out. Now it looks like the Virgin has chronic dandruff. Is snow really like what's in those plastic bottles? Like what's on Christmas cards?"

"Snow is softer and whiter and quieter than it could ever look like in pictures. Why have you never gone to see?"

"I'm afraid. That it won't be as good as how I imagine. Shark and

I would talk about snow for hours when we were children. We made a pact we would go and see it together."

"We'll go and see snow together," Robin says. "When Shark gets better, we'll all go. We have so much to do." She kisses him on the cheek.

"I have to go buy us an Easter egg coloring kit."

"Will you pick up my shots for tomorrow?"

"Sure."

"You're my knight in shining armor," she says, laughing.

"Sleep, baby, sleep," he says, kissing her eyes. "Tomorrow."

"Tomorrow," she sings.

Chris waits for her to shut her eyes. Then he gets off the bed carefully, in case she's asleep. He grabs Robin's cancer shot cooler, walks across the street to the cancer clinic. The sign on the door reads,

ONLY PATIENTS AND THEIR COMPANIONS ALLOWED ENTRANCE.
ALL OTHERS KEEP OUT.

He pushes the door open. People stare at him and then look away. He searches the faces. All new and full of hope. Did all the other patients die? he thinks. He shakes his head, cuts off the thought. He joins the line for shots, trying not to make eye contact so he won't have to talk. A short black man with a short Afro dressed in a white doctor's coat shuffles officiously down the hall toward him. Chris looks closer. "Tweed?" he asks.

The man stops, smiles. "But you is sight for sore eye. What you doing here?"

"Tweed, you playing carnival or what?" Chris asks, touching his hair where the eraser hairdo used to be.

Tweed sucks his teeth. "It's Doctor Tweed now," he says proudly.

A man gets in line behind them. "How do you feel today, Mister Burrows?" Tweed asks with an American accent.

"I'm in a lot of pain, doctor," the man answers, gritting his teeth.

"We'll fix that," Tweed reassures him. "Don't worry."

"Where did you get that freshwater Yankee accent?" Chris asks, smirking.

"Shush mon, come to my office," Tweed says to Chris.

Chris follows him. The sign on the door says, DR. TWEED LIGHT-BORN, A.A.N.D. Tweed sits behind his desk. Chris stares at the diploma, with a gold seal and Tweed's name printed in fancy writing, from the American Association of Nutrition and Dietary Consultants.

"So what's the scoop, Tweed? The diploma."

"I's head of security and assistant dietitian and I's taking correspondence course to be doctor of metaphysics. The cancer doctor gets me dat diploma fair and square. It cost he fifty bucks." He winks. "I's also in charge of delivering green to the politicians so dey don't shut us down."

"You don't deal anymore?"

"Coke the bread dat the devil knead, and all dat other shit," he says, laughing. "I's been to Operation Hope. I's squeaky clean." He picks up a pencil, chews.

"You don't rhyme anymore?"

"I don't need dat, now dat I straight. I learn to talk my feelings and say I love you and all dat other stuff."

"I miss your rhyme, Tweed."

He looks sad. "So what you doing here?" he asks.

"I came to get the shots for my girl."

"I'll get dem for you."

Chris follows Tweed through a room full of microscopes and computers. He opens a fridge. "What's her name?" Tweed asks.

"Robin Wilke."

"Here," he says, handing Chris a package.

"How's Shark?" Tweed asks.

"The same. Sleeping and mumbling."

"He'll come back badder than ever. Worse only get better."

"I got to go now, Tweed," Chris says, shaking his hand. Tweed gives him a straight businessman's handshake.

"What kind of shakes dat is, Tweed?" Chris asks, imitating his old rhyme. "You hip starting to drip? You turning square on me, man? You turning queer?"

He laughs. Before Chris shuts the door, he yells, "Keep cool, don't be fool."

Chris laughs, walks down the street, walks into the market. It smells fruity and green and fresh. Chris is walking among impossibly colorful piles of mangoes, oranges, pumpkins, corn, guavas, cassavas, dasheen, eddoes, soursops, peas, limes, lemons, sugar apples, star apples, pineapples, passion fruits. A teenage girl with melon-sized breasts yells and winks at him, "My juicy melons will make you juicy. Come and give them a squeeze." A black hand juts from behind a stack of sugarcane and slaps the girl's head. "Watch you yard-fowl mouth, gal. Quit cutting you tongue at the mens or I gonna cut you backside." The lady connected to the slapping hand stands up and her face is round and mad. She stares at Chris and asks, "What you staring at, like you never see human like yourself?"

Chris walks away laughing to the sound of laughter, to Pa Beah's Lookman Obeah booth. The booth is crammed full of candles shaped like black women and white men, black cats and white skulls. There are plastic bags full of dried things: roots, bats, seahorses, blowfish and small bottles of oils marked Jinx Removing, Bouquet 666, Desire Me. A bowl of artificial eyeballs marked EVIL EYES stare at a line of glass jars with sun-cooked egg whites floating in them.

"Oui papa, look trouble here," Pa says, smiling his one tooth. He pushes his frail body up off the stool.

"Don't stand up, Pa," Chris says.

His head is tied in black cloth. Around his neck is a necklace of little skulls and two green-white plastic, glow-in-the-dark rosaries.

"I's standing up to get one hug so I can suck you young sap." Chris hugs Pa Beah gently, like hugging twigs. His Golden Syrup-colored skin, stretched over bones, so tight it looks like it could snap.

"A farmer should never do he planting sitting down. He crops won't flourish," Pa says.

"You look like you're flourishing to me," Chris says. "You know what I'm here for?" Chris asks.

"He who ask question can't avoid answers. Common sense before book sense," Pa says, opening a drawer, taking out an Easter egg coloring kit. "Dis the last. I save it for you."

"Thanks," Chris says, paying Pa five dollars.

"Dere something else, aye boy. Come, boy."

Chris follows Pa to the back of his booth, behind a black curtain. He sits across from him at a round table covered with a black cloth. He places a white plate on the table and then a white candle on the plate. He lights it, holds Chris's hands below the table and stares at him through the winking candle flame. Chris looks at Pa's eyes, feels hot, then cold.

"It Shark. He swimming in puddle of blood. And a white gal trying to dance on break-up waves."

He takes two rosaries from around his neck, places them around the candle, holds Chris's hand over the candle flame. Chris feels the heat, then the burn, but it feels very far away. He smells burning as Pa Beah chants,

> Illness, badness, go away
> Burnup in a higher wellness ray
> Bring them relief from they pain
> Make them whole again.

Pa pushes Chris's hand down onto the flame and it smothers out. Smoke rises. He rests two rosaries on Chris's palm and shuts his hand around it and the burning stops. "Now get younna head mark up with Ash Wednesday ash and put the rosary crosses against the cross on you head and den hang the rosary round Shark and the gal's neck. Remember dat sickness come on horseback, but it does walk to go. Have patience. One-one does fill basket."

"Thanks, Pa," Chris says, grabbing the Easter egg kit, walking out of the market into the street, clutching the rosaries. He hears ringing, turns around and walks toward the sound. And he's in the church and it's cool and moist and he smells wax and sees candles twinkling and streamers of rainbow light from the stained-glass windows piercing the dimness. He stands at the end of the line, not thinking, following the line of people. When he reaches the front, he stares at the gold cross with the life-sized, flesh-colored Jesus with the piercing blue eyes and blood dripping from his hands and legs and chest and head. He stares up at Monsignor O'Conner, breathing through his mouth so he won't have to smell his stale monsignor smell. Monsignor flips him plastic pious eyes as he sticks his shaking finger into the golden urn full of ash. "Remember that you are dust, and to dust you will return." Then his cold fingers are marking the sign of the cross on his forehead.

Chris walks out of the church into the bright sun. A crowd has gathered. A mass of angry voices. The people move together, surrounding, following something in the center, like a swarm of ants carrying a dead slug. Chris pushes into the crowd, hearing the chant "The chief is a thief!" Chris reaches the center of the crowd, sees the prime minister surrounded by bodyguards. A ZNS reporter shoves a microphone in the direction of the PM. "It is true that you accepted bribes for allowing major South American drug kingpins to operate in the Bahamas?"

"No," the PM replies, looking around in shock. "No comment."

"You shame we whole country. We a God-fearing people," a woman yells. A man yells, "Never mess in the road cause you gonna pass back and mash it!" "What sweet in goat mouth sour in he ass!" another woman yells.

The prime minister is pushed into the back of his white Rolls-Royce by his bodyguards. He looks out at the crowd through the window as if he's trying to figure out what's happening. An egg hits splat against the window, blotting out his face. The car pulls out in a hail of flying curses and food.

Chris gets into his car, drives, looking at his reflection in the rearview window. He sees the black ash cross on his forehead, remembers how he and Shark used to duel and would stand back to back and then walk five paces and take turns shooting spitballs through a straw at the ash crosses on each other's forehead. And they would try to see who could keep the black cross on their forehead the longest, so they wouldn't wash their faces for days and Chris would always win and Shark would say, "It cause you skin is white and the ash show up. I still got ash on me head but it the same color as me."

Chris sits on the boat making a sign that says, WELCOME HOME, ROBIN, I LOVE YOU. He finishes the YOU, coloring the U with pink, the marker making a squeaking sound against the paper as he fills

in the lines. The magnum of Dom Perignon cools out in the fridge.
The Easter egg coloring kit sits on the coffee table. He hangs up the
sign.

He places clumps of bougainvillea like crepe paper—red, white,
rose, orange, pink, purple—all over the boat. Next to their bed he
puts the bird-of-paradise plant, as he thinks, The hospital, the cage
and tomorrow. Released. Tomorrow.

Chris gets into bed, tries to sleep. But he can't sleep away from
her. He thought tonight would be different, knowing she was coming home. He rolls around in the bed, on his back, his stomach, no
position comfortable. He's at the starting line of a race. He tries to
see sheep, to count them, but only sees Robin. The final count-
down, he thinks, looking at the arms of the clock on the wall to
make sure they're still moving. Big hand on the twelve, little hand
on the three. He can't take it anymore. He untangles himself from
the sheets. Gets up. Leaves.

Chris walks into Robin's room quietly. She sleeps on her back,
her drawing pad, open to the *Butterfly Kisses*, over her chest, her
heart. He picks the pad up, kisses the paper, rests it on the table
next to her bed. He touches the rosary cross to the ash cross on his
forehead and places it around her neck. Then he walks down the
hall and enters Shark's room.

Shark sleeps quietly. His chest moves up and down. His head is
no longer swollen. They have removed the old bandage and re-
placed it with a smaller one. Chris sits on Tantie's cot, wondering
where she is, anticipating tomorrow. He fantasizes Shark waking up
and being fine. He lies down, rests his head on Tantie's pillow,
smells her thatch smell, shuts his eyes. Chris sees all the blood dripping out of Shark as he ran with him in his arms. Then he sees the
five pails of chicken blood scum and he and Shark are fighting the
shark, taking turns. Each of them fight the fish until they have
reeled the reel a thousand times. And sometimes the turns went by
fast because the line was slack and it was easy to reel. And sometimes, just when they thought they had lost the fish, the line raced
out again. And they were back at the beginning again, fighting the
shark for the precious line, inch by inch, second by second. And
Chris's muscles were so tired that they jerked around by themselves

and he said, "I don't think we'll ever get it in." Shark followed the line with the flashlight, the beam of light spotlighted the end of the rod, then out and down, following the line until it disappeared into inky black oblivion. He replied, "Don't put goat mouth on it. Don't give up. Nothing can beat us!" As the sun came up, they saw the huge black spot in the distance. It looked like a clump of reef, only it was moving slowly toward them. Chris yelled, "Mother fuck," and Shark yelled, "Holy shit." Then they saw other black spots, smaller, erratically moving around and around and around the big spot. And as they pulled the shark in, these shadowlike spots took on the shapes of outlines of sharks. Then they could see fins above the water, sharp dark knives cutting. And now all the line had been reeled in and they were reeling in the metal leader. Slowly, a click at a time, the shark at the end of the dock, bigger than the dock, so big that Chris couldn't believe it really existed, and he was so tired he thought he was dreaming as Shark tied a rope lasso to slip over the shark. Then Chris felt a jerk and then another and another and he was jerked forward and then released by the rod, over and over and over again. And they watched as the water around the dock came alive with slashes and flashes of black-and-pink foam and red as one shark after another attacked the giant shark at the end of their line. Then they were attacking one another. Chris watched the tears form in Shark's eyes as he reeled up the empty line. Chris gets up from the cot, walks up to Shark and takes the other rosary from around his neck. He thinks of his mother and pictures her lips kissing the cross on the end of her gold rosary, and he brings the glow-in-the-dark plastic cross to his lips and kisses it. He bends down over Shark's bed and puts the rosary around his neck, whispering, "Shark, it's all right. Nothing can beat us. Don't give up hope. Get better so we can go see snow." He kisses Shark on the lips.

Shark's eyes open as Chris's eyes open. Chris jumps back, watches Shark's eyes squint and try to focus like he's searching for a boat on the horizon in the noonday sun. Chris anticipates the delirium, the malformed, distorted words like before. Lines and then small beads of sweat form on Shark's forehead and Chris thinks of the rosary beads in his mother's hands as she prayed, her lips moving rapidly as she said, "The first glorious mystery, Jesus rises glorious and immortal three days after His death." He prays, "Hail Mary, make Shark be all right. Please, Mom, make Shark be all right."

Shark's eyes stop moving. They focus on Chris. Something's there, Chris thinks, as he stares, trying to convince himself, like waiting for another nibble on the end of the fishing line to make sure there's a fish.

"Chris," Shark says, confused.

Chris is too surprised to answer. He's not sure whether he heard or is imagining things. He tries to talk, opens his mouth. Nothing. He can't. He's too excited.

"Chris," Shark repeats, softly.

"Yes." Chris forces. And Shark looks at him, a puzzled look on his face.

"You're in the hospital. You've been in an accident," Chris says.

"Tired," Shark says as his eyelids close. "It hurts."

"I know," Chris says, feeling the excitement bubble through his body. He tells himself it really happened. He didn't imagine it. Shark recognized him. Shark spoke to him. And his heart beats so hard he wants to yell and scream and dance. But he just stands there staring at Shark. He hugs himself. And it's like the end is finally there and everything is really going to be all right and he's not just telling himself this. Shark came back. Robin is coming home tomorrow. The high. So high. He stands, not knowing what to do. "Thank You, God," he says as Evalina walks into the room. He hugs her. "He spoke. He spoke. Recognized me," he says, trying to keep his voice down as he hears the loudspeaker, "Code blue. Number three, STAT." Not another one. At least we are getting out of this death factory tomorrow. Tomorrow, he thinks.

Chris hears the footsteps. He opens the door to Shark's room. They stop. Turn. Enter. Chris's feet are moving before his brain registers.

He bursts into the room as the electrodes are placed on her chest. The electricity is turned on. Her drawing pad on the floor. *Butterfly Kisses* being trampled. Robin's body moves like a slice of bacon on a hot griddle.

22

"Mon, I can't believe I'm out of here today," Shark says happily. He sits on the bed, dressed in yellow polo shirt, aquamarine pants. "I ain't checking out till dis afternoon, but I couldn't wait to put on real clothes. I's so sick of my ass hanging in the wind."

Chris forces a smile, sitting on the floor next to the bed, hugging his knees. "It's about time somebody gets to leave," he says, shrugging, resting his head on his arms, thinking, It's three months since Easter, three months since Robin was supposed to get out.

"I's going to stay with Mama till I fix up proper. I hope all she Bible talk don't send me crazy." He crosses and uncrosses his legs.

"You can stay on *Paradise Overdose* whenever you need a break," Chris says, handing his keys to Shark. "I got another set in the car."

"Thanks," Shark says, catching the keys. "I'm gonna buy me a boat. A tourist boat. When I start to deal, I tell myself dat all I want is a boat so I can make a decent living taking tourist on trip. I set the money aside to buy it. All I got left is dat same boat money." His dark eyes gleam.

"That's sounds great," Chris says, and he doesn't know whether to believe him but he wants to, wants it to be happily ever after for him.

"I gonna have the bestest beach party and booze cruise and snorkel trip . . ." Shark stares at him. His smile dissolves. He picks at the Band-Aid on his head. Chris sees him struggle as he says, "Mon, if it wasn't for you . . ."

"You too," Chris says, pausing. He takes a big breath.

"I's sorry bout Robin," Shark says sadly.

Chris forces himself not to feel. "Fuck all this sensitive shit." He shakes his head.

"We'll punch dem waves together," Shark says, standing up, reaching out his hands. Chris grabs them, thinks of Robin, feels a sting, and he fights it, but it spreads. Shark pulls him up.

"I have to go," he says, leaving Shark. He walks down the corridor slowly, thinking about how long the three months since Robin's attack seem. An endless wait for the moments when her eyes opened, sitting on the floor next to her bed watching her heartbeat on the monitor, counting the seconds between each gasp. He would breathe in and out with her, each breath she took filling him with relief that she was still alive. And then, suddenly, like a fish striking bait, her eyes would snap open. Her heart would skip on the monitor. Her face full of fear until he brought his face up to hers. She would try to smile and he would try to tell her that she didn't have to smile. He remembers a month ago.

"Your face is flickering, like in a movie," she said.

"Movie?" he asked.

"A sad movie."

"A love story," he said, forcing a sterile mask on his face.

"I want to be cremated. Scatter my ashes in the sea by Mangrove Cay."

He ignored her, interrupted her. "You're not going to die," he said, grabbing her hand and holding it to his lips.

She didn't answer, her silence like a drawn sword.

"What's wrong?" he asked, the silence screaming. "How do you feel?"

"Like someone who's dying." Her voice crackled. The sword stabbed. He tasted the salt from his tears. She shut her eyes. Her eyelids trembled.

He hugged her, hearing and feeling her heartbeat.

"Promise me you won't let me be a vegetable. Promise me you'll make them let me die. Promise me you'll let me . . ."

"I promise," he said softly. And then he nestled his head, held his breath, felt her warmth, heard his mother saying, "Don't breathe hot air on me."

"Breathe," Robin whispered, and he breathed in and out. He felt the tumor pushing out of her body, against his forehead. And that was the last word she said because that night, a month ago, when he went home, she stopped breathing. And they stuck the tube in her mouth, down her throat, to pump air into her lungs, like a tire pump, to join the other one that sucked greenlike sludge, the color of frozen spinach, that clumped in the tube, from her lungs, up out of her nose.

Chris walks into Robin's room. He looks, focuses on the tubes and wires, in and out, out and in. He imagines them slithering and crawling like snakes, and he's trapped in a game of snakes and ladders, and instead of climbing he's sliming, slipping. And it's like all the moisture is slipping out of her no matter how much they pump in. She's drying up before his eyes.

He walks to the sink, turns on the tap. He puts his mouth to the water and drinks and drinks and drinks, imagining the water is going into her. He pushes his head under the tap. The water is ice cold. He imagines he's an ice cube, frozen, numb, refusing to melt.

He forces his head out. Water drips down. From his head, from his hair. It's sopped up by his shirt. He remembers trying to make Easter eggs so he could take them to her. He poured the boiling vinegar water into the glass bowls. The vapor rose as he dropped in the colored dye pills. He swirled the color into a uniform shade, took a candle and wrote "Robin" on her egg and drew eyes and nose and a smile mouth on it, remembering when she was completely bald, and she said, "My head is so ugly."

"It's beautiful," he replied.

She smiled, grabbing the red lipstick she made from the gnawed bits of fat, the lipstick she gave him as a present. She stood in front of the mirror, drew a smile and then a dot nose and two eyes on her scalp. He walked up to her and grabbed her head, kissed the smiling, drawn-on mouth. She laughed.

He remembers his hand shaking as he held the egg in yellow dye, and then something dropped into the yellow bowl, a clear drop like a tiny raindrop hitting a sun-filled puddle. It got all blurry. He couldn't see. He couldn't stop his hand from shaking. The egg dropped into the yellow, splashing yellow all over the spread-out *Freeport News* on the table. He wiped his eyes and looked at the yellow spots and splats and the egg floating in the yellow dye. He slammed his fists on the table. The bowls flew, staining the carpet and his white Speedo and his skin red and blue and green and purple and orange.

Chris shakes his head back and forth, his wet hair flying in the air, flicking water droplets through the air. He picks up the disposable lollipop toothbrush from the sink, walks up to Robin's bed, forces himself to look. Closed eyes, her nose clogged with tubes, blood sticks to her mouth. The blood turns from red to brown to black, forming black half-moons on the tops of her teeth like the little white half-moons on each of her fingernails. He sticks the toothbrush into her mouth, swabs the blood out, removing some of the dry white lip dandruff. He rubs her hair, her forehead, with a wet cloth soaked in Limacol. Flakes fly, clear, like fish scales. He flicks the green sleep out of the corner of her eyes with his fingers and he feels so sleepy, so exhausted, but he hates to shut his eyes in case she might open hers. Chris strokes her face gently, avoiding the strips of tape that stick the tubes to Robin's face, distorting it. The respirator tube forces her mouth open. A frozen scream. He feels trapped in this hospital, trapped watching the respirator blow her lungs up and down, watching her chest rise and fall mechanically. He looks. The more time, the more machines, the less Robin. It's like a part of him is being lopped off. Slowly. Sadistically. And he refuses to feel. He thinks how her head and brain keep getting bigger, demanding more as her lungs get stiffer, accepting less.

He hugs her carefully, hears-feels the bubbles hissing inside of her fizzing—she's dissolving. And he thinks of Double-Breasted Cay, the sand dots outlined in froth. He threw the froth into the air—billions of bubbles.

Chris touches the blue beach glass earring she made for him, feels her lips and tongue on his earlobe after she pierced it, licking away the blood drop. He aches for her. The tubes stick into her, making him feel sick, like the nightmare he keeps having in which he tries to penetrate her, only to find she has grown balls. They hang down between her legs. He kisses her left hand, the one with no connections, the one without the plastic heart monitor on the finger. He looks at the ring on his pinkie with the five diamonds. Thinks of his father giving the ring to his mother and saying, "You shall be my wife." Thinks of his mother giving the ring to Evalina to give to him. Thinks, I love you very much. He pretends he's slipping the ring onto her finger as he kisses her hand. He smells-feels-tastes antiseptic. He remembers three weeks ago, the last time she came back. He was asleep on the floor. Something cut through. Robin kicked, rolled, pulled. "No," he yelled. Her eyes pierced. Pink froth bubbled from her mouth as she tried to pull the tubes out. A clump of black sluglike scum slipped from her nose as he grabbed her hands, stopping her. And her hands felt dead in his hands as she choked. He put a pillow under her chin to hold her head up so the tube wouldn't cut her throat. Robin tried to touch him, but her arm just flopped. A gargling sound escaped from her mouth as she struggled to talk. He grabbed her drawing pad and a pen, put the pen in her hand. She held it in her fist. He watched her strain as she tried. The pen slipped from her grasp. She touched her hand to her heart, pushed it towards him. Her eyes pleaded, then closed.

He picked up her pad. It was sweaty. A scribbled line, like the line waves make on the beach.

Chris sits on the floor by the side of her bed. He shuts his eyes. Just fall into it. Relax. Let it all go blank, he tells himself as he thinks of himself like a shark, which has to swim ceaselessly in order to push water past its gills so it can breathe.

It's over, he thinks. She's gone. It's back to the beginning. Again. All alone again. Just forget. Just for a second. But it runs through his head on autopilot. Alone. He can't get the needle off. He can't stand it. His head falls against the side of her bed. He feels the cool steel frame against his forehead, feels as if someone shot a speargun through his chest. He slams his head into the frame, over and over until everything spins. Black dots, and the dots have wings and they're flying, circling. Vultures waiting for death below. His head is flying away from his body, flying away from her, separate. He grabs his head with his hands. He hears himself laughing. He doesn't know why he's laughing but he can't stop and then the burning behind his eyes. Then wet and warm in front, filling his nose with snot. He snorts. He tastes his blood in his mouth.

He stands up, looks at her through his tears. A smudge. He refuses to see her as she is now, seeing her as she was at the beginning, at his beginning. But the image in front of him, of her in the hospital bed, keeps breaking in. He gasps for breath, like her. His face cringes in pain. Distorting his face, like hers. His head pounds. Inside his head pounds. He rubs his temples, remembers Evalina rubbing his feet with cool aloe gel. Down and up. Because his head ached. Up and down. And his feet felt so good that he forgot the pain in his head. He looks at Robin's feet. They're the same. All that's left. He looks at the blue socks they put on her feet with the holes on both ends. He can't let her go. He focuses on the toes. Seeing only them, hearing her laugh when he would tickle them, saying, "This little piggy goes to market and this little piggy goes all the way home." He touches her toes lightly with the tips of his fingers. And with each touch a memory pops into his head. The astonishingly beautiful look on her face when she made art. The sound of their skin unsticking. Her hands muted shades of pink, aqua, yellow, purple, red. The way she listened. The summery taste of her underarms. Their legs intertwined after making love. The rainbow beach. *Butterfly Kisses.* He strokes each toe. Pink. Plump. Alive. Gently, her left foot and then her right. In his head each toe is a different part of her. He smiles, lets the happy memories play, and he thinks that he has these memories and they're his and no one can take them away. I haven't lost her. She's still with me, inside. And feels better. He peels the little socks off her feet, like peeling the skin off a mango. The feeling stirs. He can't give it up, can't give her up. He spreads some of Evalina's homemade aloe jelly onto his hand. Hears Evalina say, "Dat she mama taught she dis medicine, who learn it from she mother-mother, who was slave, and the plant did come with the slaves from Africa and in the Bible dey does use aloe to clean up the bodies of the dead. Aloe was the only ting dat God did let dat good-for-noting Adam take out of Eden. And all the aloe come from dis little plant. Dat is why it's called the Shoot of Paradise."

He spreads it onto her feet slowly, tenderly, concentrating on the pattern of her skin. He looks at the tiny translucent bubbles floating in the aloe jelly, floating on her skin like eggs clinging to a lobster. It smells of tropical coconut and pineapple mixed with briny, blossoming Bahama breezes. The sun beats down. Hot. Their brown skin sweating, gummy with salt as he spreads it on her. Each toe a different part of her. Her face, big sparkling brown-black eyes, thin eyebrows, thick eyelashes, the cloud of freckles on her nose, her perfect pink lips, her long neck, her collarbone jutting out, her round breasts, her shallow belly button, a trail of invisible hair, the black triangle, then more tasty pink lips.

"Do it," he remembers her saying. "Please, you promised."

"I didn't say when," he answered.

"You can't."

"Watch," he said, pulling off his bathing suit, crouching up into the fetal position, muscles stretching, stretching, reaching with his mouth, getting harder, harder, tongue touching the tip, then on it, around it, sucking, up and down, and he was in himself, and she was watching and she pulled off her top and sucked her own breast as he sucked himself and he felt as if they had become a work of art, one of her works of art, and he feels such a lonely passion for her. Bubbles melt gradually. He hears her asking, "If I die before you, will you come and feed me like the natives do?" Hears himself answering, "Not only will I feed you, I will think of you and come for you." His mouth opens, just a slit, then wider, tongue exits, tip of tongue touching and he's kissing her and tasting her. And he imagines her alive and wet and moving and happy, responding, alive at last. And he's so lost in the feeling he forgets to breathe and he hears her whisper, "Breathe," softly into his ear. He gulps down air as his lips touch her toes. They turn to nipples in his mouth. He strokes his left nipple, imagining her mouth on him. He reaches down slowly, lightly, touches himself, imagines her touching him. Tongue between each toe, the skin so soft and supple. He picks her up and carries her to the hard sand where the ripples are hitting the shore. He anticipates the feeling of it inside her as a wave breaks over him and he enters with the flow. He's finally at home. Whole again. Home at last. Tasting her. The softness meeting hardness, hardness disappearing into softness. Going down and up on him, in her. Finally, making love with her. He pumps harder and harder, the dolphin swims faster and faster, sensation stronger and stronger, and the feeling rushes. He surrenders as he feels it in his stomach, and he doesn't fight the feeling, and he forgets to breathe, to think, he forgets if he's alive or dead.

"Don't die," he gasps. He breathes. In and out.

He arrives back into the hospital world, jerked back into reality, focuses on her skeletal body. So many tubes going in and out, violating her like rape. He feels as if they're going in and out of him. He shuts his eyes so he won't have to see them, feels as if a trap door has opened beneath his feet and he's falling and falling.

"No!" he says. "Come on, Robin, we have so much to do. We're gonna make babies together. And we're gonna give them so much love. And we'll grow old together. And I will love every wrinkle. I will love your hair, each hair as it turns grey. And we will never have to be alone. Come on, Robin, we have so much to do."

He opens his eyes, looks at her open mouth. And he hears her saying, "Promise me you'll let me go." He hears his mother saying, "People don't put people to sleep because they aren't brave enough."

"Robin, Robin, Robin," he chants softly, as he turns off the machines one at a time. As easy as turning off a lamp. The noise stops. Silent, so silent.

He lies on the bed. Hugs her. Places his head in the spot beside her breast and underneath her arm. He holds his breath. And it's like he's underwater, in the ocean beneath the storm, flowing with the flow in the bluest blue. "Please die," he prays, over and over.

He hears a noise. He ignores it. And then the noise again. And he feels a hand touch his head, his hair, stroking. He turns over. Opens his eyes. Bright white light. Spinning. He tries to focus. Sees Shark standing above him. His eyes glistening. Shark holds his hands out. Chris grabs them, stands, falls into his arms. They hug each other stiffly like men.

23

Chris lies naked on the white hammock on the flying bridge. His head rests on the connect-the-dot sheet, on her smell mingled with his smell, sun-warmed. He breathes it in, sits up. The ocean is flat calm. He feels very calm. He stares at the cloudless sky. The sun, a setting red glob, stares back at him, burning. A sweat drop drips down his chest, drops into his navel, where a pool of sweat is accumulating. He picks up his pad, writes: "The huge red snapper hangs in the crystal water."

His touches the urn sandwiched between his legs up against his groin. He strokes it, caressing the slick hot metal. His sweat wetting it. He picks it up, holds it above his head. Sunlight soaks it. Gold beams bounce off the golden urn into his eyes. He shuts them, sees the golden chalice in church held up. Hears, "Take this all of you and drink from it: this is the cup of my blood, the blood of the new and everlasting covenant. It will be shed for you and for all men so that sins may be forgiven. Do this in memory of me."

He gets up, walks to the side of the boat, stares out at Mangrove Cay. The wrapped mangrove banyans. Sun-bleached muted colors. No longer brilliant, like faded memories. He looks at his reflection in the water. Stares. Through his reflection he sees a conch shell at the bottom, resting on the sand. He unscrews the top of the urn, looks at the grey dust inside. He sticks his finger in, wet with sweat.

The ring with the five diamonds flicks slivers of multicolored light. The ash coats his finger and the ring grey. He makes the sign of the cross on his forehead. "Remember that you are dust and to dust you will return."

A tear leaves his left eye as the final tip of sun dips below ocean. Green flash. He turns the urn over. A cloud of dust floats down. He jumps. After it. Into it. Seeing Robin's face, his mother's face. The spot next to her arm, beneath her breast.

"Krick krack,

Monkey break he back

All for piece of pommerac.

E-bo ben

My ole story en—

I'll never tell a big lie

like dat again!"

About the Author

Brian Antoni divides his time between Miami Beach, Florida; New York City; and Freeport, Bahamas. An attorney, he also rehabs historic buildings.